WITHDRAWN

Praise for

shannon stacey

"Books like this are why I read romance."
—*Smart Bitches, Trashy Books* on *Exclusively Yours*

"Shannon Stacey's books deliver exactly what we need
in contemporary romances.... I feel safe that every time
I pick up a Stacey book I'm going to read something
funny, sexy and loving."
—Jane Litte of *Dear Author* on *All He Ever Needed*

"I'm madly in love with the Kowalskis!"
—*New York Times* bestselling author Nalini Singh

"*Yours to Keep* was a wonderful,
sexy and witty installment in this series....
This was a truly a magical book."
—*The Bookpushers*

"This contemporary romance is filled with charm, wit,
sophistication, and is anything but predictable."
—Heart to Heart, *BN.com*, on *Yours to Keep*

"One of those books
that simply makes you feel good and happy."
—*Smitten with Reading* on *Yours to Keep*

cey

all he ever *needed*

HARLEQUIN®
entertain, enrich, inspire™

Recycling programs
for this product may
not exist in your area.

ISBN-13: 978-0-373-77755-6

ALL HE EVER NEEDED

Copyright © 2012 by Shannon Stacey

www.Harlequin.com

Printed in U.S.A.

For Jaci and Angela
because when the nights are dark and stormy, I can
always depend on you guys to drag me out from under
the bed…or join me, with books, flashlights and snacks.

all he ever
needed

CHAPTER ONE

MITCH KOWALSKI WAS doing sixty when he blew past the Welcome to Whitford, Maine, sign, and he would have grinned if grinning on a Harley at dusk in a shorty helmet wasn't an invitation to eat his weight in bugs.

He was home again. Or he would be after he passed straight through town and nursed the bike down the long dirt drive that led to the Northern Star Lodge. As eager as he was to get there, though, he eased up on the throttle as the first lights of Main Street came into view.

It had been three years since he'd visited his hometown, but he could have navigated the road with his eyes closed. Past the post office where he'd landed his first real job, then lost it because old man Farr's *Playboy* subscription was a hell of a lot more interesting than sorting electric bills. Then the Whitford General Store & Service Station, owned by Fran and Butch Benoit. Junior year, he'd taken their daughter to the prom and then taken her up against the chalkboard in an empty classroom.

Mitch downshifted and executed a lazy rolling stop at the four-way that passed for the town's major intersection. To the left were two rows of ancient brick buildings that housed the bank and town offices and an assortment of small businesses. To the right, the police department—which had had its fill of the Kowalski boys in their youth—and the library, which had been fertile hunting grounds for a teenage boy looking to charm the smart girls out of their algebra homework.

Yeah, it was good to be home, even if everything was closed up tight for the night. The people of Whitford knew if they had business in town, they'd best get it done before the evening news.

He went straight through the intersection, but he didn't go far before the old diner caught his eye. Or the sign did, rather, being all lit up. Last time he'd passed through, the place had been closed up tight—driven out of business by a bad economy and an owner who didn't care enough to try to save it. But now there was a new name on the sign, a couple of cars in the parking lot and flashing red neon in the window declaring it open.

His stomach rumbled, though he felt it rather than heard it due to the loud pipes on his bike, and he pulled into the parking lot. Josh, his youngest brother, wasn't expecting him—unless the boxes of clothes and other stuff he'd shipped ahead had arrived—and he would have already eaten anyway. Rather than go rummaging for leftovers, Mitch decided to grab a quick bite before heading on to the lodge.

The first thing he noticed when he walked through the door was the remodeled fifties decor, with a lot of red vinyl and black-and-white marble. The second thing he noticed was the woman standing behind the counter—a woman he'd never seen before, which was rare in Whitford.

Mitch put her at maybe thirty, seven years younger than him, and it looked good on her. She had a mass of brown hair twisted and clipped up into one of those messy knots that begged to be let loose. Jeans and a Trailside Diner T-shirt hugged sweet curves, and her ring finger was bare of either a gold band or a fresh tan line.

A little plastic rectangle was pinned above the very nice mound of her left breast. Name tags were a rare thing in a town where relationships were formed in playpens and cemented in the kindergarten sandbox, so it caught his attention. By the time he took a seat on a red padded stool at the counter, he could read it. *Paige*.

He deliberately sat with his back to the two other couples in the place in the hope they wouldn't recognize him right off. One, because he'd rather Josh heard he was back in town from him, not the grapevine. And, two, because he was a lot more interested in maybe getting acquainted with Paige than getting reacquainted with whoever was in those booths.

"Coffee, sir?"

"Please." Her eyes were brown, even darker than the coffee she poured into an oversize mug for him. "You're new here."

She gave him a look over her shoulder while setting the carafe back on the warmer. "I've been here every day for almost two years, but I've never seen you before. New's relative, I guess."

He plucked a menu from between the condiment rack and the napkin holder, wondering if the food choices had gotten an update, too, along with the sign and the vinyl. "I had my first taste of ice cream in that booth right over there."

She leaned her hip against the stainless steel island

the coffeemaker sat on and looked him over. "Tall, dark and handsome, with pretty blue eyes. You must be one of Josh's brothers."

Usually a guy didn't like being told he had a *pretty* anything, but he'd learned a long time ago having pretty eyes led to having pretty girls. "I'm the oldest. Mitch."

Her smile lit up her face in a way that elevated her from just pretty to pretty damn hot. "Oh, I've heard some stories about you."

He just bet she had. There was no shortage of stories about him and his brothers, but he couldn't help wondering if she'd heard the one about the backseat of Hailey Genest's dad's Cadillac since it was a Whitford favorite. Rumor had it when old man Genest finally traded the car in for a newer model, it still had the cheap wine stains in the carpet and the gouges from Hailey's fingernails in the leather.

Even though he'd only been seventeen at the time—to Hailey's nineteen—he still heard about those gouges if he got within speaking distance of Mr. Genest. Since Mrs. Genest's looks came off as a little more speculative than condemning, he tended to avoid her altogether. Not easy in a town like Whitford, but he could be quick when he needed to be.

"So you're the one who blows stuff up?" she asked when he didn't offer up any comment about the stories she'd heard, as if there was anything to say. While there might be a little embellishment here and there, most of them were probably true.

"You could say that." Or you could say he was one of the most respected controlled-demolition experts in the country. His education, hard work and safety record never excited people as much as the thought of him getting paid to blow stuff up, though. "You still got meat loaf on the menu?"

"First thing the selectmen told me when I applied for a permit is that you can't have a diner in New England without meat loaf."

"I'll take that, and I'll pay for an extra slab of meatloaf and a bucket load of gravy."

"How about I give you the extras on the house as a welcome-home present?"

"Appreciate it," he said, giving her one of his charming smiles—the one that made his *pretty* eyes sparkle, or so he'd been told. And since he'd been told that by women in the process of letting him slide into second base, he was inclined to believe them.

He could tell by the flush creeping up from the collar of her shirt she wasn't immune to him. Nor was he immune to the subtle sway of her hips as she walked to the pass-through window and handed the order to a young man he was pretty sure was Mike Crenshaw's oldest boy. Gavin, he thought his name was.

Dropping an old casino in the middle of crowded Las Vegas to make way for a grander one was an intense job, so it had been at least a couple of months since Mitch had blown off steam between the sheets. And a six-week cap on the relationship was perfect. He could enjoy the getting-to-know-you sex and the know-you-well-enough-to-push-the-right-buttons sex, but be gone before the I'm-falling-in-love-with-you-Mitch sex.

He checked out the sweet curve of her ass when she bent down to grab a bucket of sugar packets, and he grinned. It was damn good to be home.

HEARING THE STORIES—AND, oh boy, were there some good ones—hadn't prepared Paige Sullivan for the reality of Mitch Kowalski taking up a stool in her diner. With his just-long-and-thick-enough-to-tousle dark hair and the blue eyes and easy smile, he could have been a star of the silver screen, not a guy who had just happened in looking for some meat loaf.

And maybe a little company, judging from what she'd heard. Supposedly, he was always in the mood for a little company. Unfortunately for him—and maybe a little for her—all he'd get at the Trailside Diner was the blue plate special.

"So where you from?"

Paige shrugged, not looking up from the sugar holders she was refilling. "I'm from a lot of places originally. Now I'm from Whitford."

"Military brat?"

"Nope. Mom with a…free spirit." Mom with a few loose screws was more accurate, but she wasn't in the habit of sharing her life story with her customers.

"How'd you end up here?"

"That old cliché—my car broke down and I never left." She topped off his coffee, but she was too busy making desserts for table six to stand around at the counter and chat.

As she built strawberry shortcakes, she grew increasingly aware of the fact Mitch was watching her. And not just the occasional glance because she was the only thing moving in his line of sight. No, he was blatantly checking her out. Since she was out of practice being an object of interest, it made her self-conscious, and the fact he was the best-looking guy to pass through the Trailside Diner since she'd opened its doors didn't help any.

No men, she reminded herself. She was fasting. Or abstaining. Or whatever-*ing* word meant she wasn't accepting the unspoken invitation to get horizontal in any man's eyes, no matter what he looked like. No. Men.

Gavin called her name a few minutes after she served up the desserts, and she grabbed the hot plate of meat loaf from the window. Mitch gave her a *very* appreciative smile before picking up his fork.

Ignoring the zinging that smile caused—because she wasn't zinging, dammit—she turned her back on him and started a fresh pot of coffee. Normally she wouldn't so near to closing on a weekday night, but she didn't have enough for one refill each should her customers be in the mood to forgo sleep in favor of caffeine and small talk.

Once the coffee was brewing, Paige pulled a clean bus pan out from under the counter and went from table to table, pulling the ketchup bottles and trying not to think about the man at the counter. She knew Mitch Kowalski had a dangerous job, and he certainly looked the part of the bad boy, in faded blue jeans and a black T-shirt hugging an upper body that screamed of physical labor.

Come to think of it, she knew a lot about the oldest Kowalski. While all the brothers were practically heralded as golden boys around town, there was a special gleam in the eyes of the female population when Mitch's name came up. Right on the heels of the gleam came the details, and if there was one thing she knew about the man, it was that he didn't disappoint.

Using her butt to push through the swinging doors, she took the bus pan of ketchup bottles back to the walk-in cooler. She wouldn't refill them until the morning, but she took a minute, hoping the chill would cool her overheating face. Okay, and maybe her body.

If a seventeen-year-old Mitch could make a young woman dig her fingernails into the leather seat of her dad's new car, just imagine what an experienced, thirtysomething Mitch could do. Not that he'd be doing anything to *her,* since she was abstaining, but *imagining* was an *-ing* word that couldn't really hurt.

The strangest thing about the Mitch Kowalski stories was the lack of animosity. It didn't seem possible a man could romance a healthy percentage of the young women in a small town without leaving a trail of jealousy and broken hearts, but it seemed to her he'd managed. Dreamy-eyed nostalgia was the legacy he'd left behind.

By five minutes of closing, the place was empty except for Mitch and an older couple lingering over their lukewarm mugs of decaf, so she went ahead and turned off the Open sign. Her part-time waitress, Ava, who usually did the closing shift, was sick, so Paige had done the whole shebang, from 6:00 a.m. to 9:00 p.m., and she was ready to collapse into bed.

Mitch met her at the cash register with his bill and cash. "What time's breakfast?"

"Six a.m." At least she managed not to groan out loud in dread of the four-thirty alarm.

He chuckled and shook his head. "Let me rephrase that. How *late* can I get breakfast?"

It hadn't occurred to her she'd be seeing *that* much of

him. It was a lot easier to resist temptation when temptation wasn't sitting at her counter, watching her work. "Breakfast all day, but no poached eggs after eleven."

He looked as if he was going to say more, but the couple from table six had figured out it was closing time and were on their way to the register. After giving her a smile that jump-started the forbidden zinging again, he walked out and she focused her attention on cashing out her final customers of the very long day.

When she went to twist the dead bolt on the door behind them, Mitch was at the edge of the parking lot, getting ready to pull out onto the road on what was a very big bike. The motorcycle rumbling between his legs was a black beast of a machine. While the leather saddlebags hid her view of his thighs, she couldn't miss the way his T-shirt stretched across his broad shoulders.

As he revved the engine and pulled into the street, Mitch turned his head and for a long moment they made eye contact. Then he smiled and hit the throttle, disappearing into the night.

No men. Paige flipped off the outside lights and turned away from his fading headlights. For two years she'd avoided having a man in her life. But temptation had never come in a package like Mitch Kowalski.

MITCH STOOD NEXT to his bike with his arms crossed, his pleasure at being home eclipsed by the condition of the Northern Star Lodge.

How could things have gone so downhill in just three years? The front of the lodge—what he could see by the landscaping lights—looked, if not quite run-down, at least a little shabby. Paint on the porch peeling. Weeds growing around the bushes. One of the spindles on the stair railing was missing. He didn't even want to imagine what the place looked like in the full light of day.

His great-grandfather had built the lodge as a family getaway back when the Kowalskis were rolling in dough, and it had started its life as a massive New Englander with a deep farmer's porch. It was painted the traditional white, and the shutters, originally black, had been painted a deep green by his mother in an effort to make it look less austere. He could see one of those shutters was missing and several were slightly askew. They all needed painting.

At some point his great-grandfather had added an equally massive addition in an L off the back corner, with the downstairs becoming a large kitchen with a formal dining room, and the upstairs being the servants' quarters.

His son, Grandpa Kowalski, hadn't fared well with the stock market, though, being a lot more of a risk taker than he was a savvy businessman and, when the old family money was gone, along with the big house in the city, he'd reinvented the vacation home as an exclusive gentleman's hunting club, and the Northern Star Lodge was born. The servants' quarters became the family quarters. With the next generation, the hunters eventually gave way to snowmobilers and now Josh ran the place, but the five kids owned it together.

The boards creaked under Mitch's feet as he climbed the steps to the heavy oak front door, which squeaked a little on its hinges. The place was going to hell in a handbasket.

The great room was lit up, and his youngest brother,

Josh, was sprawled on one of the sturdy brown-leather sofas, one leg encased by a glaringly white cast from foot to knee. There was a set of crutches on the floor, lying across the front of the couch. Josh had a beer in one hand and an unopened can sat on the end table next to Mitch's favorite chair.

He sank into it and popped the top. "How'd you know I was coming?"

"Mike Crenshaw saw you walking into the diner on his way home from the VFW. He told his wife, who called Jeanine Sharp, who called Rosie at bingo. She called me."

Rosie Davis was the part-time housekeeper-slash-surrogate mother at the lodge and had been since Sarah Kowalski died of an aneurism when Mitch was twelve.

"You come to babysit me?"

By the look of his baby brother, he could use a nanny. And a shower. Their father had stamped his build on all of his children—all of them, even Liz, pushing six feet and lean—but there were differences. Josh had a rounder face with their mother's nose, and Ryan and Sean a more square jaw and their grandfather's nose. Josh and Mitch had their father's dark hair, while the others were more of a dark-blondish like their mother. Mitch's face was strong, with the Kowalski nose, and he was the best-looking of the bunch, naturally. They all had their father's eyes, too. A brilliant blue that made people, especially women, take a second look.

Not many people would take a second look at Josh right then, though, unless they were trying to figure out if they'd seen his picture hanging in the local post office. His hair was a train wreck and it looked like he hadn't shaved in a couple of days. Worn-out sweat-pants with one leg cut off at the knee to accommodate the cast and a T-shirt bearing the stains of what looked like spaghetti sauce didn't help.

"Do I look like a babysitter?" Mitch took a long draw of beer, considering the best way to handle his brother. Head-on didn't tend to work well with Kowalskis. "Heard a rumor there was a hot new waitress in town. Thought I'd check her out."

"Yeah, right. Rosie call you?"

"'Course she did. Your cast probably wasn't even dry yet and she was on the phone. When's the last time you took a shower?"

Josh snorted. "No showers for me. I get to take baths, like a woman, with this damn thing propped up on the side of the tub."

"Got some fruity-smelling bubbles?"

"Screw you. How long you staying this time? Three days? A whole week?"

Tired. His brother looked tired more than anything else, and Mitch felt a pang of worry. His little brother just flat out looked like hell. "Rosie said you were limbing that big oak out front and fell."

"Didn't fall. The ladder slipped." He shrugged and sipped his beer.

"Probably because you had the ladder footed against your toolbox in the back of your pickup."

"No doubt. Didn't have a tall enough ladder."

"Why didn't you call in a tree service?"

"Gee, Mr. Fancy Engineering Degree, why didn't I think of that?"

Rather than rise to the bait of his brother's tone,

Mitch drank his beer and waited for Josh to realize he was being an ass. Mitch wasn't the one who'd been stupid enough to foot a ladder in the back of a truck or too stubborn to ask for help, so he wasn't going to sit and take crap where crap wasn't deserved.

"Fine. I should have called a tree service. I didn't. Now my leg's fucked up. Happy?"

"Don't be an asshole." Mitch drained the last of the beer and tossed it into the wastebasket somebody—probably Rosie—had put next to the couch for his brother's substantial collection of empties. "How many of those are from today?"

"Not enough." Josh knocked back the last of his can and crumpled it in his hand before dropping it into the basket with the others.

Mitch wasn't sure what was going on, but whatever Josh's problem was, it wasn't a busted-up leg. Every time Mitch came home—which, granted, wasn't as often as he should—Josh's attitude seemed to have climbed another rung on the shittiness ladder.

"Why don't you get cleaned up in the morning and I'll take you out for breakfast," Mitch said. "We can sit and watch the new waitress work."

"Paige? She's the owner, not a waitress, and she's not interested."

"She was interested."

"Every single guy in Whitford's taken a shot with her and, I'm telling you, she ain't interested. She's lived here like two years and hasn't gone on a single date that anybody knows about. And in this town, somebody would know."

Mitch thought of the way her gaze kept skittering

away from his and how she'd blushed, and decided she'd just been waiting for the right guy to come along. There was no lack of interest on his part and, as long as she understood he was only Mr. Right in the *right now* sense, he was more than willing to break her alleged two-year dry spell. They could have a little fun while he got the Northern Star in order and then he'd kiss her goodbye and go on to the next job with no regrets and no hard feelings. Just like always.

CHAPTER TWO

AT FIFTY-SIX, ROSE Davis had better things to do than run herd on the Kowalski kids. Things like knitting a stockpile of blankets for the grandbaby her daughter Katie didn't seem to be in a hurry to give her. Maybe take a nice, long trip down to that fancy casino in Connecticut with her friends.

But she'd been looking after the kids since they were twelve, eleven, nine, seven and five, and she couldn't walk away from them yet. Probably never would, or at least not until they found special someones of their own willing to marry them and keep them from acting like idiots. After their mother died, and with their father trying to keep the lodge going well enough to feed his five kids, it had taken damn near everything Rosie had to keep those kids on the straight and narrow. She'd had her own Katie to raise, but with the help of the kids' aunt Mary—who lived in New Hampshire and was raising four kids of her own—Rosie had managed to help them grow into reasonably well-adjusted adults.

Reasonably well-adjusted and lazy adults, considering it was eight in the morning and Mitch had yet to drag his butt out of bed and say hello to her. Since she'd given her friend Darla a ride to bingo the night before, where she heard Mitch was back, she hadn't been able to leave until Darla had finally given up hope of winning, and the boys had already gone to bed by the time she got home. And, when she'd given in to the temptation of pressing her ear against Mitch's door, she'd heard him snoring, probably tuckered out from the long ride to Maine. Despite wanting to, she hadn't woken him.

But it had been three years since the boy had been home and she wanted to see him, so she broke out the vacuum. It was an ancient beast with a noisy motor and she didn't take as much care as usual to avoid bumping the walls in the hall outside his room.

It wasn't much more than ten minutes before Mitch emerged from his room with mussed hair and a scruffy jaw and a sleepy smile. "Hi, Rosie."

She barely had time to hit the vacuum's off switch before he enveloped her in a warm bear hug. His chin rested on the top of her head and she knew if she allowed herself to remember when it was the other way around, she'd come undone.

"Three years is too long," she told him as she gave him a good squeeze.

"I know. I keep meaning to get home for a holiday, but most of my top people have wives and kids and I got in the habit of picking up the slack so they could be with their families. Before I knew it, there's three years gone by."

She released him and stepped back so she could give him a stern look. "You have a family, too, even if you haven't found a wife of your own. And don't think I haven't been praying you do."

He grimaced, as always, and changed the subject. "Speaking of family, is Josh up yet?"

"I heard the tub running before I started vacuuming and he was swearing up a blue streak, so I'd say he's in the bath right now."

"What's going on with him, Rosie? He's so tired and angry. And this place is falling apart."

"Things have been tight, Mitch. Very tight. With the economy the way it is and gas prices and all that, fewer people can drive all the way up here to spend a week, or even a weekend, snowmobiling. If the snow's good enough, they'll ride locally. If not, they don't ride."

"Why the hell hasn't he said anything? He's been making the deposits like usual. How were we supposed to know the lodge is in trouble?"

"You weren't."

"But we're in this together."

"No, you're not." She gave him a warm smile, hoping to take a little sting out of the words. "You all went off to lead your own lives and Josh was left to carry this place. He was here when you and then Ryan went off to college and Sean joined the army and Liz ran off with that useless waste of a man. And he's been carrying it alone since your father died."

"He hasn't needed us."

"'Course he has."

"Then why hasn't he said so?"

"Pride, maybe? You decide to go into demolition, and now look at you. Northern Star Demolition is one of the top companies in the country. Ryan goes off to pound nails for a living and now he makes custom, million-dollar homes for people with too much damn money. Sean and Liz may not be as well-off financially, but they're out there in the world, doing what they want to do."

Mitch couldn't really wrap his mind around it. Josh had always been more interested in the lodge than any of them. He'd shadowed their dad and tried to run the place since he was old enough to walk, and he'd never mentioned wanting to do anything else. "I'm taking him out for breakfast today. Maybe I can get him to talk to me."

"Tread lightly." Rose put her hands on her hips and pinned him with one of her looks. "And why aren't you staying here and letting me make your favorite French toast for you?"

"It'd do him good to get out. We'll just go to the diner and get reacquainted."

As if she didn't know how the male Kowalski mind worked any better than that. "You leave Paige Sullivan alone. She's a sweet girl and she's made a nice life for herself here. She doesn't need you turning it all upside down before you leave again for who knows how long."

He grinned at her, even though he had to know by now his charm was lost on her. "What's her story, anyway?"

"Her story is her business, and you stay out of it. You've got enough to do here, helping your brother, without toying with that woman." A bang and a curse from down the hall let them know Josh was out of the tub and probably trying to get dressed, so she pointed her finger at Mitch. "I mean it."

"I need to jump in the shower. Don't let Josh get into the beer before I'm done."

"He's not that far gone," she said, shaking her head as Mitch went into his room and closed the door. "Yet."

Since she'd called Mitch less for help around the lodge and more for help dragging Josh out of the funk he seemed to be sinking into, Rose could only hope Paige Sullivan didn't become a distraction.

FOUR-THIRTY IN THE morning had royally sucked.

Paige had slapped at the alarm clock until it stopped beeping so she could close her eyes again. A few minutes later, though, it started beeping again, and she made herself sit up and swing her legs over the side of the bed before shutting it off. She was so not a morning person, especially when it was still dark.

As she stumbled into the tiny kitchen toward her not-so-tiny coffee mug, she reminded herself for the umpteenth time if she wanted to sleep in, she shouldn't have bought a diner in a town full of early-rising Yankees. Being slow to wake up wasn't helped any by the fact she'd covered Ava's shift and hadn't even left the diner until after she was usually in bed.

Then, when she'd finally crawled between the sheets, she'd lost some precious sleeping time to thinking about Mitch Kowalski and how he'd looked back at her from the edge of the parking lot. It was a look that promised…something. Something good and maybe naughty and she wasn't sure what else. But pondering the possibilities had kept her tossing and turning until she wished she'd never met the man.

Once she was dressed—and, no, she didn't primp any more than usual just because she might see the man in question again—she left her *very* small mobile home and walked the twenty or so yards to the back door of her diner.

They'd been a package deal—the closed-up, outdated restaurant and the small, even more outdated trailer—and the price had been right. More importantly, the town had been right. Sure, it might have been nice to buy a little house for herself, with a yard consisting of more than a few feet of sorry-looking grass between the trailer and the parking lot. But she'd sunk almost every last penny into renovating and reopening the restaurant.

The important thing was the fact they were hers. Her name was on the deed for the diner and the tiny trailer and, no matter what, they were home. She'd finally put roots down and, while they may not go very deep, they were taking hold.

Carl, her first-shift cook, parked his pickup in the lot as she was unlocking the door, and he gave her his usual morning grunt. Carl didn't say much, but she'd practically wept the first time he cooked her a perfect over-easy egg, with just a little golden crunch around the edges. When he'd followed that up with French toast and pancakes that were better than anybody's grandma had *ever* made, she'd readjusted her budget, tightened her belt and paid him the slightly higher-than-average wage he needed to provide for his wife and help his daughters through college.

At six exactly, she unlocked the door, and by six-thirty the seats at the counter were mostly full and a few of the tables, too. Paige had gone over the num-bers—her personal budget as well as the cost of doing business—crunching them hard so she could find the lowest menu prices she could charge and still make enough profit to support herself. As a result, she'd done what she'd set out to do. The Trailside Diner, with its affordable prices and great food, was more than a place to eat. It had become the social center of her adopted town again, and people gathered before work to share the latest news. Unfortunately, today's news was all Mitch Kowalski, all the time.

"Did you hear Mitch Kowalski's back in town?" Katie Davis asked Paige when she paused long enough to refill Katie's coffee cup.

"I met him last night when he stopped in for dinner."

"Oh, that's right! You'd never met him. What did you think?" Under the brim of her Red Sox cap, Katie's eyes crinkled when she smiled. She'd run the town's barbershop since her father died, and Paige was sure her picture was in the dictionary as the definition of *tomboy*.

What did she think? She wasn't about to share her late-night thoughts about Mitch with the daughter of the Northern Star's housekeeper. Everybody was connected to everybody else somehow and, in Whitford, they didn't make it as far out as six degrees. She'd learned very quickly to mind what she said.

"It's nice of him to help out while Josh's leg heals," she said, thinking that was an honest and yet noninflammatory thing to say.

Katie scowled. "Yeah, yeah. He's a great big brother. But what did you think of *him?*"

Since the blush was giving her away anyway, Paige leaned down and lowered her voice. "I thought, *Oh. My. God.*"

They were both laughing when the bell over the door rang and Paige looked up. Straight into those blue eyes.

Crap. Even though he couldn't possibly know what she and Katie were laughing about, she turned her back so he couldn't see her blush.

Thankfully, Carl barked her name to let her know she had an order up, and she had a moment to compose herself while delivering food. And then she had time to refill coffees and start a fresh pot, because half the people in the place had to say a few words to Mitch as they made their way to an open table. She heard him make a comment about Josh's leg and they were finally left alone long enough to sit down.

"Morning, Paige," Josh said as he worked to get his cast tucked under the table and out of the way.

"Morning." She had a brief respite while Mitch went to stick the crutches in the corner with the coat hooks and umbrella rack, but then he was sliding into the booth and smiling up at her.

She had no idea why it knocked the breath out of her. His smile wasn't so different from Josh's. Their eyes were the same blue and they were built a lot alike. But Josh's flirtation had done nothing for her and they'd settled into an easy friendship once he figured out she wasn't going to go out with him. But all Mitch had to do was smile and she went all mushy inside.

Was that the way her mother always felt?

Just that one stray thought about her mother was enough to firm up the mushy spots, and she was able to respond to Mitch's greeting with a bland, professional smile. "You both want coffee this morning?"

They nodded and she left to deliver the food Carl was putting in the window and do some quick refills before she carried two fresh mugs to the Kowalski brothers.

"You know what you want?" she asked, sliding her order pad out of her apron pocket.

"Mitch does," Josh said, and he smirked at his brother in such a way that Paige was pretty sure she was missing an inside joke. Then he scowled and reached under the table, and she wondered if Mitch had kicked him. Hopefully *not* in the broken leg, if he had.

"I'm starving." Mitch looked down at the menu. "I'll have two eggs over easy and three pancakes, with a side of hash. Oh, and home fries. With a large orange juice, please."

"That sounds good," Josh said. "Ditto."

She took their menus and tried not to feel too self-conscious as she walked away, even though she suspected Mitch might be watching her, if last night was anything to go by. Then again—knowing him, if only by reputation—he might have turned his attention to any one of the other women in the diner.

After pinning their order up in the carousel hung in the pass-through window to the kitchen, Paige made her rounds, checking on customers and refilling coffees and handing out change at the cash register. Every so often she'd catch herself glancing toward the table where the Kowalski brothers sat.

They weren't doing a lot of talking, other than to the people who occasionally stopped by their table, probably to welcome Mitch home or ask after Josh's leg. Left to themselves, though, they didn't seem to have a lot to say, and she wondered if Mitch's long absences were at the root, or if there was something more specific going on.

When she brought their food to them, they both

thanked her, but she didn't get so much as a smile from Mitch, which was probably for the best. She'd already been far too distracted by him and, as the piece of paper taped to her refrigerator door at home said, men were a luxury and not a necessity.

It had been her new motto in life since the day a lawyer had contacted her to tell her a man she barely remembered had left her a nice bit of money when he died and, as long as she remembered that motto, she'd be just fine.

THE COMBINATION OF too much feeling sorry for himself and pain meds took a toll on Josh, so, after breakfast, Mitch drove him back to the lodge. After handing him over to Rosie's care, Mitch turned around and drove back into town.

Breakfast had been a total bust. His brother had responded to everything he said with a grunt or one or two words, and Mitch didn't think the diner was the place to shake the crap out of him and demand to know what the hell his problem was. There was time enough for that.

After finding a parking space, Mitch grimaced as he walked through the front door of the Whitford Police Department. Not necessarily because it brought back some of the less fun memories of his youth, but because the first desk he saw was occupied by Officer Robert Durgin.

Bob was older than dirt and blessed with a perfect memory when it came to the population's youthful indiscretions, especially anything involving the Kowalskis. Ryan had busted his window (accidentally), Liz had broken his grandson's heart (in as nice a way possible) and Mitch had caused Bob to wreck the department's shiny new cruiser he'd been so proud of (though it wasn't Mitch's fault he was a better driver). Josh and Sean had had their share of run-ins with Bob, too, and the fact they'd all been teenagers at the time didn't seem to count for much.

Mitch forced himself to smile and nod as he walked by, but Bob just kept staring at him as though he was expecting Mitch to grab the petty-cash box and make a run for it. The old cop was just one of the many reasons that, no matter how glad he was to see Josh and Rosie and a few others, being in Whitford started to chafe after a few days.

People always seemed to think a place where everybody knew your name was a good thing. Maybe it was. But they also knew every damn thing you'd ever done wrong, even stuff you couldn't remember yourself, thanks to moms sitting around talking about their babies and toddlers. Hell, the first thing the teacher said to him on his first day of school was, "I hope your aim's gotten better or the janitor's going to lock you out of the bathroom."

Everything from potty-training mishaps to late-night teenage joyrides were fair game in a town like Whitford, and that's why, no matter how happy he was to be back in his hometown, he was always happier when it was time to leave. In this town, Mitch Kowalski wasn't the man behind one of the most successful controlled-demolition firms in the country. Hell, maybe even in the world. Here he was just one of those damn Kowalski kids.

Through the big window in his office, Police Chief

Drew Miller saw him coming and waved him in. Mitch grinned as he closed the door behind him, meeting his best friend halfway for a handshake that become a quick man-hug.

"It's damn good to see you," Drew said as he sank back into his fancy leather chair.

Mitch tried to make himself comfortable on the hard, wooden chair on the other side of the desk. "Chief, huh? What the hell were they thinking?"

"They were thinking you'd come back eventually, so they'd better have somebody in charge who can keep your sorry ass in line."

Mitch snorted. "You know what pisses me off? Old Bob's out there glaring at me like I'm a pillager come to plunder his doughnut box, but they made you chief of police. You were in the car that night, too."

"Yeah, but I wasn't driving. I told him I was a helpless passenger who was too afraid to jump out, but kept screaming at you to stop the car."

"You're so full of shit."

"Maybe, but Whitford trusts me with their doughnuts, my friend."

Mitch shook his head. When he'd opened the email from Drew a few months back with the subject line "You won't believe this shit," he'd had to agree. It was hard to believe his old friend, who'd been riding shotgun on more than a few Kowalski capers, had been promoted to chief of the Whitford Police Department.

Hell, the night old Bob had wrecked the new cruiser, it had been Drew who goaded him into running rather than stopping when the lights started flashing in the rearview mirror of his old Camaro. Mitch was used to flying down the maze of dirt roads surrounding the town and Bob wasn't, so when Mitch turned off his lights and trusted the moon and his instincts to guide him, he'd easily given the officer the slip. Bob Durgin, however, was determined to catch Mitch in the act that time and ended up sliding into a ditch and rolling the cruiser onto its roof.

Luckily, Officer Durgin was too honest for his own good and, when questioned by the chief, he'd admitted he'd never gotten close enough to read the license plate. Since there were two other Camaros in town close enough to Mitch's to be easily mistaken for it in the dark, no charges had been pressed. Bob had never forgiven him, though, and he'd dogged Mitch's footsteps until the day he'd gone off to college. And Mitch had no doubt the man was just waiting for him to screw up now.

"How's Josh?" Drew asked, dragging Mitch out of the past.

"His leg's not bad, but his attitude about it sucks. His attitude about everything sucks right now, actually, and I can't figure out why. And he's not taking care of the lodge worth a damn."

"How long you staying?"

"The six weeks he's supposed to have his cast on. Rosie told me things have been getting pretty tight, so hopefully that'll be long enough to not only get my brother back on his feet, but have a look at the books, too."

Drew leaned forward in his chair, resting his elbows on his desk. "You think he's skimming?"

"Down, cop. No, I think business has been going to

shit and he didn't want to tell anybody he's hanging on by his fingernails."

"Everybody's taking a hit financially. We've seen an increase in thefts, for sure. People stealing small shit they can sell easily. And metals. Catalytic converters. Copper piping. You name it, people are stealing it."

"That sucks. So, tell me about Paige Sullivan."

Drew didn't even blink at the abrupt subject change. Just smiled and leaned back in his chair again. "She's a tough nut. Not sure even you can crack that one."

"What's her story?"

"Was driving through town and her car broke down. Ended up staying and buying the old diner."

Mitch snorted. "I know that much. What I don't know is why she doesn't date."

"Interrogating the women in town about their sex lives is beyond the scope of my job description. Maybe she was a nun before she moved here."

"If a woman was a nun and then stopped being a nun, wouldn't she want to do some catching up, so to speak?"

Drew shook his head. "I'm not going to risk burning in hell to answer that."

"I'm not talking about a nun having sex, moron. A post-nun."

"I'm pretty sure Paige was never a nun, so let's move on just in case."

"I'm going to be in town six weeks. Might be nice to have some company."

Drew shrugged. "I'm sure you won't have any trouble finding a woman. Hell, you can walk into any place in town and half the women in the room will swoon, for chrissake."

"I don't want swooning women."

"Good luck with that, man. Half the women in this town have had you and want you again, and the other half want to know what the fuss is about."

"Not getting a swooning vibe from Paige."

"Good for her. Be good for you to be told no. Builds character."

Mitch grinned. "She'll say yes. And, speaking of women, how's Mallory?"

Drew's mouth flattened out at the mention of his wife. "You'd have to ask her, since she's currently not speaking to me."

"Cold in the doghouse?" Mitch smiled. "It's good to fight once in a while. Can't have makeup sex if you've got nothing to make up for."

"I don't think there's going to be makeup sex. I think there are going to be lawyers and a For Sale sign on the front lawn."

Mitch dropped the smile and shook his head. "I'm sorry, Drew. Are you sure? Have you tried…something…counseling or anything?"

"We've talked it through so many times we've run out of words. I don't think counseling will help." Drew walked over to his personal single-cup coffee brewer, which was probably a perk of the office, and brewed them each a mug.

Mitch waited while his friend made the coffee, thinking he was probably deciding what he did and didn't want to say, and how to say it. Drew and Mal had been high school sweethearts, but they'd gone their separate ways when it came time for college. They'd both ended up back in Whitford, though, and they'd just had their ten-year anniversary.

"Mal doesn't want kids," Drew finally said, after he'd set their mugs on the desk and sat back down.

"Right now?"

"Ever."

"Wow." Mitch didn't know what else to say. Drew and Mallory had always talked about having kids... someday.

"It was always not yet and not right now and some-day. I told her someday had come, and she said the only someday that had come was the someday she was going to tell me she didn't want to have kids."

"You guys were together all through high school and you've been married ten years. How can you not have had this conversation before? I mean, it doesn't even make sense. I remember you guys talking about kids. She wanted a daughter named...something. Hell. It was a flower."

"Daisy." Drew snorted. "She was afraid I wouldn't marry her if I knew, so she said what she thought I wanted to hear and then just kept on saying it. Now I'm heading toward forty and I've got no kids and I may not even have a wife anymore."

"I'm sorry, man. Why did she decide to tell you the truth now?"

"Because I told her it was time. Neither of us are getting any younger, her pregnancies would be higher risk and I didn't want to need a walker to get to my seat at the kid's graduation. Over the years I brought it up more and more often, but I finally told her I didn't want to put it off anymore. I want a baby. She doesn't want a baby. We haven't talked since."

"How long ago was that?"

"Five weeks."

"Jesus, you and Mal haven't spoken to each other in five weeks? I thought you said you guys had talked about it so much you ran out of words."

"That was in the months—hell, *years*—leading up to five weeks ago."

"Are you still living together?"

Drew nodded. "She got pissed off and went to sleep in the guest room. Since we haven't spoken, she hasn't come back."

Mitch couldn't even wrap his head around it. "You mean you haven't talked about kids."

"No, we haven't spoken at all. At first it was awkward and uncomfortable, but now…it's just our new normal, I guess."

"That's messed up." Maybe Mitch had never been married, but he knew enough about healthy relationships to recognize an unhealthy one. "Maybe you should rethink the therapy."

"When I brought it up, she said suggesting therapy was like saying there was something wrong with her for not wanting to be a mother. It went downhill from there."

"How long are you going to keep on not talking to each other?"

"I don't know. There are only two possible outcomes—divorce or I tell her it's all right if we never have kids. And I'm not okay with either one." Drew gulped down some of his coffee. "Jesus, listen to me.

You didn't stop in to hear me whine about my problems. Sounds like you've enough of your own to deal with."

"Trying to get into Paige's pants is nothing like you maybe losing Mallory."

"I meant the lodge and Josh, actually, but a hundred bucks says you won't have any better luck with Paige than I am with Mal."

Mitch laughed. "If I was an asshole, I'd take you up on that. Wouldn't mind your hundred in my pocket. But I never bet on a lady. They *always* find out, sooner or later."

"Like you're ever still around for the later."

"One of these days, I'm going to surprise everybody and stick with one woman forever."

Drew smiled, but Mitch could see the sadness around his eyes. "Just make sure you both want the same thing in life, because it hurts like hell when you find out years into it that you don't."

While he hadn't been as many years into the relationship as Drew had, Mitch had already learned that lesson the hard, messy way. A man and a woman wanting two different things ended up in two different places, as a rule, which could only lead to misery.

He was a lot better off when he and a woman wanted the same thing—orgasms not of the do-it-yourself variety. Maybe only one or maybe quite a few, but then they went their separate ways with no hard feelings. With the exception of that one doomed relationship, it was a plan that had served him well and he hadn't yet found a second woman worth detouring for.

CHAPTER THREE

By two o'clock the following day, when Ava showed up to take over until closing time, Paige was exhausted. She even thought about going home and taking a nap, which was something she rarely did, but that would only make it harder to sleep at bedtime, and that four-thirty alarm wasn't very forgiving.

Instead, she stopped by her trailer and grabbed her library tote bag, since she'd finished the last book three days before and, tired or not, she was getting itchy for more books. The weather was nice—not too hot and no humidity—so she walked to the library, exchanging waves with others as she went.

She still found it exhilarating, the way the town's people made her feel as if she was one of their own. They called to her by name and asked her how business was going, and she'd ask after their kids or an aging parent. It was what she'd been looking for her entire life—that sense of belonging—and she'd finally found it in Whitford.

Dragged around from place to place growing up, Paige had always been the new kid in school. There had always been a new man of the house, some who became stepfathers and more who didn't. And she'd done it a few times herself. More than once, she'd given up who she wanted to be in order to be what a man wanted her to be.

Her car breaking down in Whitford had changed that. Changed *her*. It was an opportunity to start a life in a town that had welcomed a stranded stranger with open arms and, to make sure she kept that life on track, she was abstaining from men. When she was sure she was who she wanted to be and had her life the way she wanted it, she'd think about letting a man share it. For now, she wasn't going to risk falling back into behavioral patterns she'd learned from her mother. No men.

The library was quiet when Paige stepped inside, but she knew she didn't have long before school let out and kids started showing up, looking for a safe place to kill some time, doing homework or reading before their parents got home from work.

Hailey Genest, of gouged-leather-seats fame, was behind the circulation desk, where she always was, from ten in the morning until five o'clock Monday through Thursday, until eight o'clock on Fridays, and three hours every other Saturday afternoon. She wore jeans and a T-shirt, with her blond hair in a ponytail, looking like anything but a librarian.

Fran Benoit, with her thick gray hair pulled back in a braid, was checking out a stack of books, and she grinned when she saw Paige. "You're too late. I grabbed all the ones with the good sex in them."

"Guess I'll have to settle for the ones with the good murders." Paige wasn't sure she could handle having Mitch Kowalski *and* sexy books in her life at the same time.

"Not having the first could lead to the second, you

know," Hailey said, giving Paige a pointed look. "Gotta release the tension or it builds up and then—*wham*—somebody's calling nine-one-one."

All three of them laughed while Paige unloaded her tote, lining the books up on the counter to be checked in. Hailey didn't tend to be very subtle in her worry about Paige's lack of a sex life. Or maybe not so much worry, as a determination to fix what she perceived as broken.

"Speaking of sex," Fran said, "how did Mitch like your meatloaf?"

Paige shook her head. "How does speaking of sex lead to meat loaf?"

Fran snorted. "Speaking of sex leads to Mitch Kowalski."

"That it does," Hailey agreed, smiling that silly, nostalgic smile that was practically a universal female reaction to the man's name being said out loud.

"I'm sure he liked the meatloaf just fine or he wouldn't have brought Josh in for breakfast yesterday morning."

Hailey shook her head. "Nobody cares about the meat loaf, Paige. Mitch is in town for six weeks and you could do with a little less tension. Don't want you killing anybody."

"So what you're saying is that I have to have sex with Mitch to save lives?"

"Absolutely."

Fran nodded. "Yes."

Paige couldn't believe either woman kept a straight face. "Nice try. Not interested."

And she said *that* with a straight face, which was even harder to believe. Of course she was interested in having sex with the man. Didn't change the fact it wasn't going to happen.

"Besides," she said, "nothing says he's interested in me, either."

Fran scooped her books off the desk and gave her a look. "Honey, if you got an innie and not an outtie between your legs, he's interested."

They all laughed again, until a gruff, exaggerated throat-clearing sounded from the reference section, and Hailey shushed them. "You guys are going to get me fired."

"They can't fire you," Fran said. "You're the only person in town who knows the Dewey decimal system."

After Fran said goodbye and despite her gloating, Paige found a nice selection of sexy romances left on the shelves. She took a couple, along with a few cozy mysteries, a political thriller and a horror that looked like it would keep her up at night. Terror was probably a healthier reason to lie awake than thinking about sex with Mitch.

As she was checking out, a couple of patrons lined up behind her, so Hailey couldn't say anything more embarrassing than have a nice day.

The three hardcovers made her tote a little heavier than usual, so Paige stopped to rest in the cute little park with the benches, lilacs and wild roses. And rather than think about whether or not Hailey's comments about sexual tension were exaggerated but grounded in truth, she pulled a paperback out of the bag and settled in to read for a few minutes.

M ITCH WEDGED THE pickup into a parking space on Main Street and went around to help Josh out. His brother didn't like having to accept a shoulder to lean on, but it was a long way to the ground for a guy with a bum leg.

Once Josh had his crutches tucked into his armpits, they walked thirty or so feet down the sidewalk and Mitch held open the door to the Whitford Barbershop.

It wasn't a fancy name, but it wasn't a fancy place. There were a few salons in Whitford now—places you could get a haircut and your nails buffed and your body tanned if you so desired. Maybe get a little dermabrasion, which sounded to Mitch like taking a sandblaster to your skin. He avoided salons, as a rule.

This was a barbershop. A shave and a haircut and, if she was in the mood, you could talk to Katie Davis about almost anything under the sun. But she wasn't touching anybody's naked feet and if you asked her about tanning, she'd tell you to go lie out on the sidewalk and roll over every fifteen minutes.

"You really look like crap," she said in greeting, and Mitch was glad she was talking to Josh.

"Can't wash my hair in the bathtub. I wash it in the kitchen sink, but it's awkward because I'm tall and can only put my weight on the one leg." He took his hat off as he spoke, revealing the mess that had inspired Mitch to talk him into a trip into town.

"In the wash chair," she said, snapping open a clean cape. After Josh settled into the chair, she handed Mitch the crutches, draped the cape over Josh and turned on the water. "Lean back."

Mitch grabbed a tattered snowmobiling magazine

from 2008 out of one of the chairs and sat down, but he glanced over at the wash chair as Katie worked up a thick lather of shampoo in his brother's hair. Josh made a low moaning sound in his throat, and Mitch watched as heat in the form of a rosy blush crept up Katie's neck. Interesting.

And not his business. He'd always thought of Katie as an almost-sister. Rose had started working at the Northern Star the year Katie was born because his mom didn't mind if she brought the baby along in a sling. She'd practically grown up at the lodge with them.

But it didn't look as though she thought of Josh as an almost-brother, that was for sure. And he didn't want to know any more about it, so he stood and tossed the magazine back on the chair. "Looks like you're going to be a while."

Katie snorted. "I'm going to wash his hair twice, then give him a good trim. I'll give him a nice hot towel shave, too, and maybe he'll look human again."

"I'm going to take a walk, then. If I'm not back when you're done, text me."

She nodded and Josh ignored him, so he stepped out into the sunshine and debated on a destination. He could walk down to the Whitford General Store & Service Station to say hi to Fran and Butch Benoit. Or he could walk to the bank and transfer some funds into the Northern Star Lodge's account. Maybe take some of the weight off Josh's shoulders.

He hadn't built a successful business, though, by throwing good money after bad. If the lodge was really in trouble and it wasn't going to be able to support itself in the long run, a monetary transfusion was a temporary fix. They needed a plan, and then they could work out how to pay for it.

Aimlessly walking down the sidewalk to avoid standing in one spot like an idiot, Mitch let his mind wander to the Northern Star. And to Josh. He'd changed since the last time Mitch had seen him, and not in a good way. And, while a broken leg wasn't exactly fun, the change in his mood and general outlook on life went deeper than that. More important than helping out while Josh healed and figuring out the lodge's finances was figuring out why his brother was turning bitter.

When he got to the town park—the small one tucked in next to the hardware store, not the big one with the playground equipment and bandstand—he spotted Paige Sullivan sitting on a bench, and he pushed Josh to the back of his mind temporarily.

She was sitting sideways, with her feet tucked under her and one arm hooked over the back of the bench. In the other hand was a paperback, and she didn't look up until he sat down next to her. "Mind if I join you?"

When she almost dropped her book, he felt guilty for startling her, but then she smiled. After marking her page with her library card, she tucked the book into a canvas bag on the ground next to her. It had the Whitford Public Library logo on the front and appeared to be straining at the seams.

"I only meant to sit here a minute, but it's so nice out and I pulled out a book." She looked at her watch. "And there goes an hour."

"There are worse ways to spend an hour. Did you leave any books for the rest of us?"

She laughed. "I don't have cable, so I read while everybody else is watching TV."

"I don't read as much as I'd like to. There are a few thriller writers I like, so I download their books to my phone and sneak pages when I can."

"My cell phone makes calls and that's it. I have to have internet for the diner and, since I spend most of my life there, I don't need to carry it around with me."

He leaned back against the bench, turning his face up to the sun. He didn't get to sit and do nothing very often. It felt good. "Tell me how you ended up in Whitford. It's not exactly a hot destination."

"I already told you. Was driving through and my car broke down and I never left."

"There's more to it than that."

She shrugged. "Not really."

"You didn't already have a home and a job or any other reason to go back to where you were before the car died?"

"I had a crappy job and a crappy apartment. Obviously my car wasn't all that hot, either."

He turned his head to look at her, intrigued by her vague answers rather than put off by them. "Most people love to talk about themselves, you know."

"Go for it."

He grinned and shook his head. "I don't think so. I want to hear *your* story. I already know mine."

"We *all* know yours," she said pointedly, making him snort. Wasn't that the truth? "I was living in Vermont, but I was notified I'd been left some money in a will. They had the check but the man's wife really wanted to meet me, so I drove to Portland."

The man's wife? "How did you know this guy?"

"Not *that* way. He was my stepfather for a while, when I was little. I barely remember him, but his wife said he talked about me a lot. I guess he tried to keep in touch with me, but my mother made it difficult and eventually he gave up and had a family of his own. She said he worried about me a lot, though, over the years."

She looked sad, as though she was sorry to have missed out on somebody caring enough about her to worry. "So he left you some money?"

"Yeah. They had kids of their own, but he did some software thing and they were pretty well-off. So I was driving back, trying to imagine how my life would have been different if my mother hadn't run off on Joel and what it would have been like to be his and raised in one place like his kids, when my car broke down."

"And you used the money he left you to buy the diner?"

She nodded. "Katie happened to drive by right after I broke down. Total stranger, but she gave me a ride into town. Butch took care of my car. Fran called Rose, and then Josh drove down and picked me up. Said I could have a room at the Northern Star until my car was fixed. And then Mallory showed up the next day because she'd heard about me and didn't want me stuck at the lodge with no way to do errands. Before my car was fixed I knew I wanted Whitford to be my home."

He looked back up at the sky. "Funny, all that adds up to the main reason I stay away so much."

"It's a great town."

"You wouldn't think it was so great if everybody remembered and talked about everything you'd ever done wrong in your life."

"At least you've always had a place to call home. It took me a while, but Whitford is that place for me now."

He didn't call anyplace home for long. Hometown, yes. But home, no, and he liked it that way. "Where are you from? You don't sound like you've always lived in Vermont, but I can't quite pin down your accent."

"That's because I don't have *an* accent. I have a whole smashup of accents. I was born in Nevada, but we left there before I was a year old and we were never in one place long. My mother's a bit nomadic, I guess."

"You keep calling her 'my mother.' Never Mom or Ma."

"I guess I call her Mom when I talk to her. Her name's Donna, but I can't quite bring myself to use it."

"Not close?"

"We're…not *not* close. But she's always been more wrapped up in her own life, so I don't hear from her a lot."

Mitch liked to think if his mom was still alive, he'd talk to her as often as he could. As it was, he never went more than a few weeks without talking to Rosie or his aunt Mary on the phone.

His cell phone chimed and he checked it to find a text from Josh. *Done.*

He didn't want his brother to be done. He wanted to sit in the sunshine with Paige and get her to tell him more about her. Like why she didn't date, as far as the good citizens of Whitford could see. And they saw pretty much everything.

"I have to go," he said reluctantly. "I left Josh at the

barbershop, and Katie's either done with him or she gave up and threw him out."

"He was looking a little ragged around the edges when you brought him in for breakfast yesterday."

"Definitely overdue for a trim." He stood. "I'll see you later."

"Enjoy the weather."

He was halfway across the park when he turned back—intending to ask her if she wanted to do something, like maybe take a ride on the bike with him—but Paige already had her nose buried back in her book. She wasn't even watching him walk away, which didn't bode well for her wanting to spend a little alone time with him after dark.

He walked back to the barbershop, wondering who else around town he could spend a little time with during his not-quite-a-vacation. But nobody on his mental list really piqued his interest. Nobody but Paige Sullivan.

THE NICE THING about living in a mobile home not much bigger than two pickup trucks parked bumper-to-bumper was the fact it didn't take long to clean. The previous owner had updated the bathroom, and Paige had replaced the linoleum and carpet before she moved in. She loved being barefooted too much to walk on flooring as old as she was.

The kitchen and the bedroom were a little on the shabby side, but every month she tried to set aside enough money to make a small improvement. This month it was replacing the ancient lauan closet door in her bedroom with a white louver bifold that brightened up that corner of the room.

She opened and closed it a few times, proud of how well it came out and how smoothly it moved in the runner, and then she flipped on the vacuum to clean up the small mess she'd made. The old door was already outside, leaned up against the skirting, and she'd have to remember to ask Carl if he'd mind throwing it in his truck and disposing of it after his next shift.

The comforting drone of the vacuum lulled her mind into roaming free and she wasn't surprised when it roamed right to Mitch Kowalski. She'd been thinking about him almost constantly since he'd sat down next to her on the park bench yesterday.

Mostly she wondered if he was just being nice or if he was actually interested in her. And then, no matter how hard she tried not to, she'd imagine what it would have been like if he'd put his arm around her and kissed her right there in the park in the broad daylight.

That definitely would have given the town something to talk about. Not that they needed much prodding to talk about Mitch, but Paige had never done anything— besides reopening the diner—that put her on the gossip hot sheet.

From what she'd heard, Mitch had an apartment in New York City, but he rarely stayed there. He traveled from job to job, either staying in hotels or renting a furnished apartment if he'd be there a few months.

That probably explained how he'd avoided any heavy relationships so far. He wasn't in one place long enough for things to get serious. Sort of like her mother, except

Donna Sullivan was usually running toward what she thought would be love and not away from it.

She wondered how it worked for Mitch. Did he stay on the run so love couldn't catch him? Or was love simply unable to pin him down? It was like a chicken-versus-the-egg question for his love life.

Laughing at herself, Paige yanked the cord out of the wall and wound it around the vacuum. Maybe he traveled because his job demanded it. Period. And she had better things to do than ponder the state of Mitch Kowalski's love life.

Her cell phone vibrated in her pocket and she rolled her eyes when she saw the name on the caller ID screen. "Hi, Mom."

"Hi, honey. How are you?"

"Good. How about you?"

Wait for it... "I've been better."

And, as expected, her mother launched into a litany of complaints revealing her growing doubt about her current relationship. Corey was five years younger than Donna, a fact which had thrilled her mom at first, but was quickly becoming a source of insecurity. "I swear, he would have forgotten the anniversary of our first date if I hadn't put it on Facebook."

Paige put her phone on speakerphone and very quietly spread some work out on the table in front of her, careful to make sympathetic noises at the appropriate times. Pulling what she thought of as the "Gavin's Specials" tally sheet out of the pile, she scanned through the numbers.

Gavin Crenshaw was young, but he loved to cook and he was good at it, so he was working at the diner until he could save enough money to move to Portland or Boston and start moving up the culinary ladder. In the meantime, Paige let him try out recipes on her customers, as long as the ingredients weren't too expensive, and Ava made slash marks on a sheet of paper by the register whenever somebody ordered one of the Gavin's specials.

Whitford hadn't embraced the eggplant parmesan. Judging by the tally marks, most of Whitford hadn't even *tried* the dish. The roast beef melt on grilled garlic bread, though, had been such a hit Ava had kept a separate tally for the number of customers who asked that it be added to the regular menu. Paige made a note to have Gavin offer it a few more times and, if the interest stayed high, she'd consider it.

"Last night he just rolled over and went to sleep. I snuggled up against him, but he started snoring before I got any further."

"He was probably just tired, Mom," Paige said. It had been a few minutes since she made a sympathetic noise, plus she wanted to waylay any descriptions of "any further." "He's five years younger than you, but he's not nineteen, either."

But that explanation wasn't the sympathy Donna was looking for, so the complaints marched on. Paige put a red X next to a couple of items and made a note to remind Gavin their fellow citizens weren't fans of gussied-up vegetables. They liked a side of green beans. Corn was okay. Caramelized anything wasn't a crowd favorite.

Another ten minutes went by before her mother

wrapped it up. "Oh, he's pulling in the driveway now. Gotta run. Love you!"

Paige hit End with a shake of her head. "Nice talking to you, too, Mom. I'm doing fine. Business is great, thanks for asking. And there's a really hot guy in town I'm not having sex with because I don't want to end up like you."

She tried not to take it personally. She loved her mother and she knew her mother loved her, too, but she'd long ago given up on being the most important person in Donna Sullivan's life. It was just the way her mother was wired and she was never going to change.

As emotionally unsatisfying as the call was, it had come at a perfect time to serve as a reminder of why Paige had a *no men* rule. She had better things to worry about than a guy forgetting the anniversary of their first date or rolling over and going to sleep.

Or whether or not one had thought about kissing her on a park bench in the sunlight.

CHAPTER FOUR

PAIGE LOVED WHITFORD'S Old Home Day celebration. A little bit of the love came from the diner not opening until noon, allowing her to sleep in until a very decadent seven o'clock. Mostly, though, she loved the strong community bond she felt while honoring her adopted hometown.

It was already warm, so she slipped on a red sundress with a snug bodice that flared into a flowing skirt. Besides being cool, it also made her boobs look great. Not that she was showing off for anybody, but she lived most of her life in Trailside Diner T-shirts and it was nice to look pretty and feminine every once in a while. As a nod to the humidity, she pulled her hair into a ponytail and skipped any makeup but a quick swipe of lip gloss.

Though sleeping in was a refreshing change, the diner being closed meant toast with jelly for breakfast, but she didn't mind. That left more room for the fried dough only available in Whitford on Old Home Day, and the incredible baked goods the PTA would be selling. If she was lucky, somebody forgot to hire the Italian sausage vendor this year, because she blamed him for her jeans being too tight for an entire week after last year's celebration.

At a little after nine, she walked down to the library

to meet Hailey. The parade didn't start until ten, but the base of the statue commemorating the founding donor of the library offered a great view and somebody would steal the spot if they didn't get there early. It didn't matter that Hailey was the librarian, either. People would shush if she shushed them, but they weren't giving up prime parade-viewing real estate.

Hailey was already waiting when she climbed the small, grassy hill, and she grinned when Paige sat on the cement slab next to her. "You look like a sexy pinup girl in that dress."

"I was going for not hot and sweaty, but sexy pinup girl works."

"From the ankles up, anyway."

Paige looked down at her worn, comfy flip-flops and wiggled her toes. "Damn. I was really hoping to snag a guy with a foot fetish today."

"There are other parts of my body I'd rather a guy be obsessed with."

"I don't know. Free foot massages. Maybe pedicures if he's got a steady hand."

Hailey smirked. "I wonder how Mitch feels about feet."

And curse the pretty sundress for doing nothing to hide the warm flush creeping over Paige's skin. "You mean the entire town doesn't already know if he has a foot fetish?"

Hailey actually looked as if she was giving the question serious consideration. "I don't think I've ever heard any stories about him and feet."

"Doesn't matter, anyway. I have no interest in Mitch Kowalski's interests."

"Aw, but you looked so cute sitting in the park to-gether the other day." Paige gave her a *you have got to be kidding me* look. She smiled. "Or so I heard. From about twenty different people."

"I was reading. He was waiting for Josh to get his hair cut. We talked for a few minutes, then he left. No big deal." Well, her imagination thought it was a big deal, especially when she was supposed to be sleeping, but she didn't think anybody else would.

"Mmm-hmm."

"Besides, he's off-limits. You had a relationship with him and you're my friend, so therefore I can't have a relationship with him." Plus there was that whole ab-staining thing, but their friendship was a handy excuse.

Hailey laughed. "We did *not* have a relationship. We were young and stupid and bored, so we got drunk and had sex in the backseat. And that was a very long time ago. So long ago drinking wine coolers was the cool thing to do."

"But still—"

"But still nothing. Trust me when I tell you there was no emotional involvement at all, for either of us, and you are clear to land, honey."

"My runway's closed." Paige frowned, then shook her head. "I'm butchering this whole airplane thing. I can't be the plane *and* the runway."

"Let me make it easy. He'll be the plane. You be the hangar."

"For a guy who's parked his plane all over town? He can taxi on down to another hangar."

Hailey laughed. "You're right. You do suck at the air-plane thing. But I don't think he's quite as free with his plane parking as legend makes him out to be, you know. I've lived my whole life here, and a lot of those stories are the equivalent of my uncle's fish stories. They just want everybody to think they landed the big one."

"I can't do planes *and* fish. You've gotta pick one."

"Reel him in, keep him a few weeks, then throw him back and let him swim away."

"You're killing me with metaphors."

"Bang the guy, Paige. Have hot, sweaty sex until you think you'll never walk again, then kick him to the curb."

It sounded good in theory—hell, it sounded *great* in theory—but Paige couldn't take the chance. All she needed was to fall for a guy like Mitch and lose everything she'd gained because she was busy chasing a guy who didn't want to be caught. She'd done it before, though she'd made the decision to change her life before it got to be a habit, as it was for her mother.

In an effort to distract Hailey, Paige changed the subject to the impending library fundraiser and it worked. Time ticked away as they talked about budgets and used book sales and the pressure the Whitford library was under to ramp up the development of their digital collection, until it was almost time for the parade.

Paige was startled when Hailey put her arm around her shoulders and pulled her close, pointing with her free hand. "Tell me again you're not interested."

She looked across the street to where Hailey was pointing and sighed. Of course Mitch had to pick a spot directly across from theirs to watch the parade from. No doubt it was the bench that had drawn them, since a couple of teenagers gave it up so Josh could sit there, but still. Did he have to be directly in her line of sight like that?

Mitch was wearing what looked like a ragged T-shirt from his high school days—probably in honor of the occasion—and cargo shorts that drew her attention to his legs. She couldn't really say she'd ever really paid attention to a guy's legs before, but she liked the look of his. He sat on the bench next to his brother without taking his eyes off his phone. Paige hoped whatever had his attention, kept it. Maybe he wouldn't even notice her in the crowd.

"If Mitch catches you looking at him like that, he might do a kamikaze dive into your hangar right here in front of everybody."

Paige laughed and shoved Hailey away. "Will you quit with the planes? Let's talk about something else. Have you seen the fried dough vendor yet? I want to be first in line when the parade's over."

If she was going to surrender to something bad for her, better junk food than a man.

"ARE YOU GOING to play with that thing all day?"

Mitch scowled at his touch screen. "I'm not playing. We're doing prelim work on a drop in Miami, and Scott's supposed to double-check the calculations on the dust cloud radius. There's a school and a health clinic close and if we need HVAC crews to cover their intakes and shit, that's gotta be factored into the bid."

"Did you tell Scott to do it?"

"Yes."

"Then he probably did it. Watch the parade."

"The parade hasn't started yet. And I sent him a re-minder email yesterday and I haven't gotten a response."

"He's probably sending your emails to his spam folder because you won't leave him alone long enough to do his job," Josh said, and Mitch was about five seconds from shoving his brother off the end of the bench, cast or no cast. Instead he ignored him. "Paige looks hot as hell today."

Mitch looked up, half-written text message forgotten, and scanned the area. It didn't take him long to find her. In that red dress she looked like one of those women from that story he'd hated in English class—the women who lured men to their doom.

She was sitting on the base of the library statue with Hailey and they were laughing. Hailey was an attractive woman, but there was something about Paige that drew his eye and held it.

"Doesn't she?" Josh said twice, and Mitch realized he was talking to him.

"What?"

"Doesn't she look hot?"

"Yeah." She did, and before the day was over, he in-tended to tell her that himself.

The crowd stirred with excitement as the police de-partment's new SUV came into sight at the end of the street, blue lights flashing. Drew hit the siren and let it wail for a few seconds, signaling the beginning of the parade.

Mitch figured they had a few minutes before it got to them, so he bent his head over his phone to fin-ish the text to Scott. The growling sound and flash of movement in his peripheral vision gave him just enough warning to evade Josh's grab for the phone. "What the hell?"

"Put the damn phone away or I'll throw it in front of the fire truck."

"You touch my phone and I'll throw *you* in front of the fire truck." Since he was done anyway, he tucked it into the cargo pocket of his shorts. "A quick text isn't going to ruin the day."

"But he'll text you back and then you'll have to respond and then you'll check your email and next thing you know, you're wandering around looking for a quiet spot to make phone calls."

Mitch snorted because he had to wait for the ambulance horn to stop sounding before he could speak. "I couldn't make a phone call right now if my business depended on it."

Hopefully, it didn't. There was a lot on Northern Star Demolition's plate, but he had to trust the people he'd hired to do their jobs. This trip home to make sure Josh didn't injure himself worse by doing too much was supposed to be doubling as his first vacation, but he wasn't very good at it.

But work matters got slowly pushed to the back of his mind as the town's rescue vehicles went by, followed by the Little League teams riding on floats advertising their sponsors. Butch Benoit's wrecker was decked out in twinkling lights, though it was the candy Fran was tossing to the crowd that made the kids shout and wave. There were a bunch of little girls from dance class twirling in fluffy skirts, and a line of antique tractors.

And a pretty blonde in a red sundress he caught watching him a few times. She'd look away if he caught her eye, but her gaze was there to be caught too many times to be incidental. Even Burt Franks's blue-ribbon-winning pulling horses couldn't steal his attention away from Paige for more than a few seconds.

"Poor Burt," Josh muttered.

"What's the matter with Burt?"

"He's so proud of those Percheron and nobody's paying any attention to them. Everybody's watching you watch Paige look like she's trying not to watch you."

Mitch glanced around and, sure enough, a whole lot of people jerked their eyes back to the horses. Whatever. He was used to these people being way too interested in what he was doing.

When the fire department's big ladder truck went by, signaling the parade was over and people were free to pour into the street, Mitch kept track of the red sundress as the women walked down the hill and into the crowd. Paige looked like a woman on a mission, and he had to walk fast to set an intercept course.

"Don't mind me," he heard Josh shout from somewhere behind him. "I'll just hobble along and hope nobody kicks my crutches out from under me."

Just a few more milling-around people to dodge and Mitch was able to put himself in Paige's path. She stopped short when she saw him. "Hi, Mitch. Enjoy the parade?"

"Not as much as I'm enjoying that dress. You look like every woman in a country song."

She tilted her head, lips curving into a smile. "So I took your dog and your truck and left you crying in your beer?"

"Not that kind of country song. More along the lines

of taking you for a ride on my tractor down to the creek for a little dip."

"Do you have a tractor?"

He had to think about that for a few seconds, but it was the creek he wasn't sure about. He'd dig a trench and fill it with the garden hose if that's what it took. "The lodge does and I think it even runs. Wanna go for a ride later?"

Despite the blush creeping up out of the neckline of the sundress, her smile was annoyingly polite. "I think I'll pass. And I'm going to get some fried dough, so I'll see you around."

She wasn't more than ten feet away when he heard his little brother snicker behind him. "A tractor ride? And we don't have any creeks deep enough for skinny-dipping, dumb ass."

"Shut up." Since they were surrounded by people who had nothing better to do than eavesdrop on their conversation, he made a big show of shrugging it off. "Plenty of women to wade in the creek with."

"I'd rather find a woman selling food. Where the hell is the bake-sale booth?"

Mitch stood on his toes, trying to see over the crowd. He felt kind of bad about abandoning Josh in his pursuit of Paige, so he put her out of his head and turned his attention to finding them some food.

BEING BUSY AT the diner helped keep Paige's mind off Mitch's surprising invitation to ride his tractor, despite it being one of the more interesting propositions she'd heard in her life. Sitting on his lap, bumping across a field, was a visual to savor later.

Ava was working her regular shift, so Paige wasn't technically on the clock. But the Whitford Historical Society was selling reusable drink bottles emblazoned with their logo to raise repair money for the Grange Hall, and the Trailside Diner was offering free water or lemonade refills to anybody who bought the bottles. It was a hot day and a lot of families were taking advantage of the offer.

Thankful she'd worn her flip-flops with the sundress rather than dressy sandals that would be killing her feet right about then, Paige refilled bottles and gave Ava a hand keeping up with the families trying to get a real lunch into their kids before they went nuts on the food vendors lining the main street.

When the initial rush was over, Ava helped herself to a glass of the premixed lemonade Paige had stocked up on for the event and leaned against the counter. "So tractors aren't really your thing?"

She wasn't surprised talk of her turning Mitch down was already spreading. "Or maybe Mitch Kowalski isn't my thing."

"Honey, those Kowalski boys are every young woman's thing."

"He certainly seems to think so."

"Wouldn't hurt you any to take a ride on the boy's tractor."

Paige laughed and shook her head. "Riding on tractors with boys isn't on my list of things to do anytime soon."

And Ava knew why, since she was one of the few people Paige confided in. More than once, she'd caught herself wishing Ava was her mother, but she tried not to think it too often. Part of making her home here was letting go of her old life and embracing the new. Resenting the choices her mom had made didn't do anybody any good.

The bell jangled before Ava could say anything else about Mitch, and Paige was thankful for that since it was him walking through the door. As her body starting zinging and pinging and slightly overheating all over again, she did her best to look as if she couldn't care less.

"It's nice and cool in here," he said, taking a seat at the counter. "Good place to sit and have a cheeseburger."

"Did you lose Josh?" He was supposed to be taking care of his brother, which he couldn't do while sitting at her counter.

"He overdid it, standing in line for cotton candy, so I took him home."

"You didn't stand in line for him?"

"Hey, I offered. He can be pretty stubborn."

Probably a family trait. "You want fries with your burger?"

"Absolutely."

Ava scratched his order down on her pad and went off to hand it to the kitchen, leaving Paige with no reason not to be standing there talking to Mitch. The way he looked at her made her self-conscious about the dress, and she wished she'd thrown a T-shirt over it before offering to help Ava.

"Did you get your fried dough?" he asked.

The reference to their earlier meeting made her

blush. "Yes. And I went back again later for a second, even though I shouldn't have."

"Old Home Day only comes once a year. It's no fun if you don't throw willpower to the wind and gorge on carnival food."

She may have gone back for seconds on the fried dough, but Mitch was the danger to her willpower. If she was going to ride any guy's tractor or land his plane or play catch-and-release, it would be with him. And that was a good reason to excuse herself.

"You've got everything under control," she said to Ava. "I was thinking about getting some hanging baskets from the garden club this year."

"Go and have some fun before things wind down too much."

She smiled and waved to Mitch as she left, and he lifted a hand in response. He didn't smile, though, which amused her. Didn't seem that he knew how to take rejection very well, but he'd have to get used to it.

With a sigh, Paige set off down the street. A third fried dough was out of the question, but maybe she could find some kind of decadent treat to pacify herself with. Her body might not think cotton candy or a caramel apple was a good substitute for a man like Mitch, but that was all it was getting anytime soon.

CHAPTER FIVE

MITCH NEEDED TO get back to work. Desperately. At Northern Star Demolition, if people didn't do what they were told, he could fire them. His employees listened to him. Family didn't listen for shit, especially Ryan. Granted, Mitch wasn't paying him, but the lodge needed a carpenter and his brother was a damn carpenter.

"I'm running a business here, Mitch," Ryan said, his annoyance coming through loud and clear over the telephone. "I can't just take off because you think the front steps are a little rickety."

Mitch tipped his head back on the couch so he could stare at the ceiling, not that he'd find what he was looking for there—which was patience with his brother—but it beat banging his head against the coffee table. "I run a business, too, Ryan. But I'm here. And the problems here go a lot deeper than rickety steps. The place is going to hell."

"Then hire somebody to do the work. Somebody who doesn't charge what I get."

"There's not a lot of money left to play with here, and us writing a check to the lodge to cover it won't solve anything in the long run. We need to get together and fix the place up and decide how we're going to keep it in the black. You can spare a couple of long week-ends, at least."

"I'll try."

That might have been fine if Mitch believed him, but he'd worked with enough building contractors to know he was being blown off. "Josh needs help. You remember him? Our youngest brother. The one that's been running the place with only Rosie to help him?"

"Sounds like he's been doing a piss-poor job of it, too."

That's just what Mitch needed. Another brother with a shitty attitude. What fun it would be to have both of them under the same roof. But the building needed some repair and Ryan was a goddamned builder, so Mitch was going to make him show up, even if he had to go to Massachusetts and drag his ass up there by force. Just on principle.

"I'll come up Friday night," Ryan said after the silence dragged on. "I'll look the place over on Saturday and we can figure out what needs to be done, and then I'll hit the road early Sunday morning. If the place is going to need more than a couple weekends' worth of work, I'll have to adjust my schedule and talk to the guys running my jobs. But I'll at least look at it over the weekend."

"I appreciate it," Mitch said sincerely. "And so will Josh, though he probably won't tell you so."

"Tell Rosie I'm coming." Which was code for telling Rosie that Ryan would be looking for shepherd's pie and at least two loaves of her banana bread.

"See you Friday. And if it's dark when you get here,

be careful on the stairs. Second step up's ready to give out."

Once he'd closed his phone and tossed it on the cushion next to him, Mitch shut his eyes. And thought about Paige. Not deliberately, but she was the first thing that popped into his head and his focus went all to hell. There were about a dozen other things he needed to be doing right that minute, but none of them appealed to him as much as remembering how Paige had looked in the sunlight, sitting on the park bench.

She'd looked hot as hell in the red sundress yesterday, too, but for some reason the image of her lost in a book, with the sun making her hair shine, was the picture that sprang to mind when he thought her name.

If he hadn't known she had a history of not looking for a good time, he might have slid a little closer to her on the bench. Maybe put his arm around her. Before he got up, he would have kissed her and gotten a promise she'd see him again later. Dinner, maybe a movie, and then he'd spend the night in her bed.

But Paige might have a good reason for not dating, and he wanted to know more about that reason before he treaded somewhere he shouldn't.

"You sleeping?"

Mitch opened his eyes and smiled at Rose, who was standing in the doorway. "Just resting my eyes."

"My husband used to say that, just before he started snoring. I made you a couple of fried bologna sandwiches for lunch. Come eat them before the bread gets soggy."

"Where's Josh?" he asked as he followed her into the kitchen.

"He's resting his eyes, too. Fell asleep in a lounge chair in the backyard and, since he hasn't been sleeping too well at night, I'll leave him be."

"Ryan'll be up Friday night. Just for the weekend, to scope things out."

"Guess I'd better make sure I've got the stuff for shepherd's pie."

"Don't forget the banana bread." Mitch sat at the table and sank his teeth into a triangle of fried bologna sandwich that was oozing mayo and juices from the thick slabs of tomatoes. He moaned and devoured a second bite before speaking. "Nobody makes sandwiches like this anymore, Rosie. I miss them when I'm gone."

"Just one of the many reasons you need a wife. One who can make a decent fried bologna sandwich."

Mitch almost choked on his third bite. "A wife is the *last* thing I need."

Rose shook her head, sitting across from him with a sandwich of her own. "I don't know where we went wrong with you kids."

"What do you mean? Ryan got married. Liz has been with that meathead, Darren, for years. And Sean's married now."

"Ryan also got divorced and, as you so delicately pointed out, Liz is with a man we don't like. Since you boys weren't very good at hiding your feelings, we rarely get to see her. And Sean may be happily married now, but one out of five isn't exactly a winning record."

"Didn't realize it was a sport," he mumbled around a mouthful of sandwich.

"Don't you get lonely?"

"Not really. I hate to break it to you, Mrs. Cleaver, but not being married doesn't mean I'm a monk."

"Don't be a smart-ass. What about kids? How are you going to start a family if you can't settle on one woman?"

In an unexpected—and unwelcome—flash, Paige Sullivan's face popped into his head. Since he wasn't looking for one woman to settle down with, he assumed his subconscious went for the one woman whose home base he most wanted to slide into.

"My job doesn't really mesh well with settling down," he said. "I have to travel a lot. And not just a few days or a weekend here and there. I'm talking about weeks at a time."

"You'll make it work for the right woman."

"Guess I haven't found her yet."

He thought he had once. Pam had not only seemed like Ms. Right, but she'd come pretty damn close to being Mrs. Mitchell Kowalski. Smart, funny and sexy as hell, she'd pushed past his habit of avoiding commitment, and it was only a few months before she moved in and started turning his apartment into a home.

Unfortunately, home was mostly a place he visited between jobs, and Pam really ramped up the nagging about him being gone all the time once he put a diamond on her finger. It had been a pivotal time in building Northern Star Demolition, and he'd kept telling her he'd eventually be able to travel less. Instead, *eventually,* she'd let another man keep his side of the bed warm and, when Mitch found out, gave him an ultimatum. Her, or his work. Even if he hadn't had contracts to honor and people depending on him for their paychecks, he wasn't giving up his business, so that had been the end of that.

Since Pam, he'd gone back to doing things the way that had always gotten him the physical pleasure without the emotional pain—letting the ladies know right up front he wasn't sticking around. A few laughs, a few orgasms and they were smiling when he kissed them goodbye.

"When you do find the right woman," Rosie said, "bring her by and I'll teach her how to make fried bologna sandwiches the way you like them."

"It's a deal," he told her, just to end the discussion.

He wasn't going to find the right woman anytime soon because of the simple fact he wasn't even looking.

PAIGE USUALLY USED the quiet time between breakfast and lunch to restock condiments and help clean up out back, as well as to recover from feigning indifference to Mitch, who seemed to be making breakfast at the diner a habit. Today, however, she was playing bartender. Not because she was serving booze—not having a liquor license took care of that issue—but because she was listening to Mallory Miller's woes.

The chief's wife worked for a law office in the city so, with the long commute, Paige rarely saw her during the week, especially on a non-holiday Monday. Mal said she'd called in sick—as in sick of her crappy life, though she hadn't told them that. And Paige poured them each a cup of coffee and offered a shoulder to cry on.

It wasn't until Carl hollered out he was going on break that Mal really got into what was bothering her, most of which Paige already knew. Drew wanted children, Mallory didn't, and they weren't speaking to each other. And hadn't been for a while.

"I think I should be enough for Drew," Mal said. "That our life together should be enough. Why do the last ten years become irrelevant and worth throwing away if we don't have kids?"

Paige, who'd been leaning against the counter, topped off their coffees and set the carafe back on the burner in a hopefully-not-too-obvious bid for more time to think. She was supposed to be listening, not being put on the spot. What the hell did she know about marriage? Not much. "Did you ask *him* that?"

"I'm not asking him anything."

"You do realize you can't fix anything if you won't talk to each other, right?"

Mal shrugged. "I said everything I had to say on the matter. I don't want to be a mother."

That's where it got hazy for Paige. It wasn't a decision Mal had suddenly come to and sprung on the police chief. She'd known all along she didn't want to have kids but had let him believe she did rather than risk losing him. The entire marriage had been built on false advertising, and Drew hadn't known it. But Mal had a point, too. They'd had ten good years of marriage. Did not having children really erase that?

"I thought I'd grow into it," Mal told her. "The idea of having kids, I mean. I thought I'd get used to being married and eventually feel the urge to be a mother and Drew would never know how I'd felt. But the urge never came."

"But you can understand why Drew's upset, right?"

Mal's lips tightened. "I understand being upset. But

throwing our marriage away? I should be as important to him as children that are nothing but hypothetical, don't you think?"

"I'd like to think so," Paige said, being honest without definitively taking sides—the key to peaceful business ownership in a small town.

The bell over the door jingled, and Paige stifled a sigh of relief. Mal wasn't going to air her dirty marital laundry if there were other customers in the place. But she'd been relieved too soon. It was Katie Davis, which meant the conversation would continue. But at least, if she could manufacture some busywork, Paige wouldn't have to be a part of it.

She liked Mallory Miller. Over the last two years, they'd grown closer than acquaintances, though most of their interaction was at the diner or as part of a group, usually with Hailey and Katie or at movie night. But if anybody asked, Paige would call her a friend.

She liked Drew too, though, and their marital problems weren't really a black-and-white issue. If Drew had cheated—or Mallory, for that matter—it would be easy to take sides. In this particular case, however, Paige wasn't sure what to say.

And she still had high hopes Drew and Mal would reconcile and, if that happened, she didn't want to be the bad guy who'd tried to talk her out of it.

"What are we talking about?" Katie asked once she'd pulled up a counter seat and Paige had made her a large vanilla Coke.

"How much men suck," Mal told her.

Katie snorted. "I don't have that much time."

Paige still hadn't figured out what the deal was with

Katie. She didn't date any more than Paige did, but she wasn't "news." The pretty blonde had a healthy number of male friends and was generally considered *one of the guys*. So much so, in fact, Paige had heard some speculation as to whether Katie Davis even *liked* guys. Paige knew she did, and she also suspected Katie had already given her heart to somebody in particular and the guy hadn't figured it out yet. Katie, however, would neither confirm nor deny that theory.

"I think I'm going to move out," Mallory said, and something in the way she said it made Paige believe she'd just that second reached that conclusion.

"Make *him* do the moving," Katie said.

"If I move to the city, I won't have that long commute anymore. And he's the police chief, so he'll be staying here. It makes more sense for me to move than him." Tears began streaming down Mal's cheeks, and Paige took the coffee mug out of her trembling hands, setting it on the counter. "I can't believe it's over."

"I still think you should try counseling before you make a decision like that," Paige said quietly.

"Yeah, I want to tell a total stranger I've been lying to my husband for ten years. And then I can listen to Drew and the therapist tell me I'm a bad person and that everything would be okay if I have a baby."

Katie stopped sucking on her straw to shake her head. "I've never been, but I'm pretty sure marriage counseling doesn't work like that."

Paige had to agree, but she was trying to extricate herself from the conversation, not dig herself in deeper, so she kept that to herself. Then, thankfully, a few guys who worked for a local construction outfit walked through the door and she had an excuse to leave the counter.

It was a little depressing, honestly, to join in a *men suck* party. She didn't think they sucked, despite her current ban on becoming involved with one herself. Especially in this case, where she didn't think Drew had done anything wrong. He was understandably upset that his wife had been lying to him since before they'd even married.

But she'd seen women in Mal's situation before. One woman in particular. Paige's mother was the master of burying her own wants and needs to please a man. Donna Sullivan never worried about the future—if she'd eventually grow to hate herself or resent the man, or what would happen if the day came when she couldn't hide her true self and the man discovered she wasn't who he'd thought she was. All that mattered was that the man not leave her right then.

A few more people wandered in as she poured sodas for the construction guys, so she didn't get a chance to drop back into the conversation before Katie had to get back to the barbershop and Mallory went on with whatever came next in her non-sick day.

She kept busy until two, when Ava showed up. Ava was almost sixty, though she was fighting a valiant battle against the years with deep-chestnut hair dye and a variety of facial creams she bought from infomercials, but she loved waiting tables and she was good at it.

When given the choice as they'd prepared for the diner's grand reopening, Ava had chosen the two-to-closing shift. Her husband had died suddenly of a heart attack the year before and she'd said those hours—the after-work, dinner and evening-news hours—were the time she missed him the most, so she'd rather keep busy. Paige hadn't had a preference, so she was the one knocking her alarm clock across the nightstand at four-thirty every morning.

"Did Mitch come see you this morning?" Ava whispered to her when they passed each other at the pie case.

"No. Why would he?"

Ava winked. "Just wondering."

As she finished cleaning her tables so she could get the hell out of there, Paige mumbled under her breath. It would be a lot easier not to think about Mitch Kowalski and his killer smile and pretty eyes if people didn't talk about him all the damn time.

"I NEED A ride into town."

Mitch looked up from the ledger book he was stuck skimming through since his brother thought Excel was something you did in sports, and saw Josh standing in the office doorway, leaning on his crutches. He looked a lot better than he had the night Mitch arrived in town and his attitude had improved a little, but he was still sadly lacking in charm. And manners.

"Please," Josh added before Mitch could call him on it.

"You couldn't have thought of that before I went to the diner for breakfast?"

"I didn't know you were going, though I should have since you go every damn day. Will you give me a ride or not?"

"Sure." Mitch could see the muscles in Josh's jaw

flexing as he closed the ledger book and set it aside, but the tension was unavoidable.

It had to burn Josh's ass a little, watching big brother go over the books when he really didn't have anything to do with the lodge, but they were all equal owners and he had the right to do it. All he could do was be as cool as possible about it and make it clear he was just getting a feel for things so he could help, rather than checking up on the operation. So far it looked pretty simple. Reservations and income were down. He could see where Josh and Rosie had worked on getting the expenses down, too, and the lodge wasn't as bad off as he'd thought. By pinching every penny, they'd kept the ledger ink black, but it was close. There was no wiggle room for hiring a carpenter or a painter.

Or a tree service.

"Where we headed?" he asked, following Josh into the kitchen where the keys to the pickup hung behind the door.

"You need to stop at the market and pick up a few things," Rose called from the pantry.

"You got a list?"

"I called Fran with the list and it'll be waiting for you."

Josh rolled his eyes. "I lose the list one time and now it's like I'm twelve and can't be trusted to remember milk."

"You only lost the list once, but you lost it the day before Thanksgiving."

Mitch laughed and held the door open for Josh. "We'll be back, Rosie."

"Leave the market for last, or the half-and-half will

go bad while you two stand around yapping with people."

Josh had mastered the art of climbing into the pickup one-legged, so at least he was spared the indignity of a brotherly boost. Mitch tossed the crutches in the back and walked around to the driver's side. The truck cranked over hard and he swore under his breath, hoping they weren't going to add vehicular issues to their list of problems.

"You didn't tell me where we're headed," he reminded Josh.

"The hardware store. I need to drop off a check to Dozer to square up for last month. I was going to bring him a check right after I was done limbing that damn tree."

He'd gone to the emergency room instead. Mitch didn't bother asking him if he had enough in the account. Josh would be insulted, and if there was one thing Mitch knew after spending the day looking at the books, it was that his youngest brother might be stupid enough to foot a ladder in the back of a truck, but he was fiscally responsible.

"I haven't seen Paige Sullivan doing the walk of shame out the back door yet," Josh said, sounding a little smug.

"I prefer spending the night in *their* beds. Keeps them from lingering after breakfast."

"Unless you've gotten better at lowering yourself out of your window, you've been in your own bed every night."

Now he sounded smug *and* amused, and Mitch

snorted. "I've been a little busy, in case you haven't noticed."

"A little busy sitting at the counter watching Paige work. And everybody saw you swing and miss at Old Home Day. You're striking out with her, just like every other guy in Whitford."

"I'm just getting warmed up," he muttered.

Fortunately, a good song came on the radio and Josh cranked it up, so they rode the rest of the way into town singing along and playing the drums on various parts of the truck interior. Mitch pulled the truck up in front of Whitford Hardware and grabbed the crutches, while Josh slowly and carefully lowered himself out of the passenger's side.

An ancient brass bell jangled when Mitch pushed open the door, and Albert Dozynski—permanently dubbed Dozer by his new hometown when he'd bought the place in the seventies—looked up from the shelf of gardening supplies he was straightening.

"I heard you were back in town," he said as he pushed himself to his feet. He was a child when his family had immigrated to America, but his parents had only spoken Polish at home and he still had a trace of their accent. "How have you been?"

"I've been good." He shook the man's hand. "How's business?"

Dozer shrugged. "Slow, but I'm not going anywhere."

"Glad to hear it."

Josh pulled a checkbook out of his back pocket, and he and Dozer moved to the cash register to settle up, so Mitch wandered off to look around. The store was a treasure trove of hardware and miscellaneous anything and everything, begging to be explored. A person couldn't go into one of those big home-improvement warehouses and find a carburetor float set from a generator made in the early 1980s, but there was a good chance Dozer had one. He could dig up a nut for any bolt and a fitting for any pipe. And maybe his prices had to be a little higher than those big-box stores' prices, but at those places a woman had to carry her purchases to her car and you couldn't borrow a pipe bender or a blowtorch if you were only going to need it once.

"You lost?" he heard Josh call, and he abandoned the crate of old tractor parts he'd been digging through. He wasn't sure their old tractor even needed any parts, but you never knew what you'd find at the bottom of a box buried at the back of Whitford Hardware.

"You do me a favor," Dozer said as they headed toward the door. "If you see my grandson, you tell him he's supposed to be helping me move things around and clean up this week."

"Will do," Mitch said as he held the door open for his brother again.

If he remembered correctly, Nick, the AWOL grandson, would be about sixteen. Just the right age for blowing off helping out at Grandpa's store. Mitch knew the boy's mother a little because she'd married Ryan's best friend, but he hadn't seen Lauren Carpenter in years. He'd have to remember to ask Rose how she was doing. He scanned the area while Josh climbed into the truck and handed him the crutches, but he didn't see any kids who looked like they might be Nick Carpenter.

"You got any other errands to run while we're in town?" he asked Josh as he pulled away from the curb.

"I was thinking about stopping in to see Andy Miller."

Andy was Drew's dad. He'd been a good friend to their dad—one of his best friends—and he'd been around the lodge a lot when they were growing up. "How's he doing?"

"I heard he was asking around for work, and we could use some help."

"Ryan's going to come up."

"Eventually. And he'll be looking a the big picture and only be able to do so much. I was thinking more about all the little things I've let slide by. I don't really want to spend any more money than we have to, but the place is starting to not look like the pictures on the website, and that turns customers off."

Mitch thought it was probably a good idea, except for one thing. One really *big* thing. "What about Rosie?"

Rose Davis didn't speak to Andy Miller. Ever. Nobody knew why and, after almost three decades, nobody dared ask, but she didn't like the man. He couldn't imagine she'd be pleased to have him working around the Northern Star.

"She works for us," Josh said.

Mitch laughed so hard he almost drove off the road. "You keep telling yourself that, Josh."

"Screw you. Just head out to Andy's place."

"No problem. I'm looking forward to watching you try to run from Rosie on one leg."

CHAPTER SIX

ROSE SAW THE dishes in the sink the second she stepped into her kitchen and shook her head. Those would be Mitch's breakfast dishes, since she'd long since trained Josh to put his dishes in the damn dishwasher rather than leaving them for her to deal with.

It was good that Mitch had eaten at home, because maybe it meant he'd given up on Paige Sullivan, but it wasn't good that the corn flakes he'd left in the bowl had hardened into splotches of whole-grain concrete she'd have to chisel off the side of the bowl. She turned the faucet on, hoping some hot water would soften them up, and looked out the window to see if she could spot the offender.

She spotted an offender all right, but it wasn't Mitch. Andy Miller was standing in her backyard with a tool belt slung slow around his waist and a tattered Red Sox hat shading his eyes. The swoosh of anger through her veins was immediate and familiar. He wasn't welcome at the Northern Star Lodge, and he damned well knew it, too.

Dropping the bowl in the sink with a clatter, she turned off the faucet and dried her hands. She hadn't spoken to the man in twenty-six years, but she was going to break that silence and give him a piece of her mind. And then she was going to chase his sorry ass out of the yard, even if she had to use the tractor to do it.

Before she could get to the back door, it opened and Mitch stepped in, smiling when he saw her. But, as he closed the door, he must have seen she was unhappy, and his gaze flicked to the sink. "I meant to rinse that."

"To hell with your dirty dishes. What is that man doing in this house?" She'd almost said "my" house, but stopped herself just in time. The Northern Star Lodge belonged to the kids, no matter how long she'd been the head of the household.

"He's not in the house. Andy needs work and we need some help."

"There are plenty of people in this town who need work. You *know* how I feel about him."

"I know you don't like him and nobody knows why. I also know Andy Miller is not only my best friend's father, but was my dad's best friend. They were like brothers."

"He's no friend of mine," she said, folding her arms across her chest.

"I'm not paying him to play Scrabble or share knitting patterns with you. I'm paying him to work."

"I really don't want him here."

Mitch's jaw hardened, and the little boy she'd raised and was hoping to appeal to was lost behind the mask of a man who'd built his own business out of nothing. "Are you going to rebuild the front steps and paint the porch?"

She shook her head. "No, but Ryan could do the building, and all you need is a high school kid for the painting."

"Ryan's dragging his ass about coming up. It's done, Rose." Mitch started to walk away, then stopped. "You're one of the friendliest and most generous women I've ever known. Why do you hate Andy so much?"

"I have my reasons," she snapped, and then *she* walked away. Out of the kitchen and up the stairs and straight down the hall to her room, where she slammed the door like a teenager in a snit.

She was stuck. Mitch wasn't going to consider firing Andy Miller unless she gave him a good reason, and she would never tell anybody why she hated Andy. She'd never tell a soul.

Maybe Mitch and Josh didn't have to take her feelings into account when it came to running their business, but they damn well *did* have to live with the consequences.

MITCH SLAMMED THE pantry door and then kicked it when it didn't close all the way. Andy Miller had started work Tuesday, now it was Thursday, and Mitch didn't know where Rose kept the extra coffee filters.

Josh didn't know. He said Rosie always made the coffee. Mitch would ask her, but he didn't want to give her the satisfaction. She was on strike…or whatever you called a woman lounging in her room all damn day, knitting and watching television. Meanwhile, the guys who actually owned the place—and signed her paychecks—couldn't make a pot of coffee.

Swearing under his breath, he grabbed the keys off the hook and started for the back door.

"Going somewhere?"

So she'd come out of her room. Holding a stack of DVDs, no less. "I'm going into town."

"Good. You can stop by the library for me. I'm done with these movies, and Hailey called to tell me she found more I'd like in a box of donations. She's holding them at the desk."

She set the pile on the table and walked out before Mitch could point out the irony of her asking him for a favor—and *asking* was a stretch—when he couldn't make a pot of coffee because she was pissed off at Andy Miller. Adding a few more creative words to his string of expletives, he grabbed the stack of DVDs and went out the door. Josh and Andy were in the back, going over a list of supplies, and he hoped to get out unseen. He wasn't really in the mood for company.

He went to the library first, just to get it over with. Hailey was at the circulation desk, as always, and she raised an eyebrow when she saw him.

"Don't see you here often," she said.

"Don't get here often." He didn't live there, for one thing, which she very well knew.

And the older he got, the more tired he grew of the *nudge-nudge-wink-wink* that followed him around this town. Sure, he'd sewn some wild oats. So had Hailey— hell, they'd sewn a few together—but everybody had accepted *her* growing up and becoming the librarian, and she wasn't subjected to innuendo and suggestive looks everywhere she went.

That was one of the reasons he embraced traveling for work. He could sew oats to his heart's content and then put it behind him. Nothing was ever behind him here.

"Rose said you had some DVDs for her."

Hailey pulled a small pile of movies out of a drawer and, after doing something on her computer, swiped each one with a handheld scanner.

"I don't have her library card with me," he told her.

"I pulled up her name in the system. We got the new computer system a couple years back and there was a learning curve, but worth it."

He nodded, waiting while she put the DVDs into a plastic bag, not sure what he was supposed to say to that.

She handed him the bag, but didn't release it when his hand slipped through the loops, holding him there for a second. "I probably shouldn't tell you this, but don't give up on Paige. If you keep chasing her, she'll let you catch her."

He wanted to deny he was chasing Paige and then demand to know where she heard that, but that seemed a little junior high, so he simply smiled. "Good to know."

"She's worth catching."

He thought so, too. "I'll keep that in mind."

His next stop was the Whitford General Store. There was probably an entire box of coffee filters in Rose's kitchen, but they didn't do him any good if he couldn't find then.

"Rose didn't call in a list," Fran informed him from her perch behind the counter. She moved to the tall stool when she had customers, but behind her there was a plush office chair, a computer and her knitting basket.

"Don't need a list, Fran. I'm a big boy."

She snorted and then he wandered up and down the aisles, wishing he had a list. Coffee filters he knew, but he couldn't remember what else was or wasn't in the pantry. He grabbed bread and milk, since everybody always needed those, then added some junk food to the basket. Just because he could.

Good enough, he decided. Later he'd go through the kitchen and make a list. Then he and Josh could take a ride into the city and hit the grocery store. Josh could drive one of those motorized carts around, and it would do them both good to get out of town, even if it was only for a few hours.

The whole time she was ringing up his purchases, Fran looked as if she had something she wanted to tell him but wasn't saying. Rose had probably called her, and the woman was holding back a lecture about loyalty or something along those lines. Or maybe Rose hadn't called. Andy working at the lodge was everybody's business by now, and it never had been a secret how Rose felt about Andy.

"I've known you your whole life, Mitchell Kowalski, and I probably know more about you than you think I do."

That sounded serious. Though she probably didn't know as much as she thought she did. If the Benoits had heard what he did with their daughter on prom night, Butch would have ripped him apart while Fran bagged up the parts to put out with the garbage.

"Wouldn't surprise me," was all he said.

"Don't break Paige Sullivan's heart."

"You're not the first person to warn me away from her." And he was getting tired of it.

"Oh, I'm not warning you away from her. I think Paige could use a little…temporary romance in her life. You have a knack for leaving women satisfied and happy when you take off, rather than brokenhearted. Make sure Paige is no different."

He wasn't quite sure what to say to that. He wasn't sure there was anything he *could* say to that. Having a woman old enough to be his mother—if not his grandmother—talking to him about his sex life was pretty high on the *awkward* list. And he didn't even want to think about Paige's reaction to hearing that Fran Benoit was trying to get her laid. By him.

Okay, *that* he had no objection to. But everybody being in everybody else's business, especially their personal business, was just one of the things about the town that put his teeth on edge.

"I have no intention of breaking Paige's heart, Fran." He wasn't going to address whether or not he had any intention of offering up some temporary romance, as Fran had so delicately put it.

"Good." She took his money and gave him his change. "She's a nice girl."

"So I've heard."

He grabbed his groceries and walked out before she could say any more. Once he was in the truck, he debated on where to go next. He didn't really have any more errands to run, but he didn't want to go back to the lodge yet. With Josh's attitude and Rosie's snit, Mitch was left being the voice of reason, so it made sense to avoid the place until he'd shaken off his bad mood and could be reasonable.

His stomach growling made the decision for him. It was late for breakfast and early for lunch, but he wanted some damn coffee. And maybe an omelet. Seeing Paige again couldn't hurt, either.

IT HAD BEEN a slow morning and, having run out of busywork, Paige was leaning against the counter, flipping through a magazine, when Mitch walked through the door, and she lost all interest in the article she'd been reading about all-natural industrial cleansers.

He smiled when he saw her and took a seat at the counter, at the end farthest from the pass-through window to the kitchen, where Carl was prepping for lunch. "Morning, Paige."

"Hi, Mitch. Coffee?"

"Lots of coffee. Lots." He gave her a wink that made her tingle in all the right places.

No, the wrong places. No tingling, she reminded herself as she poured a coffee and set it down in front of him. "Anything else, or just the coffee?"

"I'll take a hash and cheddar omelet with home fries, skip the toast, and some company."

He was looking her in the eye when he said it, and she hoped what she was feeling on the inside couldn't be seen on the outside, because it could be summed up in three words. *I want him.*

"It's pretty quiet right now," she said. "If you're looking for company, you'll have to make do with me."

"There's nothing 'making do' about you, Paige Sullivan."

Even as the tingling and zinging and other -*ing* words intensified, she laughed. "That was pretty slick. You're even smoother than the stories give you credit for."

"Is it working?"

"Nope. Sorry," she lied. "Let me go put your order in."

Since Carl had disappeared from the window, Paige had an excuse to slip out back for a few seconds. Mitch Kowalski was hell on her nerves. And not the nerves that got rattled when children ran amok in her diner while their parents sat and drank coffee. He was hell on the nerves that were connected to body parts that had been severely neglected for the past two years.

She didn't hide long though, because, after Carl took the slip from her, he gave her a funny look. "You feeling okay? You're a little flushed."

Great. "I'm okay. It's a little warm in here."

"No, it's not."

She shook her head and went back through the swinging door. Mitch was drinking his coffee, but it looked a lot like he'd been watching the door for her return. Even though there were some newspapers piled near him, he was ignoring them and, since he'd said he was looking for company, she didn't really have a choice but to visit with him.

After topping off his coffee, she poured herself an iced tea and leaned her hip against the center island. She could have sat on one of the many empty stools, but she either had to sit far enough away it would seem rude if he was looking for conversation, or close enough so those nerves might start getting ideas again.

"After Ava comes in later," he said, "you want to go for a ride with me?"

Yes. Yes, she did. "I have plans after work, but thanks anyway."

"It would be fun. We could go over by the lake. See where we end up."

It was the seeing where they'd end up that was the problem, because there was a pretty good chance if she was alone with Mitch, she'd end up in his arms. Or his bed. "Maybe another time."

Rather than taking the hint, he leaned forward and grinned. "Come on. I've even got a helmet that would fit you."

"Helmet?"

"For the bike. I'm talking about taking a ride around the lake on the bike, not in the truck."

Oh, that's just what she needed after two-plus years of self-imposed celibacy—a hot guy between her legs and a vibrator on wheels under her. "I...can't."

He leaned back again, wrapping his hands around his coffee mug, but he didn't look rejected. Curious, maybe. "Why don't you date, Paige?"

"Sorry, but details about my personal life aren't on the menu."

"I don't get it. You're beautiful. You're obviously smart and driven, since you not only brought this place back to life, but you made it better than it ever was."

The man knew how to flatter a woman, that was for sure. "Thank you."

"You seem to be in a great place in life. Why aren't you looking for a man to share it with?"

"Men are a luxury, not a necessity."

"What's that supposed to mean?" he asked, scowling as if the concept was totally foreign to him. Which it probably was.

She moved away from the island and straightened the salt and pepper shakers just to give her hands something to do. "It means I don't *need* a man in my life.

And I have that written on a sticky note taped to my fridge so I don't forget it."

"But you *want* a man, right?"

She pretended to think about it for a few seconds. "Not especially."

"Who opens jars for you?"

"I have a little gadget that does that."

"But…" He grinned. "What about sex?"

"I have a little gadget that does that, too."

He looked stunned for a few seconds, and then a naughty gleam lit up his blue eyes, and she wondered how the hell she'd gotten herself into this conversation. She was supposed to be letting him know she wasn't interested—even if it wasn't precisely true—and somehow she'd ended up talking to him about sex toys?

"I've been told," he said, "that little gadgets aren't a good substitute for the real thing."

They weren't, actually, but she wasn't about to tell *him* that. "Maybe whoever told you that wasn't using the right gadgets."

"Or maybe she was still basking in the glow of the real thing."

"Basking in the glow?" Gadgets didn't cause basking. Or glowing. "Tell me you didn't just say that."

"Oh, there's a glow. And basking. Trust me."

Trusting him was the last thing she'd be stupid enough to do. "I guess you'd know, considering the *very* extensive experience you have."

Rather than looking insulted, Mitch leaned back in the seat and smiled. "You've been listening to too many stories, I think."

"It's impossible to spend any time with the women in this town and *not* hear the stories."

His smiled dimmed a little. "And they wonder why I don't come home more often."

"You don't like it here?"

"It's a little claustrophobic. I don't mind visiting, but I'd never stay. Even six weeks of this place will be too much."

And she loved it enough to make it her home. It was enough to bolster her resistance to his charm. "You must not hate it, though. You named your company after the lodge."

"No, I don't hate Whitford." He blew out a breath. "It's just that once they pin a label on you here, you wear the label forever. When you walk into a place here, they see a beautiful woman who's made a success out of her business. When I walk into a place, they don't see a grown man who's made a success out of his business. They see every story they've ever heard about me doing something wrong, even though I've changed."

"So you're not a charming playboy who romances the ladies and leaves them smiling as he rides off into the sunset anymore?"

"Okay, so *that* I'm trying to be, but you won't let me." Oh, he was good. "You know, Paige. I'm not looking to be a necessity here. Just a temporary luxury."

"I'm not a woman who needs luxury in her life."

"I bet I can change your mind."

She looked him in the eye. "I bet you can't."

"I can be persuasive."

"Really? Because it seems to me you've never had

to work too hard at persuading a woman you're a good bet."

"I have a feeling you're worth the effort."

The man knew all the right buttons to push. "You're welcome to try."

She knew as soon as the words left her mouth they were the wrong ones to say. He nodded, his gaze hot and promising all sorts of naughty things she didn't want to think about but would no doubt dream about. "I intend to."

CHAPTER SEVEN

It was almost seven by the time Ryan's black, three-quarter-ton truck with Kowalski Custom Homes logos printed down the sides pulled up to the lodge the following night, and Mitch walked out of the barn he'd been sorting through to meet him. His brother could be a pain in the ass, but he hadn't seen him since they'd all gotten together to celebrate Sean getting out of the army.

They started to shake hands, but it turned into a quick hug. "Glad you could come. Hope you can still swing a hammer now that you're all yuppied up."

Ryan looked down at his clothes—khakis and a navy polo shirt bearing a smaller version of the logo on the truck—and frowned. "I'm not a damn yuppie."

"You look like one. All bosslike."

"I *am* the boss. But I can still swing my own hammer." Ryan looked past him at the lodge. "From the looks of things, I'm going to need to."

"Told you it was getting rough."

"You weren't lying. Right now I'm starving."

"We can drive down to the diner and grab a burger or something."

Ryan scowled. "No shepherd's pie?"

"Rosie's…on strike, I guess you could say."

"What do you mean she's on strike?"

"We hired Andy Miller to do some odd jobs around the place."

"Oh." Ryan shook his head. "So no banana bread, either?"

"Nope."

"This place is really going to shit."

"Tell me about it."

"Where's Josh?"

"He wanted to get cleaned up. Takes the poor sucker a half hour to get up and down the stairs, so he might be a while, but we can head into town when he's done."

Ryan walked toward the steps, giving them a good looking over. "I heard the woman that runs the old diner now is pretty hot."

"Yup." His younger brother liked to push his buttons, and he wasn't going to give him the satisfaction of getting territorial. Or asking him how he knew about Paige.

"Also heard you struck out."

So he'd been talking to Josh. "A swing and a miss maybe, but I'm still at bat."

Apparently finished inspecting the stairs, Ryan turned to face him and shoved his hands into his pockets. "I'll be around a bit. Maybe I'll get to know her and see if she'll let me steal a few bases."

"You take so much as one step toward first base with Paige Sullivan and I'll break every bone in your body. And I'll mess up your pretty yuppie clothes while I'm doing it."

Ryan just laughed at him. "I knew it."

"Knew what?"

"Forget it. I'm going to go rummage around the kitchen."

"Like I said, we can head down to the diner and—"

"I don't want to go into town. I'm tired and I've had enough of sitting in a truck. I'll just make some sandwiches or something."

Ryan made it as far as the front hallway before Rose came flying down the stairs. Mitch watched her hug his younger brother as though he'd been away at sea rather than in Massachusetts, growing more aggravated by the second.

Of course Rose fussed over Ryan. *He* hadn't committed the unforgivable sin of offering a good man some honest work. And Mitch didn't want Ryan anywhere near Paige. He knew Ryan had only been screwing with him, but his younger brother wasn't bad looking, he was a nice guy and—unlike the rest of them—he was as steady and solid as a slab of granite. What if Paige was willing to break her no-dating rule for him?

It would be embarrassing, for one thing. Mitch would never live it down. And Ryan wouldn't just romance Paige and move on. He wasn't wired that way. Mitch loved women in the same way he loved cheeseburgers and the *Die Hard* movies and a good football game. Ryan loved in a *forever and ever, amen* kind of way, and Mitch had never known him to be casual about a woman.

"I made you shepherd's pie," Mitch heard Rose tell Ryan, and he followed them toward the kitchen.

"Mitch said you didn't."

"Mitch doesn't know everything. Of course I made you shepherd's pie. And there's banana bread, too."

"I told you I smelled banana bread and you said it

was an air freshener," Mitch said, trying not to sound too pouty.

"I lied," she said, opening the oven door to show a huge glass casserole dish of shepherd's pie.

"Is that all for Ryan, or do we get some, too?"

"Of course you can have some," she snapped. "I'm not twelve."

Biting down on the variety of smart-ass responses that popped into his head, he started setting the table while Rosie continued to fuss over the golden boy. He was almost done when Josh showed up and rescued Ryan from the maternal smothering. More backslapping and jokes ensued, but Mitch knew there were some tough conversations in their future.

They only made it halfway through the first helping of shepherd's pie before Ryan turned serious. "Josh, why didn't you tell us things were getting tough up here?"

"Why didn't you ask?"

Mitch winced. Under the belligerent tone was a hard truth. They hadn't asked. They'd lived their lives and run their businesses and just assumed Josh was holding down the fort. "We should have. And we should have come back more often and we didn't, but we're here now and—"

"Temporarily."

"We're here *now* and we'll work together to get the place back on track."

Josh snorted. "You've got some magic fix for the economy and the gas prices? Because that's what it's going to take."

"We're going to prioritize. Sink some time and money into what needs to be fixed first and slap some bandages on the rest. I was thinking I could ask Chelle, the woman who handles the website for Northern Star Demolition, about revamping the lodge's site. Maybe boost it on the search engines and build a Facebook page. Get the name out there a little more."

Ryan was nodding. "People don't pick up pamphlets at restaurants or rest stops anymore. They pull up the information on their freakin' phones."

Mitch waited to see if Josh would contribute, but he was busy stuffing shepherd's pie into his mouth. Instead of looking encouraged, their youngest brother looked even more sullen. "We're going to step up, Josh."

All that got him was a shrug, and Mitch took a big bite of mashed potatoes, hamburger and corn to keep from pushing at Josh. It wouldn't get him anywhere, and he didn't want to escalate dinner conversation into a shouting match when Rosie had gone to so much trouble to welcome Ryan home with a nice supper.

Tomorrow they'd start getting truly hands-on, and Josh would come around when he saw that his brothers truly intended to pull some of the weight for a while.

"Are you seeing anybody?" Rosie asked Ryan in an obvious bid to change the subject.

"Nope. I heard the woman that bought the diner is pretty hot, though."

Mitch glared at him across the table, but he didn't say anything because nothing he wanted to say could be said in front of Rosie.

"Stop pushing your brother's buttons," she chided Ryan, who just grinned at him.

He could grin all he wanted, but he wasn't touching Paige. Paige was his. Maybe not quite yet and maybe not for very long, but it was enough to make her off-limits to his brother. But since she didn't know that, the best thing to do was keep Ryan busy at the lodge until he went back to Massachusetts.

Then he'd start working a little harder on the whole *Paige being his* thing.

"JUST WRITE DOWN 'kerosene and a match' and call it good."

Mitch tossed the clipboard onto the tailgate of Ryan's truck. "We're supposed to be making a list of supplies to fix the place up."

"Like I said—kerosene and a match."

"You know what?" They were only a little more than halfway through the day, but he'd already had about enough of Ryan's shit. "Go home."

He started to walk away, but Ryan grabbed his elbow and would have spun him around, except Mitch yanked his arm free. "What the hell is that supposed to mean?"

"You don't want to be here. You don't want to help. Fine. Go home."

"I'm here and we're supposed to be making a supply list."

Mitch put his hands into his pockets to keep from swinging on his brother. "Kerosene and a match? You think that helps?"

Ryan blew out a breath and shook his head. "Sorry. I'm just in a shitty mood today."

It wasn't just *today*, though Mitch decided against saying so. Ryan tended to be in a shitty mood whenever he was forced to visit Whitford, and Mitch was pretty sure he knew why. Back when they were in college, something had happened between Ryan and Lauren Carpenter—Dozer's daughter—that had changed the way Ryan felt about coming home to Whitford. And he apparently hadn't gotten over whatever it was yet.

He almost asked his brother about it, which he'd never done before, but Andy Miller came around the corner of the lodge, with Josh not far behind him. Probably for the best, since it wasn't his business and it probably wasn't a good time to poke at his brother's sore spots. Not that it ever was, but especially not when the last time he'd seen all three of them in as foul a mood was the day they'd talked Liz into taking a stupid risk on the toboggan. After Rosie got her inside with a bag of frozen peas combating the egg on her forehead, she'd made the boys shovel every bit of snow out of the yard—not the driveway, but the actual backyard. It had taken the four of them more than three hours, and they'd been cranky as hell. Right now, they were worse.

"When you start breaking it down, it's not that bad," Andy said, seemingly oblivious to the tension between the brothers. "A lot of small projects that take more time than money, with only a couple bigger ones."

"How big?" Mitch asked.

Andy shrugged. "With the way the boards have weathered and are tweaking, I'd recommend replacing the porch rather than piecemealing repairs, and then scraping and painting the whole thing. And it's well past time to upgrade the windows and doors to something more efficient."

"I got an estimate on replacing the windows with low-E glass," Josh said, "but, after I was through shitting bricks, I tossed it."

"I'll do the windows," Ryan told them. "Not right now, but before late fall hits. For now, we should fix the steps and focus on the smaller things and, when I free up a crew, we'll come up and replace the windows, doors and the porch."

"A crew?" Josh looked skeptical.

"Couple of the younger guys. Maybe they'll learn something, and I pay them less than the experienced men."

"What are you calling smaller projects?" Mitch asked Andy.

"Gotta mix of a little bit of everything. The siding's not bad but, if Ryan's going to pop in replacement windows—" he paused and looked at Ryan, who nodded "—then we won't replace the window trim, so it should all be scraped and painted. The stairs, as he said. Some landscaping stuff—some trees still need limbing and shit like that. The barn floor's starting to sag pretty good, and storing the sleds and the four-wheelers in there's a lot of weight. Most of the planks can be flipped and reused, but we need to get down there and reblock it. Some other stuff. Like I said, more elbow grease and time than money."

"One guy's only got two elbows and a certain number of hours in the day," Josh said defensively, as though he'd been accused of something.

"The important thing is that we have a plan," Mitch said. "Which means now we can *finally* have some lunch."

They all started toward the house, except Andy. When Mitch looked back, he said, "I should probably go…do some things. I'll be back later this afternoon, though."

"Rose doesn't own the lodge. We do," Mitch said. He managed to sound authoritative, but he mentally had his fingers crossed she wasn't eavesdropping. "We're taking a lunch break and I'm inviting you in to eat with us."

Andy smiled. "You may own the place, but if my feet cross that threshold, her temper will level the place around your ears."

That was probably true. "Let's go into town, then. A burger sounds better than a bologna sandwich, anyway."

"Sounds good to me," Ryan said, while Josh shrugged and started toward the truck. "Give me a chance to meet the new owner."

Mitch forced himself to keep walking and not give his brother the satisfaction of rising to the bait. Josh got to ride shotgun by default, because of the cast, so after Ryan and Andy crammed themselves into the not-quite-a-full-backseat of the truck, Mitch got in the driver's seat and fired the engine. When the dash came alive, including the clock, he was a little relieved to see it was almost two o'clock, which not only explained the hunger, but also meant Paige would already be gone by the time they got there and, therefore, wouldn't be meeting Ryan.

Except, as luck would have it, she was the first person Mitch saw when he stepped through the door of the Trailside Diner. She had her apron off and was leaning against the center island, as usual, talking to Ava. Paige turned her head to look when they walked in and she smiled at him, which was the best damn thing that had happened all day.

The urge to puff himself up like a rooster took him by surprise, though. Women smiled at him all the time. They smiled a *lot,* and he'd never gotten any kind of thrill at being the guy who'd put the smile on their faces. But, when Paige smiled at him, he wanted to pound his chest and let out a Tarzan yell.

Andy and Josh had continued on toward a table, but Ryan stopped next to him and waited. Mitch scowled at him, but he just grinned and made a none-too-subtle gesture with his head. *Gonna introduce me?*

Probably because they were standing in the doorway like idiots, Paige started toward them. "I was just on my way out. Stopping by for lunch?"

"Yup. This is my brother, Ryan. Ryan, Paige Sullivan. She's owned the diner for two years now."

Ryan laid on the charm with the smile and the handshake and the pleased-to-meet-you, but Paige turned her attention back to Mitch the second Ryan released her hand. "How are things going at the lodge?"

"Good. We're making up a list of things to do, and it's not too bad."

"Glad to hear it. I have to run, but give my best to Rosie. Oh, and, if you're really hungry, try Gavin's special today—caramel apple pork chops and they're so good."

She was gone before he could form an opinion on the pork chops or even say goodbye, and Ryan's low chuckle made him wish they were still young enough to get away with slugging his brother.

"Hate to break it to you, but that woman's not into you," he said before walking off to join the others at the table.

Mitch might have believed him and even found that thought a little depressing if Ava hadn't paused on her way by with some menus. "Brothers. Can't believe a word they say."

THERE WASN'T MUCH to do in Whitford on a Saturday night, so they all tended to make their own fun. And the first Saturday night of each month was the most fun for Paige because it was movie night with the girls. They rotated houses, though Paige never got to host since she had neither a television nor anyplace for more than two people to sit.

Tonight they were at Hailey's, which was Paige's favorite movie-night spot. Hailey had a cute Cape on the outskirts of town and no husband grumbling about being banished for the evening or kids who wouldn't stay in bed. They didn't have to worry about the movie's rating and they could laugh as loudly as they wanted, which could grow more and more rowdy as the night went on, depending on who was mixing the drinks.

And, true to form, Hailey had chosen yet another romantic comedy based on how hot the leading man was rather than critical praise or word of mouth, never mind whether or not it was any good. If anybody asked what it was about, she'd hold up the DVD case and say, "Look at this guy!"

Paige wasn't about to complain, though. Lauren had been on a Nicholas Sparks kick lately, which led to a shortage of tissues and a decrease in attendance. Fran was pushing for a *Thelma & Louise* rerun and the previous month, when Mallory had hosted, they'd sat through

War of the Roses, which, considering her marital situation, made everybody a little uncomfortable.

"Funny movie, Fran's nachos and a full rum-and-Coke," Jilly Crenshaw, Gavin's mother, said as she sank onto the couch next to Paige. "I love movie night."

"Me, too." Her drink was a lot more Coke than rum, but it wasn't the booze that appealed to her. Or even the movies. It was the friendship. The sense of belonging and *knowing* these women of all ages, shapes and sizes. And they knew her, which was more than she could say for most of the people whose lives she'd moved in and out of like a temporary shadow. Some of these women already, in two years, had come to know her better than her own mother did. Because they *wanted* to.

"Gavin says business seems good."

Paige nodded. "Better than I anticipated it would be two years ago, actually. Weeknights are still pretty quiet for dinner, but breakfast and lunch do pretty well. And the weekends are busy."

"Good. I think Waters went out of business because he only gave a damn during snowmobile season," Jilly said, referring to the diner's previous owner. "Of course it's nice to have all the sledders coming through, and you can always charge a little more when they can sled right to your door, but he never adjusted after the snow melted. None of us were willing to pay tourist prices for a cheeseburger and a soda, you know?"

Paige nodded, because she did know. Back when she'd first started asking around about the old, closed-down restaurant, she'd gotten quite an earful about Waters's business sins, which only strengthened her conviction that the old diner should serve as the social heart of the community and not just a place to eat. She catered to the snowmobiling crowd somewhat, serving up big steaks and sirloin burgers and the like during the winter, but her priority had always been good food for reasonable prices for her neighbors.

"Five-minute warning," Hailey yelled over the buzz of the multiple conversations taking place.

There was a mad rush to top off drinks, refill paper plates and hit the bathroom before the movie started, and Jilly stood up. "I need to grab some more of Rose's banana bread before it's gone."

Since she already had two slices on her plate plus a great end seat on Hailey's love seat, Paige didn't move. A couple minutes later, Rose sat down next to her, juggling a full plate and a coffee mug.

"I went with the hot chocolate," she told Paige after she'd set the mug on the end table. "I don't know how she does it—and she won't tell me—but Hailey makes the best hot chocolate."

"How are things at the lodge?"

"Not too bad." Paige thought Rose's face tensed up a bit before she relaxed it into a smile again. "Ryan's home, which has been nice. They settled in with beer, chips and the ball game, so I decided to come to movie night."

"I met Ryan this morning. I'm surprised he's not around more since he lives so close. Well, not really close, but it's only a few hours."

"Getting that boy to come home for a visit's harder than getting an invitation to the White House. He says he's always working, but I don't see the point in having the headache of owning the company if you can't take a long weekend now and then. Look at Mitch. He's taking a whole six weeks off. Mostly. He sneaks off to use the computer a lot, and that fancy phone of his is getting a workout."

Hearing Mitch's name seemed to jack up the temperature in the room, and Paige hoped her sudden flush wasn't so pronounced this woman, who was practically a mother to him, would notice. "How often are they all home at the same time?"

"Almost never. I don't even know how many years it's been. Maybe even since their dad passed away." Rose shook her head. "We all got together when Sean got out of the army last year, but we all went to Ryan's house because it's close to the airport and, with Sean and Mitch and Liz all flying in, it made more sense. It's not the same as coming home, though."

Paige remembered when Rose and Josh had driven down to Massachusetts to welcome the middle Kowalski brother home. "How are Sean and his wife doing?"

"Wonderful." Rose practically beamed. "No baby news yet, but I pray for one every day. Lord knows Katie doesn't seem interested in giving me a grandbaby, so it's up to one of the other kids. At the rate they're going, Sean and Emma might be my only shot."

Paige lowered her voice as the movie started. "You never know. One of them might meet the right person, fall in love and have you knitting baby blankets before you know it."

The way Rose looked at her made Paige feel like the woman was reading more into her words than what she'd meant. "Maybe. It won't be Mitch, though. Mitch doesn't settle down."

Paige forced herself to laugh and shrug. "Maybe it'll be Ryan, then."

Rose just smiled and turned her attention to the television, so Paige did the same. The other woman didn't need to worry that Paige had her sights set on being the one to settle Mitch down. The eyes and the smile and the flirting might weaken her knees, but she wasn't going to let them weaken her resolve.

CHAPTER EIGHT

MITCH DELIBERATELY TIMED his arrival at the Trailside Diner on Monday for that window between breakfast being over and lunch not yet started. He wasn't really hungry, but a coffee never hurt. And he wanted Paige Sullivan all to himself. Or mostly, anyway. Carl would be in the kitchen, prepping for lunch and getting things ready to hand over to Gavin in the afternoon.

He'd stopped at Dozer's to get a belt for the old tractor, which had led to rummaging around in boxes that hadn't been rummaged through in quite a while, so he detoured straight to the men's room to wash up first. He was surprised to find the door propped open with a bucket and even more surprised to find Paige up in the air, with one foot on the sink vanity and the other on a step stool.

Rather than risk scaring her and making her fall by shouting, "What the hell do you think you're doing up there?" he tapped gently on the open door and cleared his throat.

She'd been so intent on trying to pop out the translucent plastic panel that covered the fluorescent ceiling light, he still startled her, but not so badly she toppled off her precarious perch. "Mitch! What are you doing here? Wait. Never mind. That's a pretty stupid question."

"I wanted to wash my hands before I sat down. I had to go digging at Dozer's for a belt for the tractor."

She laughed. "Get a little dusty?"

He wanted to put his hands around her waist to steady her as she climbed down, but he settled for holding the ladder instead. "Why isn't Carl doing this for you?"

"Because he's the cook, not the handyman, and he's busy with cooking." With her feet back on the ground, Paige wiped her hands on her apron. "It's my lightbulb and I'll change it, just like I changed the one in the ladies' room a few months ago."

"You're lucky you haven't broken your neck."

"Because of the sink, I can't quite get the ladder in the right position, so I have to kind of use both."

"Step out of the way and I'll do it. You can hand the new ballast up to me."

"I can do it."

God, he loved that stubbornness in her voice. "I know you can. But I'm here and I'm taller and it'll take me about two seconds."

It was tough logic to argue against, but she looked as if she might try. Then she sighed. "Okay, but your lunch is on the house."

"Why can't it just be a favor?"

"It's still a favor. Your lunch will cost me nothing compared to having an electrician change the ballast."

"Which you wouldn't do."

"Not if I can do it myself, which I can, even if it takes me longer."

"Okay, you can spot me a sandwich," Mitch said.

The important thing wasn't a battle of wills, but rather keeping her from breaking her neck by way of unsafe ladder habits. He shifted the ladder off to the side a little, since he had enough reach to do it properly. "You know, my brother's in a cast for six weeks because he was stupid with a ladder."

"It's really charming, this whole *make her feel stupid* thing you've got going on. Does that usually work for you?"

He popped the light cover out and handed the panel down to her. "Right now I care more about you not hurting yourself than I do about getting in your pants."

"The ladder was steady. I made sure my balance was good and the ladder wasn't going to shift before I started trying to pull that down."

"Josh made sure he footed the ladder, too." He pulled out the old ballast and handed it down to Paige in exchange for the new one.

"Gee, however did I manage to run this place for two years before you blew into town?"

That made him laugh. "Part of being good at your job is knowing your limitations and finding people who can help you shore up the weak spots. For instance, I know Carl and I'm willing to bet he doesn't know you're in here doing this and, because you're stubborn, you won't ask him to do a fairly simple task he wouldn't mind doing."

"I prefer being self-sufficient." When he reached down, she handed him the plastic panel. "I bet you're not very good at admitting your weaknesses."

"Sure I am." He climbed down off the ladder and folded it up to lean against the wall.

"Name one."

He turned on the water and thought a few seconds while he waited for it to run warm. "Well, I figured out in the early days of Northern Star Demolition that I have trouble selling myself. Banging my own drum, so to speak. Prospective clients would ask me why they should hire me over another outfit, and I'd get flustered and stutter and shit."

"You have trouble selling yourself? I find that hard to believe."

"Believe it or not," he said as he grabbed some paper towels from the dispenser to dry his hands, "I'm a very humble guy."

She laughed, but he wasn't offended. "So what did you do?"

"I sat at a bar with a friend of mine who was in PR and told him all the reasons Northern Star Demolition was the best company for any job. He typed it all up into a bullet-point kind of list, which I read over and over again until I had it memorized and could say it with confidence. I also don't have any patience for politics so, if there's political squabbling over a demolition, Scott—my second in command—steps in and handles all of that while I focus on the job." He tossed the paper towel and turned to face her. "Doesn't make me weak or not good at what I do because I had to ask for help."

"Point taken. And thank you for changing the light."

In a couple of steps, he was standing so close to her he expected her to back up. "Men can be handy to have around."

"While I appreciate the help, you didn't do anything for me I couldn't have done for myself."

"But it's not nearly as much fun."

She narrowed her eyes at him. "Are we still talking about fluorescent lights?"

He shook his head. "Fireworks, maybe."

After rolling her eyes at him, she grabbed the old ballast and walked out of the men's room. Since he didn't know where the ladder went and it wasn't very heavy, he left it where it was and kicked the door free of the bucket on his way out. Walking away from him wasn't going to do her any good.

She'd promised him lunch.

SHE SHOULD HAVE known she wouldn't get rid of him that easily. After taking the ballast out back to be disposed of later, Paige went back for the stepladder and saw Mitch sit at the counter to wait for her. It annoyed her, even though she'd offered him a free lunch for helping her out.

Everything about him annoyed her at the present moment. The smile and the flirting while trying to convince her he was so humble he couldn't even push his own company on people. The way he seemed so sure that if he just kept showing up and being a nice guy, she'd sleep with him. The fact she couldn't sleep at night because she was too busy thinking about how much she wanted to sleep with him.

She should throw him out. Just point to the sign that reserved her the right to refuse service and then show him the door.

It was a nice visual, but she could never follow through on it, if for no other reason than not wanting to come up with an explanation for all her other customers as to why she'd tossed a Kowalski. Instead, she shoved the ladder back into the supply closet and, after washing her hands and giving herself a stern look in the mirror, went back to the dining room to find the counter empty. The disappointment she felt only made her more annoyed with him—until she heard his voice.

He'd moved to a booth, and Drew Miller was sitting across from him. The police chief looked tired, if not downright haggard, and Paige felt a pang of pity for him. No matter who was right or wrong—if there even *was* a right or wrong—their situation sucked.

After she brought a coffee for Mitch and a soda for Drew, she gave their lunch orders to Carl and turned her attention to the two women who walked in and took a booth near the door. Jean was a dental hygienist who worked for the town's only dentist, who was rumored to be almost as old as the town charter. And Dana was a logger's wife who stayed home with two rowdy sons. Both were a little older than Paige, brunettes, and interested in checking out Mitch without being obvious.

"Morning, ladies," Paige said, giving each of them a menu and silverware wrapped in a napkin. "What can I get you to drink?"

They both wanted coffee, and she was almost back to the table with the mugs when the women giggled and she overheard part of the conversation. "There's no way you had sex in a canoe."

Paige slowed her steps, telling herself it would be rude to interrupt them, but really, who wouldn't want to know who had sex in a canoe?

"We did!" It was Dana talking. "It was his dad's and they weren't supposed to take it, but Josh and Sean helped him carry it to the pond. Ryan would have told on him, I guess. But to make a long story short, the sex was amazing and we didn't tip the canoe."

Of course it was Mitch who had sex in the canoe. Who else would the women of Whitford talk about having sex with?

Since Dana chose that moment to notice her, Paige refrained from rolling her eyes and pasted on a smile as she set their coffees down. "Have you decided what you'd like?"

A few more people were wandering in for an early lunch, and Paige was grateful for the distraction. For one thing, being busy kept her from eavesdropping to see who else in the place might be reminiscing about sex with Mitch Kowalski. That in turn helped keep her from speculating, at least during work hours, on what it might be like for *her* to have sex with him.

She was hoping it was Drew's turn to pick up the check but, after delivering the lunch special to a couple of guys at the counter, she saw Mitch waiting for her at the cash register.

"Yours is on the house," she reminded him.

"I'm paying for this one." Before she could object, he leaned closer, as if he didn't want anybody else in the diner to overhear. "Instead of a free lunch, I want a lunch I pay for, but with you."

There went the tingling and zinging again. "I'm sure my customers would be thrilled if I sat down and ate my lunch while they waited."

"We'll have a late lunch. Tomorrow. I'll pick you up here at two, when Ava comes in."

"That sounds like a date," she said suspiciously. She didn't date. No men.

"It's a favor. And you owe me a favor, right?"

"How is going to lunch with you doing you a favor?"

"I'm going to do a little shopping, too. You can help me pick out Rosie's Christmas present."

That made her laugh, which of course made everybody in the place turn and look. "It's the second week of August, Mitch."

"I like to plan ahead. Why not do it now, when I can guilt you into helping me?"

"Guilt?"

"I changed a lightbulb for you. You won't help me pick out a gift for poor Rosie?"

He was so full of it. "I shouldn't encourage you."

"But you will." He grinned as though he'd won a door prize or something. "Right?"

"Okay, fine." She rang up his check and gave him his change. "But make it two-thirty. I'd like to change out of my work clothes if you're going to drag me into stores."

"Sounds great." He paused halfway to the door and turned back. "Oh, and wear jeans."

He was gone before she could ask why, so she went back to work, trying to ignore the curious looks and the not-so-subtle whispering at Jean and Dana's table. She wanted to stand on the counter and announce that she was *not* going on a date with Mitch Kowalski.

But he was picking her up at two-thirty to take her out to lunch. No matter what the logical part of her mind said, there was a part of her that practically trembled in anticipation.

She was going on a date with Mitch.

"I HEAR THINGS are a little rocky at the Northern Star right now."

Rose wasn't surprised Fran had heard what was going on, and felt a pang of guilt for not telling her herself. She and Fran Benoit had been friends a long time, but there were some things Rose didn't want to talk about. Andy Miller was one of those things. "Not for me. I'm having a nice little vacation."

"So you're really on strike?"

Rose laughed. "I wouldn't call it that exactly."

Fran shook her head and propped her elbows on the counter. Rose had made an impromptu run to the store to restock her stash of snacks, but the place was empty, so they were taking advantage of the quiet to catch up. Sometimes it took Rose three hours to pick up a gallon of milk.

"How is it that I don't know why you dislike Andy so much?"

Because Rose didn't want her to know, but she didn't want to hurt her feelings, so she hedged. "It was so long ago I don't even remember myself."

"You're a bad liar, Rose Davis, but I'll let you get away with it this time. Tell me about Mitch and Paige instead. Everybody seems to be talking about them."

That was news to her. Maybe she was spending *too* much time in her room. "What are they saying?"

"Oh, you know how people talk about Mitch. It's pretty obvious he's got his eye on her, and we all know Paige hasn't dated anybody that we know of since she came to Whitford, so there's a lot of speculation on whether or not they're hooking up, as the kids say."

"He needs to leave that girl alone."

Fran looked surprised, either by her words or her sharp tone. Maybe both. "Most of us think he'd be good for her. You know how he is. He gives them a little romance, then kisses them on the cheek and off he goes with no hard feelings. It would do Paige good to have a little fun."

"She doesn't strike me as the kind of woman who just has a little fun. I think she had some sadness before she came to Whitford and she's really thrived here. If Mitch breaks her heart, it'll change her."

"I don't think you're giving her enough credit."

"It's got less to do with her than with him. You know I love that boy like he's my own, but he's not a man I'd ever want a woman I care about to get involved with. He's got no intention of settling down, so it's best for Paige if he just leaves her alone."

"I say a little bit of no-strings fun is good for a woman. Especially one Paige's age. She's too young to forget what good sex is like."

Rose nodded. "I agree with that, but there are plenty of nice men in Whitford who'd love to have good sex with her. Men who are part of the community and want to settle down."

"Well, I told Mitch he should go for it," Fran said stubbornly.

"You're becoming a meddling old woman."

"And you're not?"

Rose laughed. "Not yet, but I'm going to have to start if I ever want babies around, I think."

"I'm telling you, I think it'll be Mitch and Paige."

Rose wasn't up for arguing the point any further, so she simply shrugged. But Paige was a nice girl and she was smart enough not to get mixed up with a guy like Mitch. That relationship would only lead to heartache.

CHAPTER NINE

PAIGE WAS GOING to have to learn to nail down the specifics where Mitch was concerned. "You didn't say anything about a motorcycle."

"It's a beautiful day."

What was beautiful was the man sitting sideways on the seat of his big Harley-Davidson, with his arms crossed so the blue T-shirt was pulled tight across his shoulders, and his ankles crossed, which emphasized his long legs.

"You said we're going shopping," she reminded him, flailing for excuses, because she was afraid getting on that bike was going to be the beginning of the end for her resistance.

"It has the saddlebags. And I'm not planning to buy her a pony or anything. It'll work. Hell, if we find the perfect thing and it's too big, I'll go back in the truck or have them ship. And I have two helmets."

She was out of excuses, except one, and she didn't really want to tell him she wanted to take the truck so she could keep a safe distance between her body and his body. There was no distance on a motorcycle.

"Give me a minute," she said before going back into her house.

She rummaged through her purse and put her keys

in the left front pocket of her jeans. Then she slid her license and debit card into her back pocket. The rest of it she left on the table, since a purse on a motorcycle was possible, but not practical. Then she ducked into the bathroom and took a few minutes to pull her hair into a French braid, which was the only method she knew to combat helmet hair.

Mitch was still in the same position, looking like the poster child for slightly naughty boys-next-door, when Paige walked back out and locked her door behind her.

"Where are we going?" She took the helmet he handed to her and put it on, thankful she knew how to buckle it already and wouldn't have to feel his fingers brushing along her jaw.

"Thought we'd cruise the back roads into the city. More lunch options and places to shop."

And more miles with her thighs wrapped around his ass. "Okay. Do you have any idea at all what you want to get? Christmas being so close, and all."

He laughed and stood up straight so he could turn and straddle the bike. Short of clapping her hands over her eyes like a child, there was nothing Paige could do but watch and try not to drool. Then he fired the engine and kicked the stand out of the way. Once he had it balanced, he gave a little *come on* gesture with his head.

Taking a deep breath, Paige threw her leg over the short sissy bar on the back, settled on her part of the seat and set her feet on the back pegs. Then she faced the big dilemma. Hold on to the bar behind her, which became awkward and uncomfortable fairly quickly, or hold on to Mitch, which would also be awkward and uncomfortable, but immediately.

He started to walk the bike forward, cutting the wheel to miss her car, and Paige realized it had been a little longer than she thought since she'd been on a bike. As he rolled out onto the street, she put her hands on his hips out of sheer nervous reflex and, when it didn't seem to faze him at all, left them there. He gunned the engine a bit heading through town, showing off, and she hoped the helmet hid her face well enough so the entire population of Whitford wouldn't know within five minutes she was on the back of Mitch Kowalski's motorcycle.

All it took was a few miles of open road to make her forget all about whether or not people knew what she was up to. It *was* a beautiful day, with the sun warm on her back, but the rushing wind keeping her cool. She watched the scenery go by in a way she never got to from the driver's seat of her car, and breathed in the scent of fresh country air.

Her nerves had settled, but she kept her hands casually rested against Mitch's hips. She could put them in her lap—she'd ridden with one of her mom's boyfriends almost every day and he hadn't even had a sissy bar—but she liked touching Mitch and he didn't seem to mind being touched.

He turned his head a little so he could be heard over the wind and the bike's engine. "You okay back there?"

"I'm better than okay," she yelled back. Because she'd leaned forward so he could hear her, her breasts pressed up against his back and heat flooded her body, making her even more aware of the way his hips pressed against the inside of her thighs.

And that was why she shouldn't have gotten on a motorcycle with Mitch. Because after two years of being fairly content to live her life without a man in it, she was once again aware of her inner thighs in a context other than wondering if they'd rub together if she made another run at the movie-night snacks. Damn him.

She leaned back as far as she dared and turned her head to the other side, checking out the roadside foliage, in an effort to discourage any further conversation.

As the miles passed, though, she relaxed again, and when he leaned back and turned his head to ask her where she wanted to eat, she didn't bother freaking out over the close contact.

"You choose," she hollered back to him.

After a while, he pulled the bike into the parking lot for a restaurant that was a little more upscale than what she was used to. She'd been there once, for a baby shower, but it wasn't the kind of place she'd eat on a regular basis.

"Not really dressed for this place," she said after he'd shut the bike off and they'd removed their helmets.

"You look fine and they don't have a dress code." He must have seen something in her expression, because his face softened. "Look, the service here is top-notch. You're on your feet most of the day doing this, so let's let somebody wait on you for a change."

"Okay." She wanted to point out it was a little expensive, but he obviously knew that if he was familiar with the service.

She had to admit, once they were seated at a table under subtle lighting with music piped in at just the right volume, that it was nice to relax and not be the one running back and forth to the kitchen for a change.

"When you go to a restaurant, do you spend the whole time comparing it to yours?" Mitch asked after the server had taken their orders.

"Not really. I don't get out to other restaurants often, for one thing. And the Trailside Diner works well for me and for the town. That's all that matters." She took a sip of her iced tea, watching him over the glass. "When you go to a restaurant, do you spend the whole time wondering how you'd blow it up?"

He laughed and shook his head. "The last thing I do when I'm sitting across the table from a beautiful woman is mentally demo the building."

Paige felt the heat spread over her cheeks and hoped the lighting was dim enough to hide it. "How did you end up destroying buildings for a living, anyway?"

"I'd always had an interest in buildings and engineering. During college I got a part-time job with a demo company. Small stuff, mostly. But I had an eye for it—the ability to see how any action would impact the structure. After I got my degree, I signed on with a good company and built up my résumé and my skill set until I could get the loan and backing to go out on my own. I get to secretly be a math and science geek and still have the coolest job in the room."

"Do you still have to travel as much yourself, or do you have enough people now so you can relax and delegate?" When his expression changed—became a little more guarded—she replayed her words in her head and realized he might think she was fishing for signs he was heading toward settling down. "Sometimes I wonder if I'll reach the point where I can hire a morning waitress and I can just be the owner. Or if I even want to."

"I'm barely surviving this so-called vacation. It seems like I'm calling or emailing the office or Scott every half hour."

"But you don't have to, right? They're doing okay without you, so you could take more time for yourself."

"I don't want to be hands-off. Northern Star Demolition doesn't leave me a lot of time and energy for anything else, and I like it that way."

Point taken, even if that's not what she'd been going for. "How are things going at the lodge?"

He shrugged, but she noticed the lines in his face relaxed a little. "Hard to say. We can slap paint on it and fix broken boards all day long, but we haven't sat down and figured out how to make it sustain itself financially. Or if it even can."

"The economy will swing around again." She gave a nervous laugh. "And here I am grilling you about work stuff when we're in a fabulous restaurant."

"You can talk about whatever you want, as long as you keep talking to me."

Thankfully, their server chose that minute to show up with their food, because she had no idea what to say to that. She wasn't even sure she *could* say anything, since everything inside her had melted a little.

She was in so much trouble.

MITCH WASN'T GOING to make it through the day without kissing Paige. He wasn't sure how he was going to pull off the kiss, though. If there was one thing he'd figured out about Paige Sullivan, it was that moving fast would be like stomping his foot at a skittish cat. She'd flee and it would be a good long time before she let him get close again. But he wasn't going to have a minute's peace until he kissed her.

It hadn't been his intention when he'd asked her to lunch. He'd seen Jean and Dana giggling together like idiots at the diner, and he'd seen Paige hesitate as she'd approached the table. No doubt Dana had trotted out the old sex-in-the-canoe story.

It burned his ass a little, to have Paige have to hear that crap about him. He'd been sixteen at the time and they hadn't actually had sex. They'd rounded the bases in good style, but he hadn't slid into home, so to speak. But that didn't make for good lunch gossip twenty years later.

He'd made up his mind right then he was going to get Paige out of Whitford. It didn't matter if it was only for a few hours—he wanted to spend some time with her away from the grapevine.

Now he had her, in the romantic lighting with the soft music, and he never wanted to take her home. They talked about music and books and movies, though television shows didn't go far, since she didn't have cable and he didn't watch much TV.

He didn't care. She could talk to him about the weather or floral centerpieces and she'd have his full attention. Away from the diner and the people who knew everybody's business, Paige was totally relaxed, and he liked her that way.

"I can't believe I let you talk me into this," Paige said, pausing with a forkful of strawberry cheesecake halfway to her mouth.

He'd suggested the cheesecake mostly as a way of prolonging lunch, but he was glad he had. Watching the expression on her face as she slid the fork out of her mouth made him wonder if she'd gone without fine desserts as long as rumor had it she'd gone without a man.

Once he'd run out of reasons to keep her all to himself in the restaurant, they went back out into the late-afternoon sun.

"Do you have any idea of which store you want to start with?"

It took him a few seconds to figure out what she was talking about, then he laughed. Christmas shopping.

She gave him a suspicious look. "You said we were going to look for Rose's gift today."

And he didn't want to confess it had been the first, admittedly ridiculous, reason to accompany him he thought she'd go for. "I'm too full to shop now."

"I know what you mean. This may have been a late lunch, but I won't eat again until breakfast tomorrow."

"What do you say we blow off shopping and cruise around on the bike?"

When she told him that sounded like a great idea, he turned toward the Harley so she wouldn't see him grinning like a love-struck teenager. He rarely took women out on the bike—as in *almost never*. His own opportunities to ride it were few and far between, and he used the time to think things through and clear his head.

He liked having Paige on the back, though. She was comfortable enough that she didn't have a stranglehold on him, and he could enjoy the feel of her thighs pressing against his and her hand at his hips.

Mitch took a different route out of the city and cruised the back roads, pointing out interesting bits of scenery here and there. The bike was a bit loud and,

with their helmets on, talking was difficult, so mostly
he just burned up the miles and enjoyed the feel of her
behind him.

It took over an hour to reach one of his favorite spots
in the area. It wasn't much more than a wide spot in the
shoulder, but he pulled the bike in and parked it near the
tree line. Bracing his feet, he waited while she put her
hands on his shoulders to steady herself and climbed
off, then he leaned the bike onto its stand.

"Where are we?" Paige hung her helmet on the sissy
bar and pushed at the wisps of hair escaping from her
braid.

"Just wait." After hanging his helmet from the han-
dlebar, he led her to a narrow path in the trees and
reached out his hand. "It's a little steep."

With Paige's hand in his, he walked along the short
trail and a mild slope down to the river. A huge slab of
rock extended out over a brook and he stepped on it,
tugging her along with him.

"A little steep, huh?" Paige asked, amusement in her
voice.

"I just wanted to hold your hand."

She didn't pull away, which made him ridiculously
happy. Instead she looked around, so he did the same,
taking in the way the fading sun shone through the trees
and hit the water in splotches of gold. There was just
enough current in the water that it gurgled through the
rocks, and birds chirped from the cover of full summer foliage.

"It's beautiful." Paige didn't whisper, but her voice
was soft and low, as if she didn't want to disturb their
surroundings. "I bet you bring all the girls here."

"Nope." He'd never brought a woman there before, though he wasn't sure why. And he wasn't sure why he'd brought Paige. "I don't come here very often. Maybe that's what keeps it special. I came the day after my dad's funeral, though. Laid on this rock and looked up at the sky for a while."

She squeezed his hand. "It seems like a nice place to be alone with your thoughts."

It was an even better place to be alone with her, though he didn't say that out loud. There was a fine line between flirting and getting mushy, and it was bad enough his mind had even gone there. He wasn't about to share it.

"It's peaceful," was all he said, but he was in trouble. Standing in a place that he was emotionally grounded to, holding hands with a woman he was painfully attracted to, was liable to blow the foundation out from under the wall he'd built between himself and serious. He liked that wall. It kept romantic entanglements from creeping in and getting a choke hold on him when his guard was down.

What the hell had he been thinking, bringing her here?

Then she looked up at him and smiled and every logical thought in his head blew apart, leaving nothing but a driving need to know what her lips felt like against his.

Her smile dimmed a little as her expression turned to uncertainty. "Why are you looking at me like that?"

Because he seemed to have no self-control where she was concerned. "I was thinking about kissing you."

"Oh." She frowned. "You don't look very happy about the idea."

"Not sure how you'd take it. Doesn't seem very fair to just spring it on you when we're in the middle of nowhere and you have no way to get home but me."

"And they say chivalry's dead."

When Paige turned her attention back to the brook, but didn't pull her hand away from his, Mitch felt a rush of frustration. Did she want to be kissed or not? Her words certainly gave him no clues. The way she'd turned back to the water implied she wasn't interested, but then why was she holding his hand?

"Why do you want to kiss me?"

Her voice was so low he almost didn't hear her. He did, of course, but he wasn't sure what to tell her. "I don't know. Beautiful spot, beautiful day, beautiful woman. Seems like the thing to do."

As soon as she pulled her hand away and turned back toward the banking, he knew it was the wrong thing to say. "Seems like the thing to do is start heading back. I've got a lot of paperwork waiting for me at home."

Mitch caught her before she stepped off the rock, taking her arm and spinning her back to face him. "I want to kiss you because it's the only damn thing I can think about. Every time I see you, I think about kissing you. Every time somebody says your name, I think about kissing you. Every single night when my head hits the pillow and I close my eyes, I think about kissing you."

She kissed him. Bracing her hands against his shoulders, she stood on her toes and pressed her lips to his. After a second of surprise, Mitch slid his hands around her waist and took control of the kiss. He'd been waiting for this moment too long to settle for a tentative peck.

Her mouth was soft and she sighed as she surrendered to him. He kept it light at first—brushing his lips across hers and holding himself to a few quick flicks of his tongue against hers—but he wanted her, dammit, and hunger got the best of him.

He devoured her, trying to get his fill of her kiss, as he pulled her hips hard against his and her hands tightened in his hair. When their breath grew ragged and he could feel her slight trembling under his hands, he knew he could have her. Right there on the rock with the sun going down and the brook gurgling around them.

He wanted to. He wanted to so badly he was afraid his balls would explode, but some sane part of his mind—the part that usually kept him out of female trouble—pulled back. It wasn't the place. Not only because slabs of rock were a lot more uncomfortable than they were romantic, but because there was no way out after the deed was done. If things got awkward or Paige had regrets, it would be a very long ride home on the bike.

With a lot more regret than he'd anticipated, Mitch broke off the kiss and stepped back just enough to put a little space between them. Paige's cheeks were flushed and she looked as hot and flustered as he felt.

She gave a nervous laugh. "Now that we got that out of your system, you can think about something else, instead."

"If that was the plan, I think it backfired." He was already thinking about kissing her again.

"Oh." After a couple seconds of awkward silence, she waved a hand in the direction of the road. "We really should get back."

As he followed her down the path through the trees, he wished she wouldn't walk so damn fast. He needed another minute or two before he could straddle the Harley's wide seat. And it was going to be a long, painful ride home.

On Friday after work, Paige stopped by Whitford Hardware to get some advice on her current home-improvement project. She'd put off dealing with her bathroom sink's reluctant drain, but it seemed like a good way to distract herself from wondering if Mitch would stop by. He hadn't, and the job had turned into a bigger one than she'd anticipated.

Dozer popped up like a groundhog from behind a display of garden gloves as Paige closed the door behind her. "Paige! How did your closet doors turn out?"

"I love them. They make a huge difference in how the bedroom looks."

"And what's your new project?"

She sighed, shaking her head. "My bathroom sink won't drain. Well, it will, but if I put some tadpoles in the water, they'd be frogs by the time the water was gone."

"Ah. You tried the chemicals?"

"Didn't help much. The book says I need to clean out the trap, but I can't get the connectors loose. Do you have any stuff that'll loosen the PVC glue or something?"

Dozer shook his head. "The book says? You can't do plumbing with a book."

"I replaced the toilet last year by the book. Unfortunately, all the knowledge in the world won't make me strong enough to break the pipes loose."

"Sounds like you need a man." She turned at the

sound of Mitch's voice just as he stepped out from behind a dividing wall covered with a variety of hand
tools. Seeing him made that kiss flash through her head,
and the temperature in the store seemed to spike suddenly.

Praying she was the only one who heard the innuendo lurking in Mitch's voice, she shrugged. "Not really. Even if there's nothing here that'll help me loosen
them, it's just a matter of finding the right leverage."

"It would only take me a few minutes to get your
joints nice and loose."

"So lame," she said, as Dozer snorted. "Thanks, but
I prefer to take care of it myself."

"So you've said."

She narrowed her eyes, but no response to that
popped into her head. She wasn't sure there *was* any
response she could make. Luckily, the phone rang and
Dozer excused himself to go behind the counter and
answer it.

Mitch took that as an opportunity to move closer to
her, and she folded her arms, as if she had any chance
at all of warding him off. Nothing had worked so far.
"You're about as smooth as a horny teenager. I'm starting to think all the stories about you must be totally
exaggerated."

"You're welcome to judge for yourself."

"I bet," she mumbled, feeling a little over her head
in this conversation.

"In all seriousness, let me help you with the bathroom sink."

"I don't need your help."

"No, you don't." That surprised her, but she tried not

to show it. "If you don't find anything to help here, I'm sure you'll figure out how to get the right leverage. Or you'll just take a saw to the pipes and put new ones in. But what will take you hours will take me a few minutes, so why not just let me help?"

Why not? Because she wasn't stupid. She knew what he was up to—trying to prove to her that she needed a man in her life. Which she didn't. He was developing a habit of being helpful, and Paige knew what came next. She'd get used to having him around and not doing things for herself. Then she'd start worrying she couldn't do it alone, and then she'd start living her life around making sure she had a man to take care of her, including putting his happiness above her own.

On some level, she knew she was being ridiculous. So he'd changed a lightbulb. He was offering to fix her sink. That was a far cry from changing her entire life and everything about herself to keep a man from leaving her. But it was a slippery slope and, even though she'd seen her mother do it a thousand times growing up, Paige had found herself at the bottom of that slope more than once. The way Mitch tempted her to just slide *a little bit* was making her paranoid.

"I'm just trying to be neighborly," Mitch said when her silence dragged on. "Isn't that one of the things you love about Whitford? How we're all neighborly and help each other?"

"Do you kiss all your neighbors?" she asked before she could stop herself. "Never mind. I already know the answer to that."

"Just the pretty ones." He winked, which made her roll her eyes. "I have to bring some primer back to the lodge, but I can come over early evening and take care of it. It'll take me a half hour, tops, and I'll behave."

"Really?"

"Promise."

She looked him in the eye. "You'll behave *how?*"

"You're supposed to leave a man some wiggle room." Wiggle room was the last thing she wanted to give him. "Okay, fine. I'll behave like a gentleman."

Paige was torn. On the one hand, it really wasn't a good idea to be alone with Mitch in her house. No matter where they were in the trailer, it was impossible to be more than a few steps from the bed, and if he kissed her again, she might be tempted to break her no-men streak. On the other hand, fixing the bathroom sink was becoming more of a job than she'd anticipated. She'd already done almost everything she could think of to get the trap free with no success. And cutting the old pipes out would not only add more time and mess, but money.

"There must be something more exciting you want to do on a Friday night," she said.

"Not really. I was planning to come into town for supper anyway, so it'll just be a little detour."

"I'll make you dinner." Oh, bad idea. "If you're going to fix my sink, the least I can do is feed you."

"And we keep things even?" He laughed before she could take offense at his cynical view of the way she liked things.

"Just to be neighborly," she told him.

"How's five sound? I can fix the sink and then you can feed me."

"Sounds great. Thank you." Dozer was still on the

phone, but she hated disappearing on him. "Will you tell Dozer I said thanks, but I'm all set?"

"Sure. See you at five."

Five wasn't that long from now, she thought as she stepped outside. Maybe she'd cheat and run back to the diner. She could get a couple orders of the special in to-go boxes and heat them up when the sink was done. And she needed to take a shower because…no special reason. She'd worked all day and, by the time Mitch left, she might be too tired to take one so close to bedtime.

It had nothing at all to do with being alone in her house with Mitch.

CHAPTER TEN

"THAT'S THE MOST disgusting thing I've ever seen."

"Women tend to have disgusting traps." Mitch laughed as he finished forcing the nasty glop from the PVC pipe into the bucket Paige had found for him. "Let me rephrase that. If a woman uses a bathroom sink on a regular basis, bad things grow in the bendy parts of the drain."

Paige snorted. "Bendy parts? Is that a technical term?"

"Absolutely." He forced his body back into a pretzel shape, wishing her bathroom was bigger than his closet. It took him only a few minutes to put her plumbing back together and, even with his focus on the job, he was aware of her hovering over him.

He'd tried to tell her she could go do something else, but she wasn't one to stand back and do nothing while somebody did her a favor. She wanted to help. Unfortunately, the only way they could work on the plumbing together would be for her to lie on top of him and... whoa, that was not something he should be thinking about while he was stuck in one position on her floor, with her staring down at him.

"Can I help you with that?"

As a matter of fact, you can, he thought before he

realized she was referring to the small pile of tools he was trying to transfer from under the sink to the floor on the other side of him, which wasn't easy from his awkward position. "Yeah, sure. Thanks."

He handed the tools to her one at a time, listening as she put each one in its place in her battered metal toolbox. For some reason he liked that she had a toolbox and thought she was probably the first woman he'd known who had one. Or maybe most of the women he'd known had hidden theirs away so they could call on him for rescue. Which sounded a little jaded, even in his own head, but it was probably the truth.

"If you're almost done, I'll go heat up supper while you wash up," Paige said.

"Sounds good. I just want to let this sit a few minutes and then run some water through it. Make sure there are no leaks."

"If you need a hand with anything, just yell."

He laughed. "We know you'll be close enough to hear me."

"Funny guy."

A couple creaks of the floor told him she'd moved away, and he grinned when he heard the fridge open. It was a good thing Paige had a healthy sense of humor, since the first words he'd said once she'd let him through the door were "Guess you're not claustrophobic."

She'd just laughed and waved her hand in a semicircle in front of them. "There. You've had the grand tour without even moving."

Except the bedroom. In a trailer the size of hers, open was definitely better, so the significance of her bedroom door being closed wasn't lost on him. Paige didn't want him in there and, since he'd promised to behave like a gentleman, there was no point in coming up with ways to change her mind.

After he'd finished with the sink, including washing up, Mitch stepped out of the bathroom and saw Paige putting a plate in the microwave. On the tiny piece of counter next to her were two to-go boxes, one open and one closed. "What's the special tonight?"

"Baked stuffed chicken breasts with garlic mashed potatoes and creamed spinach. I skipped the spinach and got us both extra mashed."

"You're a good woman."

"If that was true, I'd be offering you something home-cooked. Maybe an apple pie, too."

He moved close enough to her to see over her shoulder as she put the second helping of chicken onto a plate. "Are you saying you cheated? Maybe took a little short-cut in our agreement?"

"You still have to behave like a gentleman."

"That doesn't seem fair."

"I said I'd feed you." The microwave dinged. "I'm feeding you."

Mitch didn't move fast enough and, when Paige took a step back to make room for the microwave door's swing, her body smacked right up against his body. In reflex, he lifted his hand to steady her and it happened to come to rest at her waist. For a brief moment, it seemed that she relaxed against him—almost leaning on him—and then she jerked forward.

"Sorry," she said. "Small space. Why don't you sit at the table and I'll bring you your plate since it's done."

He wasn't sorry at all, but there was a little strain in

her voice all of a sudden, so he let it be and sat down at one of the two places she'd set out. His eyes wandered, checking out the personal touches that made the claustrophobic trailer into her home. She'd hung small baskets from the curtain rods to hold pens and mail and odds and ends, rather than having them take up the very precious counter or drawer space. On the fridge were a variety of photos taken of places he recognized around town. Not high-quality photography, by any means, but they were cheery shots. In between two photos at what would have been about her eye level, he saw a scrap of pink taped to the freezer door.

"Huh," he said. "You really do have a sticky note on your fridge that says, *Men are a luxury, not a necessity.*"

She set his plate down in front of him, then put hers in the microwave. "I told you I did."

"Why is that saying so important to you?"

She lifted one shoulder in a lazy shrug. "It's a reminder not to become like my mother."

"So…she thinks men are a necessity? And that's bad?"

"It's not *bad* when a woman needs a man. But it's not good when a woman believes she's nothing without one and will sacrifice almost anything to keep one. It was hard growing up with my mother. She needs a man in her life to be happy, so we spent most of my childhood chasing after any man who'd tell her he loved her."

"Relationships that were doomed to begin with, because you can only not be yourself and deny your own needs for so long before you get really unhappy."

The microwave dinged again and she joined him at

the table. "Exactly. You're a pretty smart guy, Mitch Kowalski."

"Just a passing familiarity with doomed relationships."

"I thought you preferred your relationships doomed. Or with a built-in expiration date, at least."

He looked at her from across the table, which was still close enough for him to be struck yet again by how dark her eyes were, and said, "At least with a built-in expiration date, a woman doesn't have to worry about keeping me. It's not going to happen, so she can relax, be herself and enjoy a very temporary luxury in her life."

PAIGE KNEW SHE should pick up her fork, scoop up some garlic mashed potatoes and shove them in her mouth. She couldn't seem to move, though, with Mitch looking at her like that and with his words starting to make sense to her.

Wasn't he the perfect guy to help her take care of those pesky -*ing* words that were pestering her—like *tingling* and *zinging* and *yearning* and, above all, *wanting?* She knew up front he'd walk away and not look back and, as he'd said, she knew she wouldn't be keeping him. He'd be the two-legged version of a loaner car.

Before she could say anything stupid, Paige took a bite of the mashed potatoes. And then another. Once he realized she wasn't jumping at the bait, Mitch went back to polite small talk about the town and books and how much he liked Gavin's garlic mashed potatoes.

But his words had gotten under her skin, which was probably why Paige took a little extra care in freshening up after dinner. She was pretty sure he'd at least try for a kiss, despite his promise to be a gentleman. After all, there was nothing particularly ungentlemanly about a kiss.

Besides, that was a promise she wouldn't mind him breaking.

When she left the bathroom, Mitch was sitting on her couch. It dwarfed the tiny living room and she probably should have gone with a love seat, but a good sofa was something she wouldn't compromise on. She laughed when he slid his butt to the very edge of the cushion and fully extended his legs. He could actually just brush the wall the room shared with the bathroom with the tips of his sneakers.

"Northern Star Demolition probably has job trailers bigger than this one," she said, slapping his feet down.

He grinned and pushed himself back onto the cushion. "Maybe, but this suits you. It's warm and cozy. Plus, it probably doesn't take long to clean."

"On the downside, if I let more than three days' worth of junk mail pile up, I look like a hoarder."

She smiled when he laughed, but inside she was jittery, and in that awkward moment, she wasn't sure what to do next. Should she sit next to him on the couch? Sit in one of the kitchen chairs?

As if he could read her mind, Mitch grabbed her hand and pulled her toward him. She was going to sit next to him, but he tugged at her while using the other hand to steer her hips until she ended up straddling his lap.

"You didn't slap my face, so I guess I'm still okay

with the whole gentleman thing," he said in a husky voice, and it had a touch of question in it.

"Gentlemen fix ladies' sinks and throw away their own paper plates after dinner. I think you held up your end of the bargain."

"So you won't throw me out if I kiss you?"

She leaned forward, bracing a hand on either side of his head. "I won't *let* you out until you've kissed me."

Mitch slid his hands up her back and nudged her forward until their mouths met. He kissed her slowly and very, very thoroughly, while he slid his hands under the back of her shirt. The feel of his hands against her bare skin was making her crazy and she wanted more.

When she pulled up her shirt, intending to take it off, he put his hand on her arm to stop her. "This is all there is. We'll have a good time and enjoy each other's company and then, when it's time for me to go, I'll just say goodbye and be gone. I won't call. I won't text. I won't write."

"That's pretty blunt." And just what she needed to hear.

"It's better to be up front about it, so we both know going in what we'll get. All the fun stuff, with none of the not-fun stuff."

She could use some fun stuff. It had been a long time, and who better to have a fling with than a man she knew ahead of time absolutely did not want to have a real relationship with her? Once couldn't hurt. Or two or three times. It wasn't as if she was going to start spinning happily-ever-after fantasies around a guy who was leaving town, which meant—just as he'd said—she'd have none of the not-fun stuff.

"Just so *you* know," she said, "once you're gone, I won't mope. I won't text. I won't sit around restaurants in twenty years reminiscing about the night we spent together."

He let go of her arm and pulled her shirt over her head, tossing it aside. His T-shirt joined it a second later. "Then let's do some fun stuff."

Without her shirt in the way, his hands roamed freely over her back as he kissed her some more. She squirmed in his lap and she moaned as, even through denim, the friction sent tendrils of delicious heat curling through her body.

"That closed door's been teasing me since I got here," he said against her mouth.

She slid off his lap and took his hands to haul him to his feet. When he pulled her against him and she found herself plastered to his chest, she laughed and then walked backward the few steps to her bedroom door with him kissing her with each stop. She groped behind her until she found the doorknob and pushed the door open.

Then Mitch stopped. He just suddenly stopped cold and, when Paige looked up, she saw his gaze was fixed on something behind her.

"You've got to be kidding me."

"What?" She turned in his arms, trying to figure out what he was looking at.

"Is that a twin bed?"

"Yes, it's a twin." He looked as if he'd never seen one before. "The room's small. I could have a big bed that I'd only take up half of, or I could have more floor space. I chose floor space."

"Is it big enough?"

She laughed. The bed wasn't *that* small. "Just how much room do you need?"

He slid his hands down her naked-but-for-the-bra-strap back and then pulled her backward by the belt loop on her jeans. Her almost-naked back pressed against his totally naked chest, reminding her of one of the many things gadgets couldn't imitate—the warm, hard length of a man's body.

"I guess that depends on what we're going to do," he said against the side of her neck before nipping at it.

"Is this the part where you ask me what I like?"

"I'll figure out what you like on my own." He slid his hands up to cup her breasts, which she liked very much. "Don't like to limit my options."

He pushed the cups of her bra down and ran his thumbs over her nipples. She sucked in a breath, pressing her hips back against his.

"I think you like that."

She did, but she liked it even more when he turned her around and bent his mouth to first one breast, then the other. Sliding her fingers into his hair, she held his head to her chest, wanting more.

When he undid her bra and slid it down over her arms, she started to unfasten her jeans, but he grabbed her wrists and held them over her head. "I'll do that."

He kissed her again, harder and more demanding than he'd kissed her before. Easily holding both of her wrists with one hand, he slid the other over her stomach, dipping his fingertips into the waistband.

Paige whimpered, torn between wanting him to torment her forever and wanting him inside her that very second. He wasn't in any hurry, though, as he unbuttoned her jeans and slid the zipper down.

When he slipped his hand down the front, under the lacy pink panties she was thankfully wearing, a low moan escaped her and she moved against his fingers.

"I think you like that, too," he said, his breath hot against her neck.

"I do." Her words were barely more than a breath.

Mitch backed her up until her knees hit the bed and then pulled her pants and panties down as she lay back on it. In seconds, he discarded the rest of his clothes, too, and Paige's mouth went suddenly dry. She did *not* have a gadget that would substitute for this.

She thought, when she heard the crinkle of a condom packet near the pillow, that Mitch was ready, but he wasn't done touching her yet. He teased her mercilessly, his mouth alternating between her lips and her breasts while his hand moved between her legs.

Paige's fingers dug into the muscles of his back and then she reached between them and took him in hand. When he sucked in a harsh breath, she smiled and whispered, "I think you like that."

"I *know* I like that."

It wasn't until after he made her come with his hand and his mouth that she heard the crinkle of foil again. Breathless and with her heart still hammering in her chest, she waited for him to move between her legs.

Mitch paused for a few seconds, his blue eyes crinkling a little as he smiled. "You are so beautiful."

"You make me *feel* beautiful."

"I'm glad. Now let's see what else I can make you feel."

It was delicious, the slow way he slid into her. She lifted her hips as he moved in an easy rhythm, urging him deeper. Coherent words would have escaped her even if she'd wanted to speak as she focused on the sensation of being filled, the friction, the way the muscles of Mitch's back rippled under her hands.

His pace quickened and he hooked his hands under her knees. Each stroke came faster and went deeper and she arched her back as the orgasm shook her. She heard him groan, felt him pulsing inside her, and then he dropped her knees and grabbed her shoulders, pushing deep as the last tremors shook them both.

When he laid his head on her chest, his ragged breath blowing hot across her breast, she ran her fingers through his hair, stroking him. After a while their breathing slowed back to normal, as did her pulse.

Mitch rolled off her, swore and lunged back across her. "Almost fell off the bed."

He tried again, rolling more slowly as she moved over against the wall. Foil crinkled again for a second, and then he lay back down, pulling her close.

"You're glowing," he murmured against her neck.

"And basking. Definitely basking."

"My feet are hanging off the end of the bed."

She laughed and opened her eyes. "Move up so your head's almost against the headboard."

"I'm afraid to move. I might fall on the floor."

He hadn't been afraid to move a few minutes ago. "You've had sex in cars and on couches and in a canoe, but you can't handle a twin bed?"

"I did *not* have sex in a canoe."

"That's not what I heard."

He snorted. "I know what you heard. I've heard it, too, but there was no sex. There was making out, but that's it."

She wondered how many of the other stories about him were embellished or even outright lies, but she was too warm and fuzzy from the basking to open that conversation.

For now she was content to lay her head on his chest and listen to his heartbeat.

IT WASN'T EVEN nine-thirty and Mitch was already sliding out of a woman's bed. That was a new one for him, but he knew Paige got up before the crack of dawn, was on her feet most of the day and needed the sleep. Unfortunately, the bed was at most half the size he was used to and it moved more than he anticipated.

Paige opened her eyes and gave him a sleepy smile that made him want to crawl back in beside her. Big mistake, he told himself. Over the years he'd learned that a woman's spending the whole night and waking up beside him changed her outlook from harmless fun to *I could get used to this*. "Are you leaving?"

"If I leave now, the argument can still be made I was helping you with the sink and dinner ran late. If the bike's still here in the morning, all bets are off."

"Do you really think we'll keep this a secret?"

She'd been in Whitford long enough to know it was already not a secret and hadn't been since he'd parked his bike in the diner lot without going into the diner. "Probably not, but at least you'll still have deniability if you want it."

"Will you be in for breakfast?"

Even though he knew Paige didn't want a relationship any more than he did, the question still triggered his *never commit* rule. "Not sure. Depends on what's going on at the lodge."

"Okay." She snuggled deeper under the light blanket and closed her eyes as he gathered his clothes and put them on. He thought maybe she'd gone back to sleep but, as soon as he zipped his jeans, she opened them again and he realized she'd been giving him some privacy to get dressed.

Once he'd dragged his T-shirt over his head and shoved his feet into his sneakers, he leaned over and kissed her—long enough to let her know he'd be back at some point, but just shy of making him want to take the clothes back off. "I'll lock the door on my way out."

"See you around," she said in a sleepy voice, which should have made him happy, because those words were anything but commitment heavy, but slightly *less* casual wouldn't have hurt.

After making sure the door was securely closed and locked behind him, Mitch pushed the Harley out into the road and walked it a few feet before firing the engine. Not that it would fool anybody in Whitford for a second, but Paige was probably on her way back to sleep and he didn't want to disturb her again.

He took it slow on the drive home, letting the night air cool him down, but since he could only go so slow on a motorcycle without falling over, he was back at the lodge way too soon. He didn't bother cutting the engine and coasting it to the garage. They knew he wasn't home yet, they knew where he'd been and, unless they'd undergone personality transplants while he was out, he knew Josh would be waiting up to give him shit. Since he was too old to climb the maple and shimmy out onto the limb that reached a window upstairs—assuming the limb hadn't been cut off or rotted to the point it would give out under his weight—he had no choice but to go in through the door. On the off chance his brother was sitting in the great room again, he went in through the back door, hoping to get through the kitchen and up the stairs before his brother could intercept him on those crutches.

"Must have been one *hell* of a hair ball," Josh said as soon as Mitch stepped through the door. He was sitting at the kitchen table, drinking a beer with his cast resting casually on a second chair, but the fine sheen of sweat across his forehead told Mitch his younger brother had had to bust ass to beat him there.

"Took a little longer than I expected. Then we had some dinner."

"What was for dessert?"

Refusing to rise to the bait, Mitch went to the fridge and grabbed a beer. "By the time the stuffed chicken breasts and double mashed were gone, I was too full for dessert. What did you have?"

"That's cold, man." Josh scowled at his beer. "I had a couple of tuna sandwiches, which sucked, and half a bag of potato chips."

"Hiring Andy was your idea."

"Yeah, yeah. You told me so and all that shit. She'll get over it soon. I hope."

"I wouldn't bet on it." It had been decades since Rose had spoken to Andy. Whatever was behind the grudge, it was a very big deal. "What's going in the morning?"

"We're going to empty out the barn so we—or you guys, I guess—can start tearing up the floor. Why? You have a breakfast date?"

"Nope. Just gauging how old a T-shirt I should throw on in the morning."

"Probably one that should have been a shop rag six months ago."

"Great." Probably not cool to be jealous of the guy with the crutches. "I'm going upstairs. Need to deal with some email and check over some reports. You all set?"

"Yeah. I'll hobble up in a few minutes."

Mitch got as far as responding to an email from Scott Burns, his second in command, before he stretched out on the bed and tucked his hands under his head. Staring up at the old tin ceiling, he thought about Paige. Sometimes, with the thrill of the chase over, the sex was a letdown. Sometimes, even if the sex was good, once was enough to get a woman out of his system.

And sometimes, the reality was even better than the anticipation and he couldn't wait to see her again. Alone.

CHAPTER ELEVEN

"YOU'RE PRETTY CHIPPER this morning."

Paige winced and told herself to dial that down a notch or two. The last thing she needed was all of Whitford wondering why she was in such a good mood the morning after Mitch Kowalski had helped her with her plumbing. So to speak.

"My sink drains now," she said. "It's a good day when the water you used to rinse the toothpaste out of the sink isn't going to still be sitting there when you get home from work."

"The plumber give you that whisker burn, too?"

Paige reached up to her face, horrified. She hadn't noticed it when she was getting ready for work, so it couldn't be that bad. But if Katie could see it...

Katie laughed. "Busted. I knew you wouldn't admit it straight out, but you slept with Mitch Kowalski last night."

"You have a diabolical mind. So there's no whisker burn?"

"No. The good people of Whitford will have no idea you were well and truly sullied by their golden boy last night. You *were* well and truly sullied, right?"

"You've heard the stories."

"Are they true?"

"It's not like we were doing reenactments, but based on last night I'm going to guess most of them are true."

Katie propped her chin on her hand and sighed. "Details, woman. I need details."

"Since the Benoits are about thirty seconds from walking in the door and I don't think *they* want details, you're out of luck. Not that I'd share, anyway."

"And you say *I'm* diabolical."

"Tell me what you want to eat so I can get your order in before the place starts filling up."

A half hour later, the Trailside Diner was in full morning swing and Paige didn't get a chance to do more than wave when Katie was ready to leave. She wanted to tell her friend not to tell anybody about their conversation because she didn't want to be added to the story roster in town, but she'd have to take it on faith Katie wouldn't spill. She might tell Mallory, though, and Mallory might tell…hell. There was a good chance everybody would know by the end of the day.

As busy as it was, though, Paige couldn't stop herself from wondering if Mitch would stop in for breakfast. And, if he did, whether she'd be able to look at him without her face turning stoplight-red, which would definitely give her customers something to chew on besides their sausage links. Speculation was the lifeblood of the town, and Paige acting like a silly, besotted schoolgirl would be something they hadn't already dissected to death.

He didn't show, though, and while she knew she should be relieved, she couldn't help feeling a little disappointed. He wasn't a man accustomed to hearing the word *no,* so maybe now that she'd said yes, he'd lost interest in her.

And that would be fine, she told herself sternly as she carried a tray of juice glasses to a back table. She wasn't going to fret about it and jump every time the door opened or the phone rang, like her mother would. It had been an exceptionally good time, but it was also temporary, like a trip to the bowling alley. A few hours of fun and then it was over. He wouldn't call. He wouldn't text. And neither would she.

After her shift was over, Paige grabbed her bag of books and walked to the library, just as she'd planned to do before Mitch had fixed her sink and then rocked her world. Nothing had changed in her life and today wasn't any different from any other day. It was basically what she'd been looking for and what he'd told her she'd get.

As soon as she got to the circulation desk and saw Hailey's face, she knew her fear that nothing so juicy as Mitch's visit could stay a secret in Whitford was justified. "Hi, Hailey. How're library things today?"

"Good. Very good, actually, now that I know the citizens of Whitford are safe from any violent sprees that might have been in your future."

There was no sense in denying it, especially if Hailey had talked to Katie. "You're all safe for a while longer."

Hailey gave a dreamy sigh as she started checking in the returned books, and Paige realized it was a little weird for them to be having this conversation. Maybe that's why Hailey didn't ask for details—she already knew them—and it seemed as if there should be at least a little awkwardness between two women who'd slept with the same man, even if one of them had done so many years before.

"Are you going to see him again?" Hailey asked, and she rolled her eyes when Paige said she wasn't sure. "That's Mitch. He won't commit to so much as a cup of coffee. He told you that, right?"

"That when he leaves he won't call, write or text? Yeah. And that works for me."

"Have you talked to him since?"

"Nope. And I'm not sitting by the phone, either."

"Good for you." Hailey looked around, as if to make sure there was nobody lurking in the nearby stacks, eavesdropping. Would have been nice if she'd thought to check that before bringing up Paige's sex life. "Did you hear about Drew and Mallory?"

"No. I saw Katie this morning and she didn't say anything."

"I'm not sure many people know. But for the last two nights, Drew's been sleeping at the police station."

"That's not a good sign." Paige shook her head. "I keep hoping they'll work it out, but it doesn't look like it. It's one thing to not talk to each other for a while, but not being able to sleep under the same roof is bad."

They had to drop the conversation as another patron approached, so Paige grabbed a few paperbacks that looked good off the new-release display and then wandered to one of the back tables, where a three-thousand-piece puzzle was about a third of the way done. She sat and lost herself in the pieces for a while, working on a tough spot it looked like the other puzzle-doers of Whitford were avoiding.

Being worried about Drew and Mal was a good excuse to call Mitch. Being friends with the police chief, he'd probably know if there was any truth to the rumors. Maybe he'd even have some ideas on how they could help. If he did, they could meet up somewhere for coffee and talk about it.

Paige tossed down a piece of cardboard foliage in disgust. Look at her, scheming up reasons to call Mitch—to see him again—and after only one night. It was just the kind of behavior she'd promised herself she was going to avoid when she'd made the decision to stay in Whitford. A couple hours with Mitch Kowalski and she was backsliding.

She waited until all was clear at the circulation desk and then went to check out her books.

"Not as many as usual," Hailey observed. "Plan on doing something else with your free time?"

Paige felt a hot blush over her cheeks, but she kept her voice level so Hailey would assume it was from embarrassment and not annoyance with the thoughts that had been running through her head. "I've got a few projects lined up to get done, plus I need to catch up on some paperwork for the diner. Or maybe I'll blow that all off and be back in two days for more books."

Hailey laughed and then growled under her breath as the phone rang. "If you run into Mal, tell her to call me, okay?"

Paige nodded and dropped the paperbacks into her tote so she could be gone before the call ended. She needed to go home and get her head on straight. Spend a few minutes standing in front of her refrigerator, reading her motto out loud. Or, if that didn't work, she could call her mother and get a reality check.

If Mitch Kowalski wanted to see her, he knew where to find her. If not, she had a bag of new books to keep her company.

ROSE WAS TEMPTED to ignore her cell phone when it rang. With all her free time, she'd discovered a channel that served up a regular TV diet of *Criminal Minds* repeats and, right now, she found the fictional FBI profilers better company than real people.

But very few people called her cell phone instead of the lodge's landline, so she checked the caller ID and saw that it was Liz. After hitting Mute on the TV remote, she answered. "Hello."

"I hear you're quite the lady of leisure now."

Since she was sitting in her room in the middle of the day, knitting and watching television, she couldn't really deny it. "Which one of your brothers complained?"

"Sean called Josh to see how his leg is doing and Josh told him about Andy Miller working there."

"Did they really expect me to be happy about it?"

"They needed somebody who would do good work for short money. Plus, he was a friend of Dad's."

He'd been a friend of Earle's, too, and look how that had worked out for Rose. "Be that as it may, he's no friend of mine and I'm not cooking for him or cleaning up after him or so much as looking at him."

A few seconds of silence followed, and Rose could imagine Liz trying to decide if she could push further on the issue or not. "That's Josh's problem, I guess. And Mitch's, who's the real reason I called. Sean said he's hung up on the woman who reopened the old diner?"

"Sean lives in New Hampshire. How did he get to be such a know-it-all about the goings-on in Whitford?

"Josh told him. And he said Mitch is really into her."

Rose sighed, unsure how to answer that. She'd have to agree Mitch seemed really into Paige, but she wasn't sure *he* knew that quite yet. Having his siblings ragging on him wouldn't help push him toward that awareness, but it might push him away.

"I know he's been spending a lot of time at the diner," Rose said. "He's probably looking for a decent meal, since he's not going to get one from me as long as he's paying that man to be on the property."

"Oh. That's probably it." Rose could hear the disappointment in Liz's voice. "It doesn't seem right that the two youngest of us are settled down and the three oldest aren't. Especially Mitch and Josh. At least Ryan tried, even if it didn't work out."

"Are you really settled? Happily?" She couldn't stop herself from asking, even though she knew it meant Liz would come up with some flimsy excuse to end the call.

"Just because I'm not married doesn't mean I'm not settled. I've been with Darren almost fifteen years."

The fact Liz hadn't addressed the "happy" part of the question didn't escape Rose's notice. "How's work going, honey?"

"Busy. I've picked up a few extra shifts in the last couple of weeks, so I'm pretty beat."

"And how many hours did Darren work?"

"Rose…" She heard Liz's exasperated sigh—a sound Rose had never tolerated from her when Liz was a teenager. "I've told you a thousand times, art doesn't work like that. It's not a nine-to-five kind of job."

"Okay. How many pieces has Darren sold this month?"

"Don't."

"This year?"

"He sold several pieces at an art show a couple of months ago and he's working on a big commissioned piece right now."

Rose swallowed her dislike of Darren and smiled so Liz would hear it in her voice. "That's wonderful, sweetie. Congratulations."

"I'll tell him you said that."

She meant it, even if it was for Liz's sake and not Darren's. Liz loved him, so what was good for him was good for her.

"I have to run," Liz said. "Call me if anything comes of Mitch liking that woman, okay? I hate being all the way on the other side of the country sometimes."

Not as much as Rose hated it. She'd much rather have all her chickens in New England. Sean was in New Hampshire and Ryan in Massachusetts, with Mitch only here temporarily, but at least she got regular visits from them. "I'll call you if there's anything juicy to report. Try to get some rest, okay?"

Rose left the television muted after the call ended, lost in thought. Liz had fallen head over heels for the young artist who'd called himself a sculptor because he was convinced rich people wanted pieces of scrap metal welded together to make "art." And when he'd decided to go out West, where he felt people were more appreciative of his kind of art, Liz went with him, despite her family's objections. Or maybe *to* spite them.

The question was whether or not she still loved him or if she was too proud to come home.

Liz was like a daughter to Rose. While her *own* daughter was off running with the boys, Liz had baked cookies with Rose and learned to knit and let Rose put her hair up in rag rollers. Under the sweet curls and feminine ruffles, though, Liz was a Kowalski through and through. She'd strained against Rose's maternal leash until she broke free.

Six kids—one of her own and five of her heart—and only one was happily married. Sean and Emma might have only six months under their belts, but Rose knew the real thing when she saw it, and they had it. Sadly, she'd never believed Ryan's marriage would last and she'd been right.

Maybe she'd been going about this Paige thing all wrong. She'd been so focused on protecting Paige's heart from Mitch she hadn't realized Mitch might be losing his to her. If Josh thought his brother was interested enough in a woman to mention it to Sean, maybe Rose had been missing the signs while hanging out in her room with the fictional FBI team.

Maybe she had an opportunity to improve her record to 2–6.

MITCH MANAGED A mere thirty-six hours. After leaving Paige's bed Friday night, he made it through all of Saturday and Saturday night, but Sunday morning found him parking the pickup in front of the Trailside Diner.

There were a few full tables, but nobody at the counter, so he pulled up a stool and waited for Paige to notice him. A couple minutes later, the door from the kitchen swung open and she backed into the dining area carrying a bus pan full of cleaning supplies. She set it on the edge of the counter, then scanned her customers to see if they needed anything.

She must have caught sight of him through the corner of her eye, because she turned to him and smiled. "Didn't expect to see you on a Sunday morning. How does Rose feel about you skipping out on her pancakes?"

"Rosie's been sleeping in lately," he said, then wondered if he'd said it too harshly when he saw the concern on her face.

"That doesn't sound like Rose. Is she okay? She's not sick or anything, is she?"

"The only thing wrong with that woman is a stubborn streak that borders on downright unreasonable."

"Oh," Paige said in a drawn-out way, as if a lightbulb had gone off in her head. "I heard something about that. She's not making you breakfast because you hired Andy Miller."

He gave her a sharp look. "You know about her problem with Andy?"

"Everybody knows she has a problem with him. But I don't know what it is."

"Nobody does."

"That seems odd. For an incident to trigger a decades-long grudge, you'd think it would have been bad enough so half the town would know."

He had to agree with her on that one, but he didn't say so out loud, because he didn't want her speculating any further. In his experience, the only thing that caused that kind of deep, secret animosity between a woman and a man was sex. He didn't want to think about Rosie and Andy and sex. She was like a mother to him and he didn't want to believe even for a second she'd cheated on her husband. He *wouldn't* believe it.

"How's Josh handling her being on strike?" Paige asked, dragging his mind back from those unpleasant thoughts.

He shrugged. "We're grown men. We can take care of ourselves."

"Out of clean laundry yet?"

He grinned. "Almost."

"Are you going to fire Andy?"

"No. I'm going to do a few loads of laundry and then head to the grocery store and stock up on more micro-wavable dinners."

Paige frowned, fiddling with the sugar packets. "You won't fire Rose, will you?"

He laughed, trying to imagine how that conversation would go. "If I tried to fire Rosie, she'd kick my ass and send me to my room."

He liked that he could see the relief on Paige's face. He liked that she cared about a woman he loved. And he *really* liked the way she leaned forward to rest her elbows on the counter so he could see down her shirt. He couldn't see much, but the hint of cleavage was enough to make him hard.

"You know," she said, "I wouldn't mind you coming over for dinner every once in a while. Save you a few microwave meals, at least."

He'd been kidding about the microwavable dinners. He could cook well enough for himself. But he wasn't fool enough to turn down an invitation to sit at Paige's table, which, thanks to the size of her trailer, wasn't too far from her bed. He'd been thinking about getting back in that bed since pretty much five minutes after he'd left it.

"I might even make you dessert," she told him.

"I like desserts with whipped cream. Lots of whipped cream."

The flush that spread across her neck and up into her cheeks made him want to take her out back right then and there and find a supply closet or something. "I just happened to buy some when I was at the market."

So she'd heard that story, too. This town was a pain in the ass. "When?"

"Tonight?"

"I can get there by six."

She smiled a flirty smile promising fun and all sorts of naughty things. "I'll be waiting."

So would he, because walking around with a raging hard-on until six o'clock was going to suck. But she was worth it.

CHAPTER TWELVE

IT WAS RIDICULOUS to spend the entire meal distracted by the upcoming dessert, but she couldn't stop thinking about the can of whipped cream sitting in her refrigerator. Maybe she should have bought two cans. One for the strawberry shortcake and one for all the things she'd spent the day imagining a man would do with a can of whipped cream and a naked woman.

"You feeling okay?"

Paige looked at him, thinking he looked more amused than concerned. "Sure. Why do you ask?"

"You look a little flushed."

"It's a little warm in here." She stood and threw her plate away—she'd made the dessert but succumbed to more carryout from the diner—then cleared his place since his plate was empty.

She should heat up the biscuits for the shortcake and take the strawberry topping out of the fridge. And the whipped cream. Paige jumped a little as Mitch's hands slid around her waist from behind. Then she leaned back against him, twisting her neck to get a kiss.

"You seem nervous tonight."

She *was* nervous. She'd felt ridiculous buying whipped cream at the store. Sure, a lot of people bought whipped cream, but how many were buying it for sex? On second thought, she probably didn't want to know.

"I'm not nervous." His hands slid up under her shirt and she suspected it might be time for strawberry short-cake, hold the strawberries and the shortcake.

"Not nerves." He kissed the back of her neck, sliding one of his hands around her body to cup her breast. "Anticipation?"

"Maybe. I happen to be very fond of strawberry shortcake."

"I happen to be very fond of this spot, right…" His hand slid down into her jeans until he found the sweet spot. "Here."

Paige would have liked to enjoy that more, but her mind was on the whipped cream. In her imagination, it was sexy and she could picture things that would make her blush. Actually, she *had* pictured things that did make her blush.

But the reality was awkward. At what point during the getting naked and the foreplay did one of them walk to the refrigerator and get the can? And wouldn't the can be very cold? Where did one indulge in whipped cream anyway? The bathtub wasn't big enough for both of them. Anyplace except the kitchen would cause a huge mess, but nobody wanted to have sex on cold, hard linoleum.

"Hey." He spun her around and looked into her eyes. "Tell me what's wrong."

"I…" There was probably no sense in lying. She wasn't very good at it, anyway. "I've never done the whole whipped-cream thing before."

"If you're not into it, that's okay, Paige." He grinned and shook his head.

"No, I am. I just don't know…how it works."

"There's no whipped-cream protocol as far as I know."

She narrowed her eyes at him. "You're making fun of me."

"Yes. Yes, I am." He pulled open her fridge and took out the can of whipped cream. After getting the cap off, he held it up. "Do you know what you do with whipped cream?"

"What I do with it is put it on strawberry shortcake."

"Open your mouth."

"Excuse me?"

He laughed at her. "Just open your mouth."

She did and, in what seemed like the blink of an eye, he squeezed the nozzle and filled her mouth with sweet, creamy foam. Then, while she tried to swallow it all without laughing or spitting it on him, he squirted some in his mouth, too.

"And that's what you do with whipped cream," he said, making her laugh. Thankfully, she'd swallowed.

"Yummy."

"Yes, it is. Be still. You've got a little bit on your mouth."

He leaned and flicked his tongue over the corner of her mouth. She felt the jolt all the way to her toes, followed by a full-body shudder as he licked her lip.

"I think I got it."

She took the can from him and squeezed a little spurt onto her finger. Reaching up, she wiped it across his bottom lip. "Oh look. You have a little bit on your mouth, too."

His breath was a little uneven and his eyes hot as she moved in. With tiny, teasing licks, she cleaned the whipped cream from his mouth. Feeling a little more brazen, she added a little more, this time to the hollow of his throat. When he threw his head back and made a groaning sound as her tongue swept over his skin, she realized she'd found one of his hot buttons.

"You might want to take your shirt off," she said in a low voice.

She'd never seen anybody take a shirt off as fast as he did. A little whipped cream on his nipples and his fingers were digging into her shoulders. And, when she got to the fly of his jeans, he actually held his breath for a second, before taking a step back.

"It's my turn. And you might want to get naked."

She did want to get naked, though maybe not in her kitchen, blinds lowered or not. But then he squirted a dollop of whipped cream onto his finger and taunted her with it.

"My couch is leather," she said. "Easy to clean."

"You have two seconds."

It probably took her more like thirty or forty, but only because she got tangled up in her pants halfway from the kitchen to the couch. They were both laughing when she collapsed on the sofa, but it didn't stop Mitch from whipped-creaming her nipple. Amusement quickly turned to desire as he leaned over her, sucking the topping off. When he turned the nozzle toward her other breast, she intercepted the stream and ended up with a serving in her hand.

When she reached out and smeared it down the rigid length of him, his breath hissed through his teeth and his hands curled into fists. Paige only had to shift a little to get her dessert.

She started slowly, with long licks that made his body tremble, and he muttered a curse under his breath. Paige took that as encouragement, running her tongue along his shaft until he unclenched his hands and buried them in her hair.

Covering him with her mouth, she took as much of him as she could, the sweet topping teasing her taste buds as she teased him. She kept the same easy rhythm he seemed to like, pausing once in a while to flick her tongue over the sensitive tip.

"Enough." His voice was raspy as he pulled free of her.

He had to fish for the condom he'd set on the floor, and then he turned her so she was kneeling on the edge of the couch cushion and bracing herself on the back. Standing behind her, he grabbed her hips and took her. No finesse and easy rhythm this time.

Mitch was on the edge of control, and knowing she'd driven him there gave her a rush of pleasure. Her fingers dug into the back of the couch as each thrust came faster and faster until the orgasm rocked her and she might have screamed.

He pounded into her, his fingertips clenching her hips until he came with a low growl. For a minute or so he held her there, breathing hard and still shaking, before he withdrew and they both flopped sideways onto the couch.

"Holy shit," he whispered.

"I agree."

"I think that should be an official whipped-cream protocol."

"I'll stock up."

After a few minutes, when they'd stopped panting, he gave her a light slap on the butt. "I think it's shower time for us."

"Yeah, I'm starting to feel sticky. You go first."

He stood and hauled her to her feet. "We can shower together. It's more fun."

"I don't think we'll both fit."

"We'll fit. We'll just squeeze in and have to rub our hot, soapy bodies together."

"I think it's a little less sexy in real life," Paige insisted, but she went anyway because Mitch's very fine, very naked ass was leading the way.

BY THE TIME they were both in the shower, Mitch was starting to think he should have listened to Paige. The tub surround was cold and a lot of his body was ending up pressed against it.

"I guess I can scratch sex in the shower off my to-do-with-Paige list."

She laughed and pushed him even more against the surround so she could reach the soap. "It's a good thing we didn't have any chocolate syrup. At least the whipped cream rinses off easily."

That's what she thought. With both of them in there and no handheld sprayer, the logistics of trying to get both of them clean kept him from enjoying Paige's slick, sudsy body to the full extent and he was relieved when they were done. Of course, they had to get out of the shower one at a time, because the bathroom wasn't big enough for both of them to dry off at the same time. Being a gentleman—and so that he had a reason to stand there and watch—he let her go first.

When he was finished drying off, he found her in her bedroom, slipping an oversize T-shirt over her head. "Hey. I'm not done with you yet."

He whacked his arm against her dresser getting across the room and almost fell on the floor when he misjudged how much room he had on the bed. "Don't take this the wrong way, Paige, but your home makes me feel like Gulliver."

"Should I tie you down and have my way with you?"

"You can have your way with me any way you want."

And she did, touching him and teasing him until he thought he'd explode and, only then, she slid down over him and it was so intense he wasn't sure he'd ever catch his breath.

After a few minutes, she stretched out in the tiny space between him and the wall, so he got up and went into the bathroom. When he came back out, he thought about putting his clothes on and kissing her goodbye, but she hadn't moved into his space and the bed, despite its size, was comfortable, and Paige had that rumpled, sleepy look he couldn't resist. A few more minutes wouldn't hurt.

He slid back into her bed, lining himself up along the edge and keeping his head close to the headboard so his feet didn't hang over, and she nestled against him. Telling himself he'd leave before he started nodding off, he turned and kissed the top of her head.

A little while later, when his phone started playing

the theme song of an old frat-party movie from some-where in Paige's living room, he realized with a start he'd actually fallen asleep. *That* he didn't do. Ever.

"Should you get that?" Paige murmured against his shoulder. It sounded as if she'd fallen asleep, too.

"That tone means it's Drew. I'll call him back on my way home." That was a natural segue to getting up and putting his clothes on, but he let himself have one more minute.

"How's he doing? I heard he's been sleeping at the police station."

"He was, but they finally talked a little bit and he's hoping they can still save their marriage, so he's sleep-ing at home again. Not together, but under the same roof, at least."

"I feel so bad for them," she said. "And it's hard to choose a side, not only because I like them both, but because their issue isn't cut-and-dried when it comes to fault."

"She's been lying to him for their entire marriage."

"True. But she's entitled to be hurt that children that don't exist are more important to him than she is."

"It's not about the kids they didn't have. It's about her lying." He really didn't want to end this night fight-ing about somebody else's relationship. "Look, Drew's been my best friend my whole life. I always liked Mal-lory, but I'm not in a position to choose sides. I've got Drew's back. Always."

"Even if he's in the wrong?"

"I don't think he's wrong but, yes, even if he was. He'd be like a brother to me if I didn't already have too many pain-in-the-ass brothers." He raised his eyebrow.

"Can you honestly say you're not just taking her side because you're both women?"

She pushed up onto her elbow so she could glare at him. "So we're all just man haters? Or are we sheep who can't think for ourselves? If you're going to insult my integrity, be specific."

This conversation was going south on him in a hurry and he wasn't even sure how it had happened. He'd try a kiss to distract her but, with that look in her eye, he was afraid she'd bite him. And not in a playful way.

Thankfully, her expression cleared and she flopped back with a sigh. "I don't even know why I'm arguing with you, since I don't disagree with you. I like both of them and there's really no right or wrong answer."

"I swear, they're the poster couple for what happens when two people who want different things in life end up together. It's not pretty."

"No, it's not."

They were quiet for a few minutes and Mitch felt her body start to relax against his. She was going back to sleep and there was no way in hell he could let himself do the same. If his phone hadn't gone off, he might have slept the entire night, and waking up next to a woman was a big mistake.

He kissed the top of her head again before sliding out of bed. "I should get going so you can get some sleep."

"Four-thirty sucks," she muttered.

By the time he'd found all his clothes and put them on, she was softly snoring, so he turned off the lights as he left and locked the door behind him. Thankful the threat of rain showers had made him bring the truck tonight, he got in and pulled out his phone to listen to the voice mail from Drew. As it went through the "you have one new message" routine, he braced himself for bad news.

"Hey, you suck. I had to go out on a nuisance call and saw your truck parked at Paige's. Just thought I'd call in a little coitus interruptus, but obviously you're having too good a time to answer your phone. Did I mention you suck?"

Mitch chuckled as he deleted the message and disconnected. But as he started the truck and pointed it toward home, his thoughts were already turning from Drew back to Paige. She wasn't an easy woman to leave behind, naked and warm and sleepy-eyed in bed.

Although not spending the night in a woman's bed was a rule he never, ever broke, he had some guidelines that were a little more fluid, like not seeing a woman two nights in a row.

He had a feeling he was going to break that rule as often as she'd let him.

"I'VE BEEN IN your bathroom and there's no way in hell both of you fit in that bathtub."

Paige laughed at Hailey's expression before taking a few hasty licks of the fudge pop she'd bought at the market. They were sitting in the park with their ice creams and, while Paige wasn't really one to kiss and tell, the bathtub story was too funny not to share.

"We were both in the tub, but I don't think we'll try it again anytime soon."

"That was Sunday night?" Paige nodded, too intent on saving every drop of melting chocolate to answer. "And he was there Monday night. And Tuesday night.

So counting Friday night, but not Saturday, you've had sex almost every night for half a week. I hate you. Seriously, you should give me your ice cream when I'm done with mine."

"He's been coming in for a late breakfast every day, too. I can't even imagine what Rosie and Josh must think."

"Knowing Rosie, she's thankful he's saving them money on the grocery bill." Hailey licked the last of her fudge pop off the stick, then scowled at it. "I need to get out of Whitford. Maybe find somebody to date."

"There are plenty of single guys in town. Josh is single and it's not like he can run away right now." Hailey wrinkled her nose. "Ryan will be back in town for a while. How about him?"

"The Kowalski guys just don't do much for me. No offense, and one teenage indiscretion notwithstanding, of course. And even if Katie doesn't know it yet, me hooking up with Josh wouldn't be cool, because someday she'll admit *she* wants to hook up with him and I don't want the *friend's ex* thing standing in the way. And Ryan? He's almost a stranger now. Even when he's in town, he's rarely *in* town."

"There has to be somebody. I'm going to start feeling guilty if I'm having amazing sex on a regular basis and all you're getting are brain-freeze headaches from all the consolation ice cream."

"I hate you a little right now. And I'm probably going to blow my entire household budget for next month shopping online when I get home."

"You do have great shoes."

Hailey rolled her eyes. "I'd rather have great sex."

Paige wiggled her toes in her raggedy flip-flops and smiled. So would she. "Once he goes back to New York, maybe I'll buy a pair of outrageous high heels and a gallon of chocolate chip ice cream. And chips, of course, because you can't have sweet without the salty, crunchy chaser when you feel like crap."

"When are you going to see him again?"

"Don't know. He didn't say when. Or even *if.* Ryan's supposed to come back today, so I think they're going to be busy at the lodge." Paige elbowed Hailey. "It'll give me time to recuperate."

"I hate you even more now. Stop before I push you off the bench and steal all your money to buy ice cream." They both laughed, but when they stood to throw their trash away, Hailey grew serious on her. "You're not getting too attached to him, right?"

"Of course not." Maybe she'd said it too quickly, because Hailey didn't look convinced. "I'm just having fun, like you said I should. Reel him in, keep him a few weeks, then throw him back and let him swim away. Isn't that what you said?"

"Just checking. Shoe shopping and ice cream might be fun, but I don't want to have to nurse you through a broken heart."

"You won't have to, I promise. No hearts are being harmed in the making of this bizarre fish metaphor of yours."

It was all catch and release where Mitch was concerned.

CHAPTER THIRTEEN

WHEN SHE HEARD a truck pull in the drive, Rosie stuffed the rag and the can of furniture polish into the cleaning tote and rushed to get it back into the closet. She didn't want anybody to know she'd been cleaning.

She knew she wasn't technically on strike if she was stealth cleaning the lodge, but once she'd made her point, she didn't want to imagine what the place would look like if she hadn't lifted a hand in the meantime. The boys were muddling through the big, obvious stuff, but she'd never catch up if she didn't sneak in some spit and polish here and there.

Thinking the truck was Ryan's, since he was coming up for a few days, Rosie went out the kitchen door and around the house. She didn't see the man or the truck until it was too late to turn around without being seen.

Andy Miller looked her in the eye and then, instead of doing the decent thing and pretending he didn't see her, he walked directly toward her. Rose wanted to turn and run, but, by God, this was her home and she was no coward.

"It's been twenty-six years, Rose," he said. "And Earle's been gone the last fourteen of them. How long are you going to hate me?"

Whether or not to answer was a struggle. She'd managed to go twenty-six years without speaking to the man, but he'd asked her a direct question this time and ignoring it would be more rude than she usually cared to be.

"Longer than twenty-six years, I guess," she told him.

"I'm sorry. You know, you've never given me a chance to tell you that."

"Because I don't care."

"You're a hard woman, Rosie Davis."

She turned on him, fighting the urge to reintroduce the flat of her hand to the side of his face. It had been a long time since she'd slapped him, but she'd never lost the urge to do it again. "Don't you dare call me that. Only people who care about me call me Rosie."

He shook his head, his expression sad and his shoulder slumping a little. "I didn't make him do anything he wasn't willing to do. He was a grown man and he made his own choice."

She almost did hit him then, because it was the truth and she didn't want to hear it. It was a lot easier to blame Andy for what Earle had done. "I want you to leave now."

For a long moment she thought he might argue with her, but then he walked past her and disappeared around the house.

Though she thought she was done shedding tears over the situation, a few gathered in her eyes and she swiped at them with the back of her hand as she walked halfway around the lodge in the opposite direction to get to the front door.

Damn him. Damn Andy Miller and his too-late, not-enough apology. And damn Earle Davis, too.

They'd gone over to New Hampshire snowmobiling, just the two guys. It was something they did every couple of years, just to see some new scenery. Earle had come home a different man and it wasn't but a few days before guilt drove him to confess he'd cheated on her.

They'd been at a restaurant, having steaks and a few beers after the mileage was done for the day, and Andy had met up with a couple of pretty women at the bar, one of whom tripped his trigger in a big way. The only way she'd go back to their motel room, though, was if her friend could go, too. A few more beers and a hot young thing jealous her friend was getting some action, and Earle had broken his wedding vows.

She hadn't left him. They had a seven-year-old and a home and she knew, at heart, Earle was a good man. But their marriage was never the same after that. His confession was like a spot of tarnish on a piece of heirloom silver. You could treasure that heirloom and shine it up and show it off, but that bit of tarnish was always there, a sore spot you couldn't rub away.

And she blamed Andy Miller for it. Not that she didn't blame Earle, but she believed in her heart her husband would never have strayed if Andy hadn't put him in the position he'd been in. The man became as good as dead to her and, if Earle and Andy continued their friendship after that weekend, she didn't see or hear evidence of it. And her husband was never gone overnight again.

Rose pulled out a chair and sat down at the kitchen table, feeling a little shaky. She couldn't put the sorrow and regret she'd seen in Andy's eyes out of her mind, and that made her even angrier. When she was being honest with herself, she knew that blaming and hating Andy had made it easier for her to live with forgiving her husband. Nothing Andy—or the woman—could have done would make Earle cheat if he wasn't of a mind to already.

And she had to begrudgingly respect the fact nobody in Whitford ever found out Earle Davis had cheated on his wife. She and Earle certainly hadn't told anybody. But she knew if Andy had told even a single soul, everybody in town would have eventually heard, and that would have made it a lot harder to pretend everything was fine during the long months—or years, really—it took for the pretense to eventually become reality again.

Because she wasn't quite ready to admit it was unfair to blame a guy who hadn't even done anything wrong back when he was young, single and stupid, Rose went back to the cleaning closet and grabbed the big basket of supplies and a pair of rubber gloves. Any dirt or stray toothpaste with the audacity to hide in one of the Northern Star's bathrooms was about to bear the brunt of her frustration. Some women indulged in retail therapy. Rose scrubbed.

MITCH WAS TIRED. He was physically tired from spending much of Sunday night in Paige's bed, followed by much of Monday night and even more of last night. He was mentally tired from worrying about the lodge while keeping his thumb on Northern Star Demolition from a distance and thinking about the fact he'd spent a good part of three nights in a row in Paige's little bed.

And he was really damn tired of wading through the mind-boggling amount of crap his family had managed to cram into the barn. He'd thought emptying the building out to redo the floors would be a quick job, but now he was beginning to wonder if they'd even be able to start replacing planks before Josh lost the cast and crutches.

A long stream of curses cobbled together to make colorful compound swearwords made Mitch turn to see Ryan trying not to lose his grip on a crate of old tools while extricating his boot from a hole rotted in the floor.

He was about to tell him to hang on a second and he'd grab the crate, when Ryan threw the thing, and decades' worth of screwdrivers and wrenches scattered. Once his foot was free, Ryan crossed his arms and stared up at the ceiling, as if praying for the fortitude not to simply burn the whole mess to the ground.

"I need a break," Mitch said. "Let's take a ride out back."

The words *out back* got Ryan's attention, but he looked skeptical. "With as much care and attention as everything else around here got, the four-wheelers probably don't even run anymore."

"I fired them up last week just to see, and Josh said he changed the oil in them not too long ago."

"Should we tell them?"

Mitch snorted. "Hell, no. They'll hear us leave and figure it out. I don't want to give anybody a chance to point out how much shit's left on the to-do list."

The four-wheelers had been parked behind the barn and it only took a minute to undo the rope and pull back the tarp that covered them. The keys were in them and they each fired one up. They were old ATVs, without the luxuries of electronic fuel injection or independent rear suspension or power steering, but they were familiar and dependable and just what they needed.

Mitch followed Ryan across the backyard and into one of the cuts through the woods surrounding the lodge. There was a little fresh growth, but the trails they'd been using since they were kids were still there, and Mitch felt some of the tension ease out of his shoulders as he thumbed the throttle and made his four-wheeler jump over a bump in the trail.

They had enough land to have multiple trails that cut back and crossed each other at unmarked intersections. Somebody else would have been hopelessly lost within the first twenty minutes, but they knew every tree, boulder and other natural landmark on the property. Growing up, they'd all rushed through their chores so they could climb on the ATVs and go adventuring in the woods. There was one for each kid, disreputable beasts held together with duct tape and Loctite, but Katie usually went out with them while Liz stayed behind to shadow Rosie.

After close to an hour of winding through trees and pounding through ruts and over rocks, Ryan pulled off into a wide spot in the trail and Mitch did the same. Off to his right was the log they'd worked for weeks to turn into a bench, but he didn't dare test his weight on it. Looking at it made him smile, though, as he remembered how close they'd all been as kids. They'd bickered, of course, but they'd been close in a way they weren't as adults, in more ways than geographical proximity.

"We probably should have grabbed a bottle of water before we headed out," Ryan said, and Mitch laughed.

"I have gum, if that helps." He fished the pack out of his pocket and handed Ryan a piece before popping one in his mouth.

"So how are things going with Paige Sullivan?"

The question was asked innocently enough, but Mitch had no doubt Ryan was digging at him. He would already have heard from Josh that their oldest brother was creeping home from Paige's place in the wee hours. "Good."

"Really? That's all you're going to give me? Lame."

"What do you want me to say? She's fun, we have a good time, and I'm leaving in a couple of weeks when Josh gets the cast off."

"And you gave her the whole 'won't call, won't text' spiel?"

"It's not a spiel, jackass. It's not like I'm selling her a used car." He chewed his gum for a minute, hands shoved in his pockets. "But, yeah, she knows there's no relationship going on."

Saying it out loud made him wonder silently what a relationship was. Enjoying time together? Check. Great sex? A giant red check. Talking about books they both loved and about people they both knew and about their lives? Check. And, whenever they were apart, looking forward to when they'd be together again?

That was the one he was worried about. He found himself thinking about Paige during the day a little too often for comfort. He'd hear something funny and want to tell her. Or see something cool and want to take a picture to share it with her. He thought she was beautiful with messy hair and no makeup, and he didn't give a damn if she'd just had onions on her burger when he moved in for a kiss.

If some guy told him he felt like that, Mitch would tell the poor sap there was no doubt he was in a relationship.

All Mitch could do was keep in mind there was going to come a time in the very near future when Paige wouldn't be there to share funny stories with or talk books with. No more cheeseburger-with-onions kisses.

"Geez, you got it that bad?" Ryan was staring at him, an eyebrow raised.

"Hell, no. I was thinking about all the crap we have left to do at the lodge."

"Uh-huh."

"Screw you." Mitch straddled his machine, ready to get moving again, but he couldn't resist a parting shot at the brother who loved to push his buttons. "Have you run into Lauren Carpenter around town?"

Ryan's expression hardened, but he didn't say anything. He flipped Mitch the bird, then fired up his ATV with a roar. Chunks of dirt and a few rocks flew up as Ryan spun his wheels taking off, and then Mitch was chasing him up the trail.

They rode as hard as the tight and windy trails allowed until Mitch was sweating and already feeling the pull across his shoulders. As they neared the far edge of Kowalski land, where it abutted Ed Grandmaison's property, he wondered if they'd have time to load up the wheelers and drive all the way around to the neighboring town—on the other side of Grandmaison—to the real trail system.

Even as he jerked the bars to avoid a rock big enough to stop the ATV in its tracks, the smallest germ of an idea for rejuvenating the Northern Star Lodge planted itself in his mind.

PAIGE WAS DRAGGING. Badly. With an embarrassingly small amount of stage makeup, she could probably win an Oscar for playing a zombie.

That's what happened when a sweet, smoking-hot man snuck out of your bed somewhere around midnight and your alarm went off at precisely four-thirty. You felt like you got hit by a freight train, but you were grinning on impact.

Folding herself into her tiny bathtub, hoping to soak as many of her body parts as she could fit in the foamy, hot water, Paige gave herself a good scrubbing before she sighed and closed her eyes. She wouldn't be seeing Mitch tonight. His brother Ryan was back in town and they had a lot to get done. And maybe, like her, he needed to catch up on some sleep.

Just when she'd relaxed to the point she was afraid she'd fall asleep in the bath—though, thankfully, there wasn't room to drown—her cell phone rang. It was on the edge of the sink, which she could reach from the tub, and Hailey's name was flashing on the screen.

After a few seconds of hesitation, she answered the call. "Hello?"

"Every night this week?"

She didn't need a secret decoder ring to figure out what she meant by that. "It's only Wednesday night, so we're only halfway through the week."

"Is he there now?"

Paige smiled. "You tell me."

There were a few seconds of stubborn silence, and then Hailey laughed. "Okay, so I know he's not. Ryan's in town and when Andy Miller stopped in at the hardware store, he told Dozer that Mitch and Josh were glad to see him, because it meant Rose would cook a real dinner and that they'd be going over plans after they ate."

"So why did you ask?"

"I don't know. I thought maybe he'd ditched his brothers to sneak over and see you."

Since the tub didn't hold enough water with her in it to keep itself hot long, Paige pulled the plug and stood. With her free hand she grabbed a towel and started blotting herself dry. "He doesn't sneak. You make us sound like teenagers."

"You're going at it like teenagers," Hailey retorted, and Paige wondered if there was maybe a little jealousy there.

"I'm going at it like I haven't had sex in two years. As for Mitch, I think he just really likes sex. A lot. And he's very good at it."

"I wonder if it runs in the family," Hailey said. "Ryan and Josh are still single."

"I think if you had any chemistry at all with them, you would have wondered that before now."

"True. So when are you going to see him again? Do you have to wait until Ryan goes back to Mass?"

"I don't know." They hadn't discussed it at all. She only knew he wasn't coming tonight because he'd mentioned Ryan being home and what they'd be doing that evening. "I guess if he comes around again, that's when I'll see him."

"*If?* You need more than that from him. You should at least know which days you don't have to shave your legs."

Laughing, Paige threaded the damp towel over the bar one-handed and then managed to get herself into her robe without dropping her phone. "Mitch doesn't like to commit to anything, even a cup of coffee, so if he comes by on a stubble day, that's his problem."

While she set up the coffeemaker so it would magically deliver fresh coffee at four-thirty in the morning, Paige tried a few times to change the subject. She didn't want to analyze what she and Mitch had, because analysis meant feelings and those were the very last thing she wanted to talk about—feelings and the fact she might be having some.

She missed him tonight. Maybe if it was a *wham-bam-thank-you-ma'am* kind of thing, she wouldn't, but he was also surprisingly good company with his pants on. They'd spent almost an hour the night before arguing over which book was Stephen King's best before they even got around to making out on her couch. And the fact he was very good company with his pants *off* went without saying.

She hit subject-change pay dirt when she brought up Drew and Mallory. The town had been all abuzz when Mallory visited her husband at the police station. An argument ensued that was rumored to shake the windows, though nobody was repeating what was said. Nobody knew quite what to make of that, though most people had their fingers crossed it was the huge meltdown that would clear the way for the couple to reconcile.

"I've left her a couple of messages," Hailey said, "but I haven't heard back from her. Mitch is his best friend. Has he said anything to you?"

"Nope." There was no reason to share their previous conversation on the matter. It was best if Hailey thought their relationship was all sex, all the time.

"If you hear anything, let me know."

"I will. And you do the same." Paige wrapped up the conversation and then put her phone on the charger for the night.

She should probably feel embarrassed about crawling into bed while it was still light out, but Paige was beyond caring. She needed sleep and lots of it. After sliding between the sheets, she closed her eyes and thought about Mitch.

CHAPTER FOURTEEN

By Friday, Mitch was ready to share his possible plan for increasing the lodge's revenue. He told Ryan about it first, and he thought it had such good potential they stopped what they were doing to go inside, where Mitch pulled out the notes and maps and projections he'd hastily sketched out, as well as the official trail-system map he'd printed off the computer.

The more he and Ryan talked through it, the more Mitch was convinced it would work, even if the Kowalskis—and he in particular—were going to have to lay on the charm like sunscreen on a blond toddler.

"What are you guys looking at?"

Mitch and Ryan had been so engrossed in the maps, they hadn't heard Josh coming, even with the thump of his crutches against the wooden floors. Mitch used his foot to shove a chair out for him. "Maps. Ryan and I were talking today and we think with a little charm, luck and money, we can get access to the ATV trails. Instead of just a stray booking here and there, the lodge could have real business all year long instead of just during the winter."

Josh grumbled what sounded like a curse as he sat, but Mitch couldn't tell if it was a response to what he'd said or discomfort from his leg. "Dad looked into it once, but there was no way to do it."

"Martha Grandmaison passed away a few years back," Mitch pointed out. "Her son owns the property behind us now and he might be more reasonable."

"Look." Ryan slid the maps toward Josh and leaned across the table to jab at them with his finger. "We've got a whole mess of ATV trails over there. If we can get Ed Grandmaison to agree to let us pass through one small section of his dozens of acres of woods, we can cut a path that connects the trail system to our land. Since we're on the sled trails, once the ATVs get here, we can get the snowmobile club to give permission for them to use the sled trails so the ATVs can get into town for gas and food. And, most importantly, lodging. It's a win for everybody."

Josh's jaw tightened. "Yeah, that's what it is. A win."

Mitch leaned back in his chair and crossed his arms. "Thought you'd be a little more on board with a plan that would help the Northern Star make money again."

He shrugged. "Maybe you've forgotten, but Ed Grandmaison isn't your biggest fan."

"We were nineteen. And she told me they'd broken up."

Josh shook his head. "You slept with his girlfriend. He's not going to do a damn thing to help us."

Ryan pounded his fist on the table. "Well, you're not doing a goddamn thing to help us, so what the hell are we supposed to do? Let the place go under?"

"Yes," Josh snapped. He struggled to his feet and grabbed his crutches. "Let it go under and then maybe I can have a fucking life, okay?"

Mitch and Ryan were both stunned into silence, but Mitch recovered first. "What the hell are you talking about?"

"Forget it." Josh started turning away, but Mitch reached out and grabbed his crutches.

"Sit down."

"Screw you."

Mitch shrugged and handed the crutches to Ryan, who leaned them against the wall behind him. "You can sit down or you can drag yourself across the floor and up the stairs, but you're not getting the sticks back until you tell us what the hell is wrong with you."

He didn't have much of a choice, so Josh sat. "You guys sweep in here with your grand plan to save the Northern Star Lodge. You'll make a shitload of work and then you'll leave again, just like you always have."

"We have businesses to run," Ryan said. "And what's this about you not having a life? You're the keystone of the family. You run this place for all of us."

Josh snorted, shaking his head. "Because there was nobody else to do it. One by one you all went off to college and didn't come back. What the hell was I sup-posed to do? Say, 'Sorry, Dad, you're on your own'? Somebody had to stay. And then he died and you all came home but, after the funeral, you all left again."

Mitch didn't know what to say and, judging by the silence, Ryan didn't either. Josh had always run the lodge with their old man, and he'd kept on running it after he died. He'd never said he didn't want to, as far as Mitch could remember.

"I think we should sell it," Josh said.

Sell the Northern Star Lodge? It was home—the one

place that was always there, no matter where he roamed. Their great-grandfather had built it, their grandfather had reenvisioned it and their father had saved it. It was as much a part of who they were as their blue eyes, stubborn streaks and last name.

And it was an albatross around Josh's neck. An anchor dragging him under. Whatever stupid expression that meant his youngest brother had been stuck in Whitford, living a life he'd been stuck with by default, while the rest of them were free to choose their own paths.

"It's not a good time to sell," Ryan said.

Mitch jumped on the excuse to resist the idea with something more than being a selfish bastard who didn't want anything to change. "Especially a commercial property like this that's barely treading water."

"It doesn't have to be commercial," Josh argued. "Maybe somebody would just want to live in it."

Unlikely, though Mitch didn't say so. It was too unwieldy and hard to manage for a single family unless they were loaded. And, if they were loaded, they wouldn't want an old snowmobile lodge.

"We'd be lucky to make a hundred bucks," Ryan pushed on, but Mitch looked at Josh and knew it didn't matter. It had nothing to do with profits or losses and everything to do with Josh being able to walk away.

"Ryan's right," he said, and Josh's whole body tensed. In order to sell, all of them had to agree and, if he thought it wasn't going to happen, what was to stop Josh from saying *screw it* and walking away? "*But, I* get it now, Josh. We both get it and we'll figure it out."

Josh's muscles relaxed and he propped his elbows on the table to scrub his hands through his hair. "It's been building a long time, I guess. I didn't realize it had gotten so bad until Rosie told me Mitch was coming to take care of things for six weeks. For a few seconds I actually wondered what I'd do or where I'd go if I could leave this place for six weeks, but then I realized I couldn't do jack shit with this cast on."

"I'm surprised you didn't just…up and go," Ryan said.

"Just abandon the place? And leave Rosie?" Josh glared at him. "I deserve more credit than that."

"Yeah, you do."

Mitch sighed and looked at all his grand plans laid out on the table. "Before we can decide if we're going to sell, somebody has to talk to Sean and Liz. And I think we should still go ahead with the preliminary legwork for getting connected to the ATV trails. If we decide to sell, being able to show prospective buyers that potential new revenue could make a big difference in the asking price."

Josh picked at the corner of a stack of papers. "But you'll consider selling?"

"We have to do something," Mitch said. "Now that we know how you feel, we can't just walk away and leave you here without a plan."

Ryan nodded. "It never occurred to me you didn't want to run the Northern Star. I don't think it occurred to any of us."

Mitch watched Josh lean back in his chair, realizing his youngest brother had the relieved look of a man who'd just unburdened himself of a long-held, dark secret. Jesus, had *any* of them ever thought about whether

Josh might want to go out and see some of the world? He was ashamed to admit he hadn't.

But as happy as he was to know what was eating at his brother, Mitch felt a few sharp pangs of sorrow thinking about the lodge being sold. He didn't get back to Whitford often and the town drove him nuts, but it was home. His *real* home, not just the apartment in the city he slept in between jobs. And now there was a good possibility the fourth generation of Kowalskis to own the property would be the last.

"So who's going to talk to Grandmaison?" Josh asked, pulling the rough sketch of land boundaries across the table to get a better look at it.

Mitch grimaced. "I'll do it. That way we'll know right off from his reaction to me if this is even a possibility."

Ryan laughed. "Who would have guessed sleeping with a girl when you were a teenager would come back to bite you in the ass?"

In this town, everything came back to bite you in the ass sooner or later.

PAIGE HEARD THE low rumble of Mitch's motorcycle in the distance and tried not to hope he turned in and parked in front of her trailer, but she was kidding herself. She wanted to see him and hadn't thought about much except that fact all day, much to her customers' dismay. White and wheat weren't close enough when it was early in the morning—you had to get to work and you didn't have time for the waitress to screw up your breakfast.

Wednesday and Thursday hadn't been bad, but for

some reason she'd really missed him today. Maybe it was because her body had gotten used to closing out the day with an orgasm or a few, or maybe she just missed his laugh. Either way, the rumble made her pulse quicken.

The bike turned in and she heard it come through the diner's parking lot. Then, through the window, she watched him park it between her car and the house. While she appreciated the effort, it wasn't much of a hiding place and this would be yet another nice, juicy tidbit for the town to chew on. And probably another phone call from Hailey.

He took off his helmet and then sat for a while on the bike, looking tired and frustrated. She moved away from the window to give him some privacy and it was at least a full minute before she heard him climbing the steps and the knock on the door.

When she opened it, the frustration and exhaustion were gone. His expression was clear and his lips were turned up in that charming smile of his. "Hey."

"Hey, you," she said, stepping aside to let him in.

"I'm going for a ride. Thought I'd see if you want to go."

She had paperwork to do for the diner—the endless, mind-numbing task of tracking what they were using, what needed ordering, what they'd ordered too much of and so on. It was her least favorite part of owning the diner, but it was a necessary evil and she was already behind.

But, relaxed and inviting smile or not, Mitch had had a rough day and he'd come to her looking for company.

The paperwork could wait. "I was just going to make a sandwich for dinner. Do you want one before we leave?"

"I could eat."

"Do you like fried bologna sandwiches?" It was a little embarrassing to have to ask that, but she didn't have a lot in the house.

He gave her a startled look she couldn't begin to decipher. "Yes, I do."

"Tomato and mayo?"

"Of course. Can I help?"

She laughed. "Thanks, but you already know the kitchen's not really big enough for two. Grab a soda if you want and have a seat."

Once he was sitting at the small kitchen table, she pulled out a pan and plopped a dollop of butter in it. While that heated, she scored a few slices of bologna and, once the butter was sizzling, dropped them into the pan. While they seared, she sliced a tomato and, after flipping the bologna, slathered mayo onto bread. A few minutes later she set two paper plates on the table, one with a single sandwich for her and one with two for him. After tossing a bag of potato chips into the center of the table, she sat as he took his first bite.

As he swallowed, he was giving her the strangest look. "Is it okay?"

"It's perfect." He gestured at his plate. "Who taught you to make a fried bologna sandwich like this?"

"I don't know. I used to make them when I was a kid when my mom wasn't around."

"So it wasn't Rose?"

She'd known he was in a weird mood, but now he

was barely making sense. "I knew how to fry bologna long before I met Rose."

"Along with the perfect thickness for the tomato slices and just the right amount of mayo?"

"If it doesn't try to run down the side of your hand, it's not good enough. Are you okay?"

He blinked at his sandwich, then seemed to shake off whatever was bothering him about it. "I guess. Dealing with some stuff. The lodge. Brother stuff."

"Anything I can help with?" Probably not, but she asked anyway.

"I have to take a ride out and visit Ed Grandmaison. You can come with me. Maybe be a witness if he tries to kick my ass."

"I don't think I know him."

"His property abuts ours, but his house is actually on the far side, so he's in the next town over. He doesn't come to Whitford often."

"And he wants to kick your ass why?" She held up her hand. "Wait. Let me guess. A woman?"

"We were nineteen and she told me they were broken up."

"One of the first things I learned when I moved to Vermont is how much New Englanders love holding a grudge."

"Will you come with me?"

"Sure. Other than the part where a guy I don't know might kick your ass for something you did when you were nineteen, it sounds like a good time."

He grinned at her, then set about devouring the fried bologna sandwiches. He cleaned up while she changed into jeans and threw on a light sweatshirt, and then they headed out of town.

She could feel the tension in his back and she wondered if it had to do with the impending visit to Grandmaison or if it was lingering from whatever the "brother stuff" was he'd referred to. She'd wanted to poke at that a little—see if that was what was really bothering him—but it seemed like a very girlfriend thing to do, so she didn't.

Instead she was silent, enjoying the ride until Mitch put on his blinker and turned down a long dirt road. She held her breath, hating the sensation of a big Harley on dirt, but Mitch had no problem bringing the bike to a stop in front of an old, but impeccably kept, farmhouse.

She followed him up the front steps because she wasn't sure what else to do with herself, so she was close enough to hear the curses Ed Grandmaison muttered when he saw Mitch Kowalski on the other side of the screen door.

"What the hell do you want?"

"Hey, Ed. I, uh…" Mitch hesitated, shifting his weight from one foot to the other in a rare display of anxiety. "I've come to ask you a favor."

"You slept with my wife."

"I did *not* sleep with your wife. I didn't even technically sleep with your girlfriend, since you were broken up at the time."

"It was just a fight."

"We were nineteen."

Paige had to work hard to keep a straight face. Not because Ed Grandmaison could seriously hold a grudge, but because watching Mitch's charm have absolutely no effect on somebody was a first.

"What kind of favor are you looking for?"

"I don't know if you've heard anything, but things are a little rough at the Northern Star right now," Mitch said, which had to be tough for him to say to a man who hated him. "We were thinking, if we could connect to the ATV trails, we could have business year-round instead of only when there's snow on the ground. But to do that, we'd need your permission to cut in a small trail across the far corner of your property."

"You're kidding."

"It's not just about the Northern Star Lodge," Paige said quickly, stepping forward so she was next to Mitch. "If we can get the four-wheelers into Whitford, it would benefit the entire town. If visitors stay at the lodge so they can access the trail system, they'll also get gas and eat and buy incidentals."

Ed looked at her, his mouth in a grim line. "Are you his girlfriend?"

"I'm Paige Sullivan. I own the Trailside Diner." She shook his hand without answering the question. "'Trailside' means the sled trails right now, but ATVs coming into town would benefit my business, as well as the Kowalskis'. And many other businesses as well."

"I'd have to talk to my *wife*," he said, with a noticeable emphasis on the word *wife*.

"Absolutely," Mitch told him. "You'll both have questions, and we'd put you in contact with the ATV club so they could explain how the insurance policy that would cover you works and all of that. But right now, I just need to know if you'll at least consider the possibility."

Ed shrugged. "I'll consider it. The economy sucks all over and I'd hate to put the screws to a whole town because you put the screws to my wife."

"I—" Mitch began, but Paige poked him in the back. "Thank you."

They left before the conversation could go downhill any further. Mitch kept a sedate pace on the dirt, but as soon as they hit the main road, he cracked the throttle and let the bike roar back toward Whitford.

THE FOLLOWING DAY, the guys set to work emptying out the last few piles of crap in the barn so they could finally start work on the floor, while Mitch's brain set to work on the puzzle of the fried bologna sandwiches.

It couldn't be a coincidence. Supposedly there was no such thing as a coincidence. And, if it had been most of the other women he'd casually dated in the past, he'd say it was somehow a deliberate ploy to get to his heart through his stomach by way of a sandwich that made him think of home, family and love.

But Paige wasn't like any of the women he'd casually dated in the past, and he couldn't imagine her playing that kind of silly game. Which meant he was enjoying the company of—and having the best sex of his life with—a woman who also happened to make perfect fried bologna sandwiches.

That wasn't good at all.

"Your girlfriend's here."

Ryan's words had Mitch picking his head up and looking before his brain could send out the message to play it cool. Sure enough, Paige's car was pulling up the drive, and he grabbed the T-shirt he'd tossed on a pile to mop some of the sweat off his face as she parked next to Ryan's truck.

Once the initial boost his system got from seeing her faded, a low buzz of annoyance hummed through him. Showing up at his home unannounced crossed a boundary. The boundaries were fluid and he hadn't spelled them out exactly, but he hadn't thought he needed to.

She looked pretty, though, with her hair up in a ponytail and her Trailside Diner T-shirt hugging her curves in a way that made his hands itch to take its place. He walked out to meet her in the drive, and she smiled with her gaze firmly on his chest.

"You're all hot and sweaty," she said.

"Sorry." That's what happened when you dropped by uninvited while a guy was working.

"Oh, I wasn't complaining." She walked around to the passenger side of her car and grabbed a basket out of the backseat.

"Um…" If his "girlfriend" had brought him a picnic lunch, Ryan was never going to let him live it down.

"Is Rose inside?"

"What?"

"Rose. Is she inside?" She held up the basket. "Mrs. Dozynski asked me to bring some plum pierogi up to her."

"Really? Plum?" He tried to peek under the cloth covering the top of the basket, but Paige slapped his hand.

"Mrs. Dozynski said you can't have any. And neither can Josh."

Now, that was just mean. "Mrs. D's pierogies are almost worth firing Andy for."

"She said you'd say that and she also said it's too late, so don't bother."

She started to walk past him, but he hadn't quite wrapped his mind around what was going on yet. "So you didn't come to see me?"

"I wasn't even sure if you'd be here. I ran into Mrs. Dozynski at the library and she was upset because she made these special for Rose, but both Dozer and Lauren were too busy to drive them out to her, so I volunteered."

"Oh." He stared after her as she carefully made her way up the stairs and went inside. So she wasn't there to see him. That was a good thing.

He went back to work, thankful but a little surprised that Ryan didn't rib him about Paige showing up, and then blowing him off. Maybe hearing Lauren's name was enough to shut him up. Sometime very soon he was going to have to get to the bottom of the Ryan and Lauren situation. Lauren had married Ryan's best friend and had a kid and, at some point, Ryan had stopped coming home on a regular basis. Though he couldn't put his finger on exactly what, Mitch was pretty sure there was a connection there.

When they'd put in another half hour of work and Paige still hadn't come out, Mitch declared it break time and grabbed his shirt. As gross as it felt, he pulled it on before he walked in the kitchen door. Rosie had rules about people running around her home not fully clothed.

Paige was sitting at the kitchen table with Rosie, a glass of iced tea in front of her, and they were both laughing. They stopped when they noticed he'd come in, which he had to admit gave him a little bit of a complex.

"Sorry to interrupt," he said, walking over to the fridge and hoping Rosie had made a fresh batch of lemonade, strike or no strike. He knew she'd been cleaning on the sly because toilets didn't scrub themselves, but he wished she'd worry a little less about shower scum and a little more about the fridge and pantry.

"Rosie was telling me about the time Liz talked Katie into cutting her hair short so she could get onto the baseball team."

He laughed at the memory as he settled for a soda from the fridge. No lemonade, dammit. "The entire thing was a mess. To start with, we all played for the team already, so I'm not sure how she was going to explain a fifth Kowalski boy."

"A troubled cousin from the city who'd been sent to live with Uncle Frank and Aunt Sarah in the country is what I was told," Rosie said.

"Yeah, that was gonna work in this town."

Paige laughed softly and Mitch's fingers tightened around the soda can. In the kitchen of the place he called home, laughing with the woman who was like a mother to him, Paige looked as though she belonged. It *felt* like she belonged.

He pushed away from the counter he'd been leaning against and headed for the back door. "I'll leave you ladies to your stories."

After he chugged down his soda and pulled off the T-shirt, Mitch threw himself back into the work. So what if Paige seemed to be a perfect fit for the lodge and for Rose and for the whole damn town? Didn't make her a perfect fit for *him*.

She stayed another half hour, which he knew because, no matter how hard he tried to put her out of his mind, he kept listening for the door. Unfortunately, when she did finally come out, she didn't head for her car and leave so he could get his head back on straight. She headed straight for him.

"You guys are really making a mess."

"It's supposed to be heated parking for the guests' snowmobiles, but I don't know how they get any in here with all the crap piled up. But we've got to redo the floor, so out it goes."

"Lucky you."

"Have you ever been sledding?" He wasn't sure why he asked, since what he really wanted was for her to leave.

"Nope. They look fun, but the winter activity I'm best at is reading."

He opened his mouth, then closed it with a snap when he realized he was about to offer to take her out for a ride. He'd probably be making a few trips back now that the lodge's future was uncertain, so he could take her out once there was snow. But that would be as good as telling her that, after he left this time, he'd be back and he'd want to see her again. Mitch didn't do that.

"Reading's good," he said.

"I should get going. I have some bookkeeping to get done and I need to review Gavin's upcoming specials. He's on probation because people found out he'd fed them tofu."

Mitch laughed, trying to imagine *that* reaction. "Bet that went over well."

"Gavin keeps telling me they liked it until they found out what it was, but I told him you can't just spring that sort of thing on people raised on meat loaf and shepherd's pie."

When she turned to leave, he grabbed her hand, threading his fingers through hers. "Ryan leaves tomorrow and I have to catch up on some work—real work—but maybe Monday night we could go out somewhere. Get some dinner or something?"

Her smile heated his body in a way the sun and exertion couldn't. "That sounds great. I'll see you then. About six would be good."

"Wear that red sundress you wore for Old Home Day." He leaned in and kissed her, not really giving a damn who might be watching. Then he stood there like an idiot, watching until her car disappeared down the driveway.

CHAPTER FIFTEEN

BY THE TIME six o'clock rolled around on Monday, Paige had managed to make herself feel utterly ridiculous. It was silly how much time and effort she'd put into her hair and makeup just to go to dinner with Mitch.

When he'd requested she wear the red sundress, she'd gotten a thrill from the realization he'd probably spent some time remembering how she looked in it. And she'd also assumed that meant they wouldn't be taking his motorcycle. She liked riding the bike, but knowing her hair wouldn't be plastered to her head by the helmet had her taking the time to style it. She kept the makeup light and put on a pair of sandals that were comfortable, but dressy enough to go someplace nice if that was what he had in mind.

The nerves took her by surprise. Even though she didn't have to worry about a good-night kiss or any awkwardness about inviting him in, her stomach was jumpy and her color was high when she checked her reflection in the mirror for the umpteenth time.

Tonight was different somehow, she admitted to herself. This was a date and that didn't mesh with the rationalizations she'd used on herself to get into bed with him in the first place. It was too real and neither of them did real.

She was in trouble. Besides offering her some temporary fun, Mitch had shown her just how lonely she'd been. Two years alone had been good for her—she owned a home and a thriving business and that sense of home she'd always craved—but it was time to start thinking about sharing that life with somebody.

And, stupid her, she couldn't fall for somebody as grounded in Whitford as she was. There had to be some nice single men in town looking for a local woman to settle down with. They'd make a life together, send their kids to the Whitford schools and watch them grow up in the community Paige had come to love. But no, she had to let her head be turned by a man who had his own life somewhere else and absolutely no interest in returning to Whitford for good.

Well, she wasn't giving up her dream, lonely or not, she told her reflection. She was going to go out and have a good time and maybe, after Mitch left town, she'd start looking for somebody who wanted the same things in life she did. And if she couldn't find another man who made her feel the way he did, at least she'd still have her home and her diner, because she wouldn't throw it all away to chase after him.

Thankfully, a vehicle pulled into the back of the lot and saved her from the chaos of her own thoughts. It was time to have some fun.

Mitch was dressed casually, in a T-shirt and cargo shorts, so she knew they weren't going anywhere too fancy. She didn't care. She felt pretty in the dress, and the heat in his eyes when he looked at her made every second she'd spent fussing over her appearance worth it.

He pulled her into his arms and kissed her until she

was afraid her hair would stand on end from the sexual energy they generated, and then slid his hand down her arm to lace his fingers with hers. "You ready to go?"

He'd brought the lodge's truck, and when he opened the door for her, she wasn't quite sure how she was going to climb up into it while preserving her modesty. When he turned her around and then lifted her by the waist to set her on the edge of the seat, she leaned forward to give him a quick kiss of thanks.

But, with his body wedged between her legs, Mitch wasn't content with a fast peck on the lips. He slid his hands under the sundress and over her thighs as his mouth captured hers and refused to let it go. With her ankles locked around his waist, he was a little too low, but if he'd just stand on the running board, he could…

A car door slammed and jerked Paige back to reality. They were in the diner parking lot, though, thank goodness, he'd parked with the passenger door facing her trailer. She shoved him away with a laugh, and then swung her legs into the truck.

"Can't blame a guy for trying," he said before closing her door.

They chatted as he drove left-handed, his right hand busy holding hers in the middle of the seat. Ed Grandmaison had already sent an email through the lodge's website telling them he'd been in touch with the ATV club and he'd probably be willing to consider letting them cut across his land.

Mitch paused in the telling to shake his head. "Made it very clear he was doing it for the benefit of both towns, not out of any love for the Kowalski family or the lodge."

"As long as he's willing to do it, it doesn't matter why. And Carl and I were talking about what it could mean for our business in the summer. More weekend customers, probably."

"At least you don't have carpeting. Those extra weekend customers will be covered in dust if it's dry or mud if it's not."

"We're thinking about offering brown-bag lunches. Premade sandwiches, a bag of chips and a drink to go. They can sit on their machines or walk down to the park or take the lunches with them if they want."

He squeezed her hand. "I think that's a great idea. I hope it all comes together, for everybody's sake."

Paige fought back the case of the warm fuzzies his words brought on, reminding herself the sense of *togetherness* was only temporary. It would be her and Josh and a few other people working with the ATV club and the Grandmaisons, and meeting with the town to get everything in place and organize work parties. Mitch would be gone before the fruits of his labor needed tending.

When he put on his blinker to turn into a fast-food joint, she arched an eyebrow and he laughed. "Trust me."

It wasn't exactly what she'd expected, but she played along. And when he drove to a public park and carried their paper bags of food in one hand as he led her out to a gazebo on the shore of a small lake, she was glad she did.

"It's beautiful," she said, watching a sailboat drift through the sun's reflection on the water.

"I was going to take you to that spot by the river where I first kissed you, but I was afraid I wouldn't stop with kissing this time, and I don't want the food to go to waste after it took somebody thirty-eight seconds to cook it. Here there are enough people around so I have to behave myself."

He managed to do just that, more or less. They polished off their meal almost as quickly as it had been made and then walked toward the shore, hand in hand. A father was teaching his son to use a radio-controlled boat and they watched for a few minutes. The family tossing a Frisbee around in what looked like a game of keep-away with the dog made them laugh. A couple stealing a romantic kiss behind a huge oak made Paige smile.

As dates went, it was almost perfect. Quiet and sweet, with an undertone of anticipation that sizzled every time he brushed her hair off her bare shoulders or rested his hand at the small of her back.

As the sun went down, he led her to a bench near the gazebo where they'd eaten and gestured for her to sit. "Just a little longer. I promise I'll get you to bed early so you don't throw your alarm across the room in the morning."

Her head was on his shoulder, his arm wrapped around her, when the first burst of fireworks exploded in the barely dark sky. Paige gasped and tilted her head to look at him. "Did you know that was going to happen?"

"Of course I did." He grinned. "Well, I knew it was going to happen. I wasn't sure if we'd be able to see them, though. The town across the lake has a small show every night—a tourist thing, I guess—and I thought we'd have a view from here, but I wasn't sure."

Another burst, higher this time, and then another made Paige grin like a little kid. She loved fireworks, always had, though this was her first time watching them in the arms of a sweet, sexy man.

And it was the first time she was ever kissed breathless while a grand finale flashed and boomed overhead.

MITCH HAD MADE a deal with Paige and now it was killing him, but he couldn't take it back. She was behind on work and he always had work to do, so they'd taken the big table at the back of the diner after her shift ended. They'd work for two hours and then he could have his way with her.

He hadn't known when he'd agreed to it that she sucked the end of her pen when she was thinking. And she was doing a lot of thinking, so she was doing a lot of sucking. How the hell was he supposed to read reports from his crews when she kept sliding the pen between her lips like that?

When he nudged her foot with his, she looked up from the papers spread in front of her. She must have read his mind, because she frowned at him. "Mitch, really? It's barely been twenty minutes."

Damn. The night before last he'd finally had the pleasure of peeling that red sundress off her, but last night, between Ryan calling about the lodge and Scott about work and an inspector from Chicago, it seemed as if his phone wouldn't stop ringing. By the time he was done, it had been too late to head to Paige's. He knew he kept her up too late on a regular basis, as it was.

The end result was a bad case of wanting her and not wanting to focus on work. She didn't seem to have that problem, though, as she kept on sucking that damn pen and occasionally using it to make notes on whatever she was reading.

When Ava passed through to refill their coffee mugs, Paige looked up. "Can you ask Gavin to come back here if he gets a free minute?"

"Sure thing."

The kid didn't waste any time, appearing before Paige had even finished putting cream and sugar in her coffee. Seeing the kid made Mitch feel a little old. He could remember when Gavin was little enough so his dad had to boost him onto a stool to order his ice cream. He fixed his coffee while the kid talked to his boss.

"How can so many people from Maine hate seafood?" Gavin was asking.

"I don't think it was the scallops," Paige said. "I think it was the Gouda cheese. And this veal with wine casserole you want to make… I'm a little hesitant about that. Is there any way you could substitute chicken first and see how people react to wine in their casserole before we spring for veal?"

Judging by the dramatic sigh, Mitch got the feeling the kid felt like an artist who'd been asked to paint a masterpiece with an elementary-school watercolor set. "I guess. Can I try the cold melon soup again? It's perfect for the weather if people would just give it a chance."

It was Paige's turn to sigh. "Yes, but let's come up with a different word for *soup*. People expect soup to be hot, so they're not inclined to trust the dish right from the start."

Gavin walked away muttering under his breath, but

Paige just smiled and shook her head. "He thinks it's tough now. Wait until he moves to the city and he's low man on the totem pole. When he's only allowed to cook what he's told to cook, he'll look back on this job with a lot more affection."

"I ran into his old man the other day. He told me Gavin loves working here and it's really building his confidence, along with giving him some real-world experience to take with him into culinary school."

"I'll miss him when he's gone. And the specials board won't be nearly so exciting."

Whatever Paige did next required more writing and less thought, so Mitch was finally able to focus on the laptop in front of him. His leg rested against hers under the table and every once in a while she'd rub her ankle on his, which made him smile. Not bad conditions to work under, really.

If she had a bigger house, he could see them like this—maybe at the dining room table or the coffee table. The two of them working side by side until it was time to curl up on the couch to watch television, because he'd insist they get one, and then curl up in bed. It made for a cozy picture and it worried him his mind didn't instinctively recoil from the image of domestic bliss. He didn't *do* domestic bliss.

At the one hour and forty-five minute mark, his cell phone rang and he practically jumped on it in his effort to drive the silly thoughts about him and Paige and a house out of his head. "Hello?"

"Your brother's an idiot." It was Rose and she didn't sound happy.

"You'll have to be more specific."

"Josh fell getting out of the tub and it sounds like he's stuck, if not hurt. He either can't or won't unlock the door to let me in."

"Can't Andy help him?"

"He went fishing with Drew. I guess things aren't going so well with Mallory and they needed some father-son time."

Mitch closed his eyes and rubbed the bridge of his nose. "Do you think he's hurt?"

"He's cussing up a blue streak, so I'd say he's either hurt or mad as hell. But he says he's okay, so probably not too bad."

"I'll be there in a few minutes."

Paige's concern was written all over her face. "Who's hurt?"

"Josh fell and he won't let Rosie mother him. I'm going to have to take a rain check on having my way with you."

"Anticipation makes it all the sweeter."

"Unless my balls explode in the meantime," he muttered before remembering they were in a very public place. He glanced around, but either the obvious fact they were working or Ava's interference had kept the customers at the other end of the diner.

After gathering his stuff, he leaned down and kissed her. "Your place tomorrow?"

"I'll make dinner."

He kissed her again, then went out to his truck and made the drive back to the lodge in a few minutes less than was legal. Nobody was around, so he went up the stairs, assuming Josh was still on the bathroom floor.

Rose had never looked so glad to see him as she did at that moment. "He won't tell me what's going on."

"Go find me a nail or something else long and thin I can pop this push-button lock with." After she left, he pounded on the door. "Josh, what the hell's going on in there?"

"Leave me alone."

"As soon as Rosie gets back, I'm popping the lock."

A stream of curse words that would have made a sailor proud was the only response, so Mitch waited until Rose hurried back with a knitting needle. "I think this one's small enough to do it."

"Thanks. Go downstairs and I'll let you know when the coast is clear."

She looked as though she wanted to argue, but Mitch stood firm. There was a good chance Josh's worst injury was going to be to his pride, but at least brothers didn't have much dignity between them in the first place. After another stream of curses from the bathroom, she gave Mitch a sharp look and walked away.

It only took him a few seconds to pop the lock and he opened the door slowly, just in case Josh was sprawled in front of it.

He was sprawled, all right, but not in front of the door. He was naked, wet and had somehow managed to wedge his cast behind the base of the old pedestal sink as he'd fallen. A quick inspection told Mitch he was a lot more pissed than he was hurt.

It took him a few minutes, trying a few different angles, but Mitch finally managed to get him unstuck. He had to stand in the tub and bend way over to catch

Josh under the arms so he could slide him back as he sat him up.

When Josh was finally free of the sink, Mitch tossed him a towel and sat on the edge of the tub to catch his breath. Josh draped the towel over his lap and leaned his head against the wall to do the same.

"You hurt at all?"

"Wrenched up a bit, especially my back." Which sucked, because Mitch knew his back was already twisted up a bit from the crutches. "Probably feel like I got hit by a truck in the morning, but no damage to the cast or the leg and I managed not to hit my head on the tub on my way down."

"You'll live, then. You may never live this *down,* but you'll live."

"You're an asshole."

"I'd be in Paige's bed right now if you learned to dry your feet before stepping on the tile."

"She can thank me later."

"Now who's the asshole?" He stood and hauled Josh to his feet.

Once Mitch was sure his brother wasn't going to fall over and could manage the drying and dressing process without his help, he went down the stairs and wasn't surprised to find Rose standing at the bottom, her arms crossed. "Well?"

"He's fine. Slipped and got his cast stuck behind the sink. Pissed him off to no end and he probably tweaked his back, but he'll be fine."

"I don't want either of you running around tonight, so I guess I'll make supper."

Mitch thought of Paige. He could be back in town

in no time and they could pick up where they'd left off. Although maybe a little distance wasn't a bad thing, since they'd left off with him daydreaming about them playing house.

And he knew when a mother hen like Rose needed to cluck over her chicks, if only to make herself feel better.

"You're the best, Rosie," he said, kissing the top of her head. "No matter what the others might say."

EVEN WITH OTHER things to think about—like romantic dates and kisses under the fireworks—Paige's mind kept returning to Mitch's reaction to her showing up at the lodge.

She was getting pretty good at reading his expressions, and his expression when she got out of her car wasn't a happy to see her look. It was a wondering what the hell she was doing there look. Then he proceeded to blow so hot and cold she felt as is she were going through menopause.

On the one hand, he'd committed to a real date. On the other, she'd seen his hesitation when she said she'd never been snowmobiling. It was the opening when most people would have offered to take her out for a ride, but that would have implied that, after he left, he might not call or text, but he'd come back and see her again.

And that's what she needed to keep in mind—that when he said there would be no looking back, he meant it. And since she told herself she didn't have a problem with that, she went into the Whitford General Store to pick up a few things. She was determined to cook something for dinner rather than reheating takeout from the diner.

Fran pounced on her before the bell had even stopped tinkling over her head. "Did Hailey call you yet?"

"I haven't heard from her. Why?"

"We're all heading to Mallory's in a little bit. She's leaving Drew, and after such a drawn-out process to get to this point, she wants it to be quick. We're going to have a packing party, though I guess *party*'s a bad word for it."

But Mitch was coming over and she'd made up her mind to make him dinner. "I'm sorry to hear that."

"We all are, honey. But the sooner we get her packed up and out of the house, the sooner they can both start healing."

She didn't want to spend the evening separating his and hers into piles and then putting the hers into boxes. She'd told Mitch she'd make him dinner.

But she didn't live her life around men anymore, she reminded herself. He was a temporary luxury, but her friends were a necessity and she wasn't going to turn her back on one because Mitch Kowalski was willing to make time for her tonight.

"I'll be there," she told Fran. "Just tell me when."

Three hours later, the Miller house was full of boxes and women and red plastic cups bearing Rose's infamous margaritas. Mallory, pale and quiet, moved through the chaos, pointing out things that needed to be packed and showing them what would stay, which was most of it.

"My new apartment's really small, so I can't take a lot of it," she said. "Plus, I think I'll just start fresh."

It broke Paige's heart watching Mal pull her favorite coffee mug off the rack while leaving Drew's, and sorting her books from his on the shelf in the living room. Maybe that's why, when Rose stepped into the bathroom Paige was going through and handed her a drink, she took it.

"Only this one," she warned. "I have to get up at four-thirty."

Rosie nodded. "One might help take the edge off, though. Whether it's because of divorce or because your husband passed away, boxing up the life you thought you'd have but didn't to start a new one is sad business."

"I really hoped they'd work it out."

"We all did, but I'm not surprised it's over. Two people who want different things in life on the most fundamental level don't have much of a chance, especially if one of them hasn't been honest about it. Surprised they made it this long, actually."

Paige took a sip of the potent drink, then set the cup on the edge of the sink so she could continue sorting Mallory's toiletries from Drew's. "There are some goals and dreams you can't compromise on, I guess. Children's a big one. You either want them or you don't."

"Exactly. You can compromise on where you live and whether or not a wife will travel with her husband and all that stuff, but how you feel about family's important."

Maybe it was the first sip of liquor, but Paige had a sneaking suspicion Rosie wasn't talking about the Millers anymore. "But for some people, where and how they live is as important as whether or not to have kids."

"Can be. Or maybe the man fills the hole the woman

thought she was filling with work or friends or a community."

Paige kept her gaze on the drawer she was taking nail polish bottles out of, wanting to make sure she tempered her response to Rosie, who she adored and didn't want to offend. Maybe it was a generational thing or just the older woman's way of thinking, but that was the kind of attitude that set Paige's teeth on edge.

A man would make it all better.

"Maybe," she said quietly, "the woman doesn't have a hole to fill. Maybe she's on solid ground and she'll wait for a man who's happy to share it with her."

"Some men need a little more space to run."

"Well, that wouldn't be the man for me," Paige said, following it up with a casual laugh, as if they were only talking hypotheticals.

Rosie sighed. "Maybe not. I best get back to the kitchen and guard the blender. There's a fine line between taking the edge off and a bunch of wasted women shoving random crap in boxes."

Paige took another sip of the margarita, then grimaced in the mirror. She wasn't a big fan of the drink and, damn, she'd forgotten to call Mitch.

CHAPTER SIXTEEN

SHOWERED, SHAVEN AND packing a fresh batch of condoms in his wallet, Mitch whistled as he left his room and walked down the stairs. He had no idea where anybody was, and he didn't care. All that mattered was knowing where he was about to be, and that was with Paige.

A knock on the kitchen door took him by surprise, since he hadn't heard a vehicle pull up. And the occasional random guest looking for a place to crash for a night would go to the front door.

By the time Mitch got to the kitchen, Drew was already letting himself in. And to say the man looked like hell warmed over was putting it kindly. Only two things made a man look like that and Drew wasn't sick, so Mitch knew he wouldn't be using those condoms after all.

Drew made eye contact for a second, and Mitch could see the moisture threatening to gather before he looked down at the floor. "She's packing right now."

"Shit. I'm sorry, man." He went to the fridge and took out a couple cans of beer, one of which he handed to Drew. "I really hoped you guys would work it out."

"Maybe we could have if we ever talked about the same thing. My problem is the lying. Ten years of it.

But she thinks the problem is that I care more about kids that don't exist than I do her."

"You driving tonight?"

"I was hoping you'd spot me a room. I don't want to sit around and watch Mal leave me."

Holding his open beer in one hand, Mitch reached back into the fridge with the other and grabbed a full six-pack. "Let's go sit on the back porch and put a dent in this."

Drew took the beer. "Sounds like a plan."

"Go ahead. I've gotta make a quick call, then I'll be out."

"Tell Paige I said hi."

"Hey, it could be for work."

"Sure it is," Drew called over his shoulder on his way out.

Paige answered on the second ring. "I was just about to call you."

"Let me guess. You're helping Mallory pack."

"And I guess you're probably helping Drew get drunk?"

"Something like that. He'll be crashing here tonight and I'll be drinking a lot slower than him, so don't worry about him showing up and making a scene."

She sighed. "This sucks."

That it did. And it was proof, as if he needed any, that love didn't trump two people wanting different things in life. "If there's drinking involved in that packing, don't drive. Call if you need to and Rosie will come get you."

"Umm…Rosie's here. She's making the margaritas."

Mitch walked to the window and, sure enough,

Rosie's car was gone. "She's getting sneaky in her old age."

"I won't tell her you said that. Anyway, Fran's not drinking, so she'll do any driving that needs to be done. And I'm only having one anyway. Drinking or no drinking, my alarm's going off at four-thirty tomorrow morning."

He made her promise to call if there were any problems at Mallory's and then ended the call before he could ask what she was doing tomorrow night. He'd been falling off his game plan lately, a key component of which was not letting a woman get too accustomed to him being around, but the suffering on his friend's face had been a sharp reminder of the messy emotional stuff he wanted nothing to do with.

Drew was downing the last of his first beer when Mitch joined him on the porch, and he made a mental note to scrounge up some food in a little while. A few beers was one thing, but getting falling-down, puking drunk wasn't going to help the guy feel any better.

"I keep asking myself if I would have married her if I'd known from the beginning she didn't want kids."

There was no going back in time, and what-ifs didn't help anything, but Mitch popped open a beer and settled back to listen.

"I think I would have. I probably would have assumed she'd change her mind after we'd been married awhile. And when we first got married, it's not like having a baby was the first thing on my to-do list anyway. There's a good chance we would have ended up in the same place we are now—we just would have taken a different road to get here."

"Would that have been easier or harder, do you think?"

Drew considered the question, then shrugged. "I don't know. I think being pissed off she lied to me for ten years is keeping some of the hurt at bay. I guess there'd be a lot more hurt and sadness if it had gone the other way."

Maybe Drew couldn't feel it yet, but Mitch could see the guy had more than his share of hurt and sadness. "I thought you had it all. Respected chief of police, beautiful wife. I thought I'd get the having-a-baby email anytime."

"You have it all," Drew said, using a fresh beer can to point at him. "Your own business, plenty of money and you don't have to give a crap what women want in life. You just give them what they want in bed and move the hell on before it gets complicated."

It might be the way he lived his life, true, but the way Drew summed it up made him squirm a little.

"Look at you and Paige," Drew continued, and Mitch was pretty sure he didn't want to. "You're a big man of the world and she's a small-town girl, but neither of you are pretending you want the same shit in life. You'll just screw each other and move on. That's what I should have done with Mal. Screwed her and moved the hell on."

"No, you shouldn't have. You loved Mal."

"I still love her." He threw the can, and beer exploded all over the freshly painted railing. "Goddammit, I still love her."

"I know you do."

"I don't want to."

There was no magic off-switch, though, so Mitch

knew the only thing Drew could do was ride it out. That's what he'd done after his relationship with Pam ended and he thought he'd been upset. But looking at his best friend now, he had to admit he'd had a lot more anger and a lot less pain when they went their separate ways.

"Love sucks," Drew declared, popping the top on a fresh beer.

"I'll drink to that." Not that he was sure he had a lot of experience with love himself, but it sure had a tendency to make people unhappy.

But Mitch didn't hate love, or even mildly dislike it. He just wasn't ready for it. Northern Star Demolition was his mistress and he'd already learned the hard way she left no room for a wife. Maybe someday he could take a step back from the company, but that someday was a long time off and, in the meantime, there was no sense promising a woman she'd be his everything.

Images of Paige flashed through his mind—in the diner she'd brought back to life all by herself and in the tiny trailer she'd made into her home. Like Mitch, she knew what she wanted in life and she'd dug in her feet to get it.

He knocked back some beer and stared out into the fading light. It was a good thing they both already knew they were on two different roads in life and were just enjoying a quick rest stop together. Or so he told himself.

Maybe if he had another beer, he could convince himself he still believed it.

THEIR CHIEF OF police's wife suddenly moving out of their house when the town thought they were reconciling was, not surprisingly, the hot topic at the diner the next morning. Paige tried to keep her head down and her mouth shut, but her car had been spotted in the Millers' driveway.

"How's Mallory doing?" was the greeting of the day, and Paige recognized it for what it was. Probably twenty percent genuine concern and eighty percent conversational gambit, meant to open the door to spilling everything she knew about the poor woman. While, as the owner of a town gathering place, it was probably expected she'd feed them gossip along with cheeseburgers and fries, Mal was a friend and Paige deflected and distracted her way out of feeding the rumor mill.

She'd left a little before ten the night before, about the time the serious packing was giving way to alcohol-fueled mood swings. Tears, then rantings about how all men sucked, then more tears. Paige had made her escape and fallen straight into bed, exhausted by the emotional tension of the evening.

When she went through the swinging door into the kitchen with a full bus pan of dirty dishes, Carl jerked a thumb over his shoulder. "I let a stray in the back door."

She set the bus pan on the dishwashing platform and went out into the back area. There, sitting at the tiny break table nobody ever used, was a very haggard-looking Mitch.

He looked up at her, wincing against the fluorescent lights. "I'll pay extra for my breakfast and the six gallons of coffee I'm going to drink if I can sit back here."

"That bad, huh?"

"Not good."

Sympathy tugged at her heart. He'd suffered the same emotional tension she had the night before, but it must have been so much worse. Not only had he been one-on-one with Drew, but he was his best friend. "I'll get a carafe of coffee all your own, and an orange juice. What do you want to eat?"

"Four of everything."

"You sure you're up to that?"

He nodded, then winced at the movement. Shaking her head, she gave Carl his order for four pancakes, four scrambled eggs, four slices of toast and four each of bacon strips and sausage links. It was his stomach.

After bringing Mitch a carafe of coffee, Paige went back out front to brew some more and check on her customers. Katie Davis had taken a seat at the counter, not looking much better than Mitch.

"Why did you let me drink so much last night?" were the first words out of her mouth.

"I barely saw you drink at all. You must have picked up the pace after I left."

"Maybe. Everything gets a little blurry just before midnight." She flipped through the menu she didn't need to read, and Paige got the impression she wasn't even seeing the words. "I remember somebody asking Mom straight out why she didn't like Andy Miller, though."

Paige really needed to make rounds with the coffeepot, but she pretended not to see the empty mugs perched precariously on the very edges of tables. "What did she say?"

"She said she could barely remember and changed the subject, like I've seen her do before." Katie frowned at the menu. "Her eyes get sad when it comes up. Not that it does often, but when it does, it upsets her a little."

"Have *you* ever asked her?"

"Not in a very long time. Probably not since I've been old enough to converse with as an adult."

"If it bothers you—if you think it's important—maybe you should ask her again."

Katie shoved the menu back in the holder and looked up at her. "What if she cheated on my dad? What if she cheated on my dad with his best friend?"

There was a reason Katie ran the barbershop in Whitford, and it wasn't any great passion she had for hot lather and electric trimmers. It had been her dad's business, and Paige knew she'd taken it over rather than see it close. They'd been close and she could see why Katie might be afraid of Rose's answer.

"I think you should ask her," she said. "Even if it's as bad as what you're thinking, talking it out together will be better than stewing about it on your own."

Katie nodded and Paige took advantage of the lull in the conversation to refill everybody's coffee cups. Food started appearing in the window and customers came and went, so it was a while before she could slip out back to check on Mitch.

He looked better with a stack of empty plates in front of him and an almost empty carafe of caffeine. "Thanks, Paige. Drew, the poor sucker, had to go into work and I was going to go back to bed, but there was hammering and vacuuming and I was pretty sure I might die there for a while."

"Is Drew okay?"

"Not really, but I think it'll be a while before he tries to drown his sorrows in alcohol again."

Paige remembered Mitch telling her he'd be drinking a lot slower than Drew and wondered if he'd come up with a few sorrows of his own to drown. "I have a feeling Mal wasn't in much better shape today, if Katie's condition was anything to go by. But somebody told me Fran had Butch loading up her boxes this morning, so I guess she's still going today."

"It just sucks." Mitch stood and stretched gingerly, as though afraid of moving too much. "I guess I should head back and see what joyous thing's on the list for today. If I'm lucky I can dust or something, but knowing my demented family, Josh will have me running a power saw. You going to be home later?"

"I might," she said in a deliberately noncommittal way.

"Maybe I'll stop by."

"Maybe I'll see you then."

Carl bellowed her name, so Mitch winked and slipped out the back door, and she went back to work. But as she delivered pancakes and wiped tables, she added "clean sheets" and "smooth legs" to her list of things to do today. Hopefully, he'd regain some of his strength over the course of the day, because he was going to need it.

MITCH STRETCHED OUT on Paige's couch, which was about the only full-size thing in the trailer, enjoying the feel of Paige stretched out on top of him.

"See," she said, "if I had a TV, we wouldn't be enjoying this time together. We'd be staring at the moving pictures in the box."

"I think they stopped calling them that at least fifty years ago. And all I said was that it's too bad you don't have a TV because I actually have time to watch one right now. I could be finding out what it is the rest of the country's always talking about."

"Real people are more interesting."

"Speaking of interesting people, have you talked to your mom recently?"

She snorted. "For about five minutes. She wanted to know what I thought it meant that Corey let her call go to voice mail twice in a half hour. He claims he was doing laps in the Y pool, but she's pretty sure it's a sign he got his hands on a calculator and figured out she's older than he is."

"So this is the downward spiral?"

"I'd give them another five minutes or so. This one was a little shorter than most. Pretending to be young, hip and careless was a little more of a strain, and the facade cracked earlier."

"It's too bad she doesn't appreciate how awesome you are." He kissed the part in her hair, which was a spot he particularly liked for some reason. "She's missing out."

"How are things with your brothers and the lodge?"

"Better, actually. I was really worried about Josh, but now that he finally got mad enough to spill his emotional guts, he's more himself again."

"Do you really think you'll sell it?"

He still wasn't sure. And he still wasn't sure how he felt about it. Being able to logically understand Josh's point of view didn't squash the emotional attachment he felt to the old place. "I don't know. Maybe just having a choice will be enough for him. Maybe, if he can stick it out until the ATV crowd discovers us, we can hire a manager. We wouldn't want Rosie there alone. Or we might sell it."

"None of you want to run it?"

"I've got my hands full with my own company. So does Ryan. Sean never liked living in an inn with strangers coming and going, plus Emma—his wife—owns a landscaping design business that's pretty successful."

"What about your sister? Couldn't her boyfriend do his art here?"

"I'm not sure if Liz will ever come home to stay. I doubt it. Maybe if she ever smartens up and dumps the deadbeat loser, but he won't move back here."

Paige poked him with her elbow. "Gee, I wonder why."

"We're her brothers. It's our job to not like deadbeat losers who work her into the ground so he can afford to sit on his ass all day, staring at three pieces of scrap metal, and call it 'contemplating his art.'"

"She's been with him a long time. *She* must like him."

"I guess she loves him. But we don't."

"So…not much chance of them running the Northern Star, then."

"Her? Hell yes. *Them?* I'd burn it down first."

"We should talk about something more cheerful."

"If you had a television, we could watch cartoons."

"You're a funny guy."

Mitch slid his hands down her stomach, then moved them just a little lower. "How about we go in the bedroom and come up with fun stuff to do."

They had no trouble doing that. Paige was an incredibly fun lover and he didn't think he'd ever get tired of feeling her touch or watching her face or hearing her laugh.

Tonight she was in a particularly tender mood, so he took his time, savoring every inch of her body before making slow love to her. He loved the way she said his name, her body arching under his as she begged him for more.

Afterward, he held her in the position the size of the bed forced on them, but that he didn't mind. Lying mostly on his back, with Paige on her side. Her head rested on his shoulder and he ran his hand lazily up and down her back.

He was comfortable and tired after the night before with Drew and he liked the feel of Paige pressed up against him. "Hey."

"Mmm?" She was already half-asleep.

"I'm pretty beat. Do you mind if I stay tonight?"

She burrowed a little closer to him. "Stay."

To hell with the rules. Just this once wouldn't change anything. It was late and he'd battled a hangover all morning, that was all. The fact Paige's body molded so perfectly to his had nothing to do with it.

CHAPTER SEVENTEEN

KATIE HAD ONLY been three or four when Rose had given up on the idea of dressing her daughter in pink bows and fancy shoes. Jeans, T-shirts and ball caps. She'd played baseball with the boys in the park and the only thing she'd ever used her Easy-Bake oven for was a failed attempt to melt down some silverware she nicked from the kitchen so she could make BBs for her slingshot. Katie was born a tomboy and she'd never outgrown it.

She'd even taken over the barbershop that had been Earle's pride and joy, working hard to maintain the high standards her father had set. That's why, when Rose looked out the window and saw her daughter's ancient Jeep coming up the drive in the middle of a Wednesday, fear gripped her. Something had to be wrong.

Rose made it to the front porch just as her daughter climbed out of the Wrangler. "Hi, honey."

"Hi, Mom. Thought I'd stop by and visit for a few minutes."

"Just like that?" Something was wrong. She could sense it, despite Katie's carefree tone.

"Just like that."

"What about the shop?"

Katie shrugged. "I put the Closed sign up with a note I'd be back in an hour or two. It's a slow time and if I miss somebody, he'll get over it or drive at least fifteen minutes in some other direction to get his hair cut."

Rose led the way into the kitchen, which was where she did most of her visiting. Once she was there, she'd intended to offer Katie some lunch, but she couldn't stand not knowing what had prompted the impromptu visit.

"Tell me why you're here, honey."

Katie twisted her key ring around her finger and didn't quite look her in the eye. "Why do you hate Andy Miller so much?"

Rose's body stiffened and her mind whirled, trying to remember the words she'd used in the past to pacify her daughter's curiosity. "I don't hate him. We're just not friends, that's all."

"Why?"

"Sometimes people just don't become friends, Katie. It's not a big deal."

"You used to be friends. I remember when I was a little girl, he was always around. I called him Uncle Andy. Then it stopped. And whenever I asked about him, you changed the subject or put me off."

"It was a long time ago. Do you want something to eat? I haven't baked anything, but—"

"You haven't baked anything because you won't do anything for the boys since they hired Andy. That's a lot of animosity, Mom, and when there's that much animosity between a woman and a man, it usually involves sex."

She didn't want to talk about this with her daughter. Not now. Not ever. "I've never had sex with Andy Miller, I can tell you that."

"Then what, Mom? What happened when I was little that's made you hate him for almost thirty years?"

Rosie wasn't going to get out of it this time. Katie wasn't going to be distracted with a snack or fall for a change of subject. She took a deep breath and folded her hands in front of her. "Andy and your father went away one weekend when you were seven, to go sledding. Andy met some women at a bar and talked them into coming back to their motel room and...your father was unfaithful."

Katie sat down hard in a chair, her blue eyes—the same shade as Earle's—wide in the shadow of her cap's brim. "Are you sure? Did he tell you that?"

The last thing Rosie wanted to do was say anything hurtful about Katie's dad. They'd been so close and Katie treasured Earle's memory. "He did. Shortly after they got home."

"But you forgave him. I mean, you stayed with him and you seemed happy together."

Rosie sat down and reached across the table for her daughter's hand. "We *were* happy, honey. We really were. And, yes, I forgave him. It was hard at first, but your father was a good man and he beat himself up so badly about it, I was pretty sure he'd never do it again. As far as I know, he never did. Only that one time he went away with Andy."

"You blame Andy." It wasn't a question.

"He knew your father loved you and me more than anything, but Andy still practically threw a woman at him. It was disrespectful."

Her daughter didn't say anything, just stared down at their linked hands. Rose was quiet, letting Katie absorb the news. She was old enough to have outgrown believing her parents were anything but human, but committing adultery was a far cry from fibbing about what had happened to her first dog.

"It's not really Andy's fault." Katie's voice was thick with emotion. "Dad was responsible for what he did. Nobody else."

"One thing love's not known for is making a person rational. And neither is hate."

"I can't believe Dad cheated on you."

Rosie squeezed her hand. "Don't let that change how you remember him, Katherine. Don't you dare. I went through a lot of heartache to put our family back together again so you wouldn't be hurt by what happened. We loved each other and we loved you. That's all that matters."

"If you'd truly forgiven Dad, you wouldn't still be punishing Andy."

Her daughter's words cut through Rose like a hot knife, but she barely had time to process how she felt about them before she heard the telltale thump of approaching crutches on the back porch.

Katie straightened in her seat, pulling her hand free, as Josh came through the kitchen door, knocking it closed behind him with the end of a crutch. "Hey, Katie. Thought that piece of shit in the driveway must be yours."

"She's still got fewer miles on it than your last girlfriend."

"Bite me. Hey, did you see the game last night?"

"I told you our bull pen's not strong enough to close it out if we go deep into extra innings."

"But we put up a hell of a fight."

Rosie rolled her eyes at the familiar back-and-forth between these two, but when Josh leaned into the fridge to search for whatever he was in the mood for, she caught Katie watching him and her maternal radar pinged.

It wasn't a strong ping, though. Rosie would love nothing more than for Katie to get married and start a family. Mary's constant barrage of grandbaby pictures from New Hampshire didn't help her yearning for grandchildren any. And the thought of Josh being her son-in-law rather than just a son of her heart almost made her weep. But Josh had always treated Katie like one of the guys and he didn't seem inclined to see her any other way.

When he started hauling out the makings for deli sandwiches from the fridge, Katie stood. "I should get back. God only knows what disaster the town's come up with to explain the barbershop being closed."

"Where's the mustard?"

Rose ignored Josh and went around the table to hug her daughter.

"Think about what I said, Mom," Katie whispered into her hair.

"I will. And I love you, sweetie."

"I love you, too. See ya, Josh."

"Later. Hey, Rosie, did you hide the mustard?"

Once Katie left, she found the mustard, which was hiding next to the ketchup in the door, and then, because she was feeling a little soft at the moment, she made him a couple of sandwiches.

"Josh, do you know what color Katie's eyes are?"

Not surprisingly, he looked confused by the question. He squinted and she realized he was trying to cheat by looking at *her* eyes. "Uh, brown?"

She shook her head and started putting the sandwich stuff back in the fridge. Katie's eyes were blue. Not as brilliant as the Kowalskis' eyes, but a pretty pale blue like her father's. She'd teased Earle more than once about their daughter being so much like him she'd even managed to buck the odds and get his recessive gene.

Josh was probably hopeless and Sean lived just far enough away to keep visits infrequent, so it looked like Rose's best bet for having a baby to hold, even if it wasn't technically her grandchild, might be Mitch. Now if she could only figure out which one of them was throwing a monkey wrench in the works.

PAIGE HUMMED HAPPY love songs as she moved through her trailer, mentally checking things off her cleaning to-do list. She'd been humming all day, actually, which had annoyed Carl to no end, but she couldn't help it.

Waking up in Mitch's arms had gotten her day off to an amazing start and nothing had been able to dent her good mood. Not even Mitch's grumbling when he realized he was awake at four-thirty in the morning.

He'd shown up for a quick breakfast about seven and then kissed her goodbye right in the middle of the diner before he went back to the lodge. Now she figured she had another two hours or so before he came back again, and she intended to put it to good use decluttering.

The cheery romantic sound track in her head came to a screeching halt when she checked the calendar to make sure she'd written "movie night" on it and noticed the date. Josh was having his cast off in six days. Katie had mentioned the date and Paige had written a note so she'd remember to ask Mitch how it went.

It was less than a week away. Of course, nothing said Mitch was going to get on his bike and ride out of Whitford the second the doctor shut off the saw, but he wouldn't stay long.

Things had changed between them, maybe enough so he'd consider asking her to go with him. Maybe even enough so she'd consider saying yes.

Nothing said she had to sell the diner. Ava could run it on a day-to-day level with Carl's help and, thanks to the wonders of modern communication, Paige could handle the administrative end of things from a distance. And it would be a good excuse to spend a long weekend at the lodge once a month or so.

The trailer she was less sure about. She couldn't sell it without going through the legal hassle of dividing the land it sat on from the diner's—assuming the property was even big enough to be subdivided at all. Maybe she could rent it out. To a single person, of course. Preferably one with no pets.

She was compiling a mental list of admirable qualities in a tenant when her cell phone rang, and the name on the caller ID screen made her stomach drop. It was her mother and the word *Donna* flashing at her was like a bucket of ice water dumped over her head.

Her mother. The woman who'd dropped everything to chase after a man more times than Paige could count. Just as she herself had been considering doing mere seconds before.

Mitch had made it perfectly clear he had no interest

in a relationship beyond his short stay in Whitford, but there she was anyway, mentally walking away from her business and renting out her home so she could follow him to New York City. Ready to drop everything for pretty blue eyes and a charming smile.

When the phone chimed its missed-call signal, Paige realized she'd been standing there staring at it. She tossed it onto the table and rubbed her palms on her jeans. Her mother could wait.

What the hell was she doing?

Before she could change her mind, she picked the phone back up and dialed Mitch's number, breathing a sigh of relief when it went straight to voice mail.

"Hi, it's me. Something came up and I won't be around tonight, but I'll catch you later." There was nothing else to say, so she hit End.

Then, before the shock could wear off, she gathered up all her paperwork and shoved it in a bag. There was a tiny closet of an office at the diner and she'd use it. The diner and the produce order and the constant debate between Styrofoam and paper were her reality, not some fling she'd overinflated into an epic romance in her imagination.

She walked across the lot, letting herself in the back door to avoid being seen. Gavin saw her, but he only waved when she gestured she'd be in her office. It was time to catch up on the important things she'd neglected while running around with Mitch.

And if she closed and locked the office door, she might even let herself have a good cry.

MITCH LEANED THE bike through the corner, letting it eat up the miles as the roar of the engine soothed his

thoughts. He'd been cruising for an hour with no destination in mind. Just taking turns as the mood struck.

Time to head home, though. Since he wasn't seeing Paige tonight, he'd spend some time going over the
plans for the lodge some more. Grandmaison was willing to let them run across the corner of his property as
long as he got to oversee the where and the how much.

If he got enough of the legwork done, there was
a possibility the lodge could start taking in a steady
stream of summer customers as early as May, when
the trails officially opened. If they had a good winter
and the snowmobilers loosened their wallets, it would
be enough to get the lodge back into fighting shape,
financially.

But thinking too much about the lodge made him
think about the possibility they'd be selling it, and that
wasn't a topic for a summer Harley ride. Neither was
Paige, who'd sounded odd in the message that had so
casually canceled their evening together.

He twisted the throttle, forcing himself to concentrate on the road instead of the people who were mucking up his life. Nothing but him and the bike and the
wind rushing past.

And the police car he didn't see in time.

He found a safe place to pull over—his days of out-
running cops long past—and leaned the bike over onto
its stand so he could dig out his wallet. *Please don't be
Bob Durgin. Please don't be Bob Durgin.*

In the bike's mirror, Mitch watched Bob Durgin get
out of the cruiser and use his gun belt to hitch his pants
up. Great. He wondered how much a ticket for eight

miles per hour over the speed limit plus everything he'd ever done wrong during his childhood would cost him.

"You in a hurry?"

"No, sir." He sat on the bike so he wouldn't tower over the old cop too much. "I was enjoying the weather and got a little carried away."

"You Kowalskis have always gotten a little carried away."

This wasn't Mitch's first traffic stop. He knew it was best to be polite to the cop, who was just doing his job, and neither offer lame excuses nor get belligerent. But Durgin was too much. "We got carried away sometimes when we were young and stupid. Most kids do. But I'll be damned if I'm going to sit here and take shit from you because *you* lost control of the new cruiser and rolled it into a ball. I'm not a kid anymore and I'm not going to be spoken to like one. Write me the damn ticket and get on with your life."

For a second he thought old Bob was going to have a stroke right there on the side of the road, and wouldn't *that* be a hell of a story to add to the Kowalski legacy in Whitford?

Durgin's face burned. "If you'd been my kids, you'd have all learned some manners and respect, but no, Sarah had to go and choose that jerk Kowalski and have a whole freakin' herd of pains in my ass."

It took a few seconds for the cop's words to make sense to him, and then it took all his composure to keep his mouth from hanging open. Bob Durgin hated them all because he'd wanted to marry their mother?

Mitch wouldn't have thought it possible, but Durgin's

face turned an even brighter shade of red. "Forget it. Slow down or you'll spend the night in a cell."

He was back in the cruiser and down the road before Mitch even had the sense to shove his wallet back into his pocket. That was unexpected. As he fired up the bike and pulled out onto the road at a much more reasonable pace, he couldn't help shaking his head. Whitford was one seriously messed-up place.

When he got back to the lodge, he found Josh in the great room with all the papers for the proposed ATV connector trail spread out on the coffee table. Mitch noticed right off that his brother was in a good mood and that the can on the end of the table was a soda and not a beer.

"Did you know Bob Durgin wanted to marry Mom and he's still pissed off she chose Dad?"

Josh looked at him as if he'd lost his mind, then shook his head. "No, but it explains a lot. How'd you find that out?"

"He yelled it at me on the side of the road before he got embarrassed and left without giving me a ticket." Mitch went into the kitchen for a soda, then joined Josh on the couch. "You trying to figure something out or you just looking at it?"

"Mostly I'm just looking at it." Josh slid the papers around, then leaned back against the sofa. "I should have kept fighting for this after Dad said it couldn't be done."

"A lot of people don't fight for something they don't want."

"It's not that I don't want the lodge. I mean, I do and I don't. It's home, you know. And what about Rosie?

She's devoted her entire life to this house and to us and we're going to what…throw her out to be homeless and unemployed when she should be relaxing and enjoying herself?"

"Nobody's going to throw Rosie out. If the new owners don't want to keep her on, or she doesn't like them, then we'll find her a place and make sure she's taken care of. And it's home for all of us, too, so it would be hard to see it go, but you get to have a life, too."

Josh cleared his throat before taking a long drink of soda, and Mitch realized his brother was actually choked up. "Josh, nobody's going to hold this against you."

"I keep thinking I could give it a couple more years. If this ATV plan works, we could more than double the lodge's income and then we could hire somebody to manage the place, leaving me free to do whatever. But I've told myself to give it a couple more years before, and the years keep passing by and here I still am."

"Do you know what you want to do?"

Josh laughed. "That's the worst part. I don't even know. I just want to get away from here and do…something. Anything."

"Give us a little time to figure it out and we'll make sure you get to go do something."

They were quiet a few minutes, then Josh jabbed him with an elbow. "No Paige tonight?"

"She canceled on me. Said something came up."

"Probably had to wash her hair."

"You're a funny guy." He might even have laughed if not for remembering the odd note in her voice when she'd left the message.

Something had been bothering her. Maybe he should have called her to make sure everything was okay. It could be her mom. Or maybe it was just a problem at the diner. She hadn't said it was an emergency.

"When are you going to admit she's different?"

Mitch glared at his brother as if he could make him take that back by sheer mental force. "Mind your own business."

"Somebody needs to get involved or you're going to blow it."

"Blow *what?* Like I've told you several times, we're just having a little fun. She's no different than…" He couldn't finish it. He wanted to, but he couldn't force himself to say Paige was no different than any other woman he'd had a little fun with. "Shit."

To his credit, Josh didn't jump on him for the admission by omission. He just sipped his soda and let Mitch come to terms with the fact he cared about a woman. A lot.

"We want different things out of life," Mitch said, clinging to the one good reason he had for not giving in to his feelings.

"So, what, you're just going to leave?"

"Am I just supposed to stay? Walk away from Northern Star Demolition and all the people I employ so I can hang out in Whitford and sleep in her damn twin bed? That company means everything to me."

"She has a twin bed?"

"Way to focus on the important stuff."

"What are you going to do?"

The only thing he could do. "I'm going to enjoy the

time I have left with Paige and then I'm going to go back to living my life and she'll stay here and live hers."

"You're an idiot."

"Says the schmuck who can't see what's right in front of him."

Josh scowled. "What's that supposed to mean?"

"Nothing. I've got to go muck through my email in-box."

He ended up mucking through his own head more than his in-box, but he couldn't reach any other conclusion than the one he'd shared with Josh—he had to go and she had to stay.

At least, unlike Drew and Mallory, they'd started out on the same page so he had nobody to blame but himself.

CHAPTER EIGHTEEN

SHE DEFINITELY NEEDED more potato chips. Staring down at her shopping basket, Paige did a mental count and, sure enough, she had more chocolate than she did salty and crunchy. There had to be a handful of chips for every chocolate.

Maybe she should shake it up with some corn chips. They were *very* salty and would balance out her comfort-food ratio nicely. She grabbed a bag and headed for the register, where she unloaded her bounty onto the counter.

"Oh, hell," Fran said, shaking her head. "I had such high hopes for that boy this time."

Paige had to bite back a bad word. She knew she should have gone down to the city and hit a big grocery store. "That boy has to go back to work next week. Just stocking up to fill the hot-sex void so I don't go on a murderous crime spree."

"Honey, I know heartbreak countermeasures when I see them."

"I think I caught it in time." Paige was impressed she'd managed to say it as if she believed it. "I'll probably end up throwing half of this away."

"Bring it to the next movie night. There's always

at least one woman wanting to drown her sorrows in chocolate with a salty, crunchy chaser."

After shoving her comfort foods into her reusable totes, Paige bid Fran goodbye and took her time walking home. She'd already been to the library, where she'd loaded up on books and magazines she hoped would be interesting enough to keep her mind off Mitch.

When she reached her trailer, she realized she probably should have waited until he was gone to start mourning his being gone. Mitch was sitting on her front step, leaning back against her door with his hands dangling between his knees. Her heart stuttered at the sight of him, but she strengthened her resolve. She wasn't going to escape with her heart in one piece, but she could keep her dignity intact.

"I tried calling, but it went straight to voice mail," he told her.

"I had to call a vendor today and I made the mistake of using my cell phone to keep the diner's line free. My phone's on the charger right now."

"I was thinking maybe we could take the bike and ride down to the city and get a nice dinner somewhere."

It sounded perfect. "I can't. I have too much work to catch up on."

He pushed himself to his feet and moved closer to her. "You were busy last night. You're busy tonight. Are you blowing me off, Paige Sullivan?"

"Of course not. It's just that I've let too much work pile up and I've lost a lot of sleep and if I don't stop and catch up, everything's going to go to hell in a hurry."

She wished he wouldn't look her right in the eye like that. Acting wasn't one of her finer skills, and she was afraid whatever he might see on her face wouldn't match the nonchalant tone she was going for.

"I miss you." He moved even closer, so she took a step back and that made him cock his head. "What's going on, Paige?"

And now came the hard part. She took a breath, then plastered a smile on her face. "Nothing. We had a good time, but it's interfering with stuff I have to get done, so it's time we move on."

"That's it? It's been fun and it's time to move on?"

"Isn't that how you do it? This is all there is and you won't call or text? I'm pretty sure it was all in the Mitch Kowalski pre-sex spiel."

His jaw tightened and then he gave a hard shake of his head. "This isn't like you at all. Why do you sound so angry?"

So she wouldn't dissolve into a blubbering mess in front of him. "You should spend what little time you have left in Whitford with your family. I'll probably see you around…someday."

She was almost to her door when Mitch caught her arm and spun her around. "Talk to me, goddammit. Tell me what's wrong."

The emotional dam broke and tears built up, spilling onto her cheeks. "What's wrong is that I realized you're leaving soon and that's going to hurt. I know it was supposed to be 'all the fun stuff, with none of the not-fun stuff,' but I blew it, okay? I'm knee-deep in the not-fun stuff, and it's time for you to do your trademark smile and wave as you ride off into the sunset before I get any deeper."

For once, Mitch didn't seem to have a charming

comeback to offer. He was so silent and still, she wasn't even sure he was still breathing until he sucked in a sharp breath and looked down at the ground.

"Just walk away, Mitch. It's what you do. I knew it before and I'm counting on you to do it now."

"We need to talk about this. You need—"

"What I *need* is to run my business and take care of my house and myself."

"And I was the temporary luxury."

"That's all you wanted to be." She waited for him to say something—anything—that would tell her his feelings for her had changed, but he stared over her shoulder with his jaw clenched and his hands shoved in his pockets. "Good luck with the lodge."

She went inside and this time he didn't try to stop her. Standing there waiting, it seemed like minutes passed before she heard the bike start and then the engine roar as he pulled onto the main street and pounded it through the gears.

Sliding down the door until her butt hit the floor, Paige put her head on her knees and let the tears come.

It was the right thing to do. She'd made a promise to herself and she couldn't break it, even for Mitch, because giving up the diner and her stupid little trailer and the friends she'd made would make her unhappy and eventually she'd hate both him and herself for it.

She'd done the right thing. She just wished it didn't have to hurt so much.

Rose watched Andy through the kitchen window. He was cutting lumber for something, using a makeshift workbench made of plywood spanning a couple of sawhorses. The guys had so many projects going on around the lodge, she couldn't keep track anymore.

She'd been thinking about him a lot since Katie's visit. She didn't like to think she'd been punishing Andy so she wouldn't have to acknowledge that deep down there would always be a little corner of her heart that would remain broken. She and Earle had a good marriage until the day he died and she'd loved him, but she could never totally forget what he'd done. Rather than risk the good life they had together and with Katie, she'd channeled that lack of forgiveness toward Andy. And it wasn't fair.

Before she could change her mind, Rose turned off the water she'd been running for dishes and dried her hands. Then she straightened her spine and walked out into the backyard.

He looked surprised to see her, but he didn't say anything as she approached. Just set the saw down and pulled off his gloves.

She stopped a few feet in front of him. "I accept your apology."

It looked as though he was going to smile, but thought better of it. "Thank you."

"That's all." She turned to walk away.

"Are you sure?" He said it quietly, but she stopped and faced him again. "I don't think that's all and, if you're going to accept my apology, I'd rather you get it all out so we can move on."

"What if he hadn't told me?" she asked, even though she hadn't gone outside with the intention of doing anything but accepting his apology. "Would you have come into my house? Eaten my suppers? Would you have been able to look me in the eye?"

"I was young and stupid, Rose. I know that's not an excuse and I'm not proud of it but, no, if Earle hadn't told you, I wouldn't have, either."

"You disrespected me. You disrespected Katie. Hell, you disrespected Earle by putting him in that position in the first place. And I know you didn't force him to do anything he didn't want to do, but if you'd both just eaten your dinner and gone back to the motel, my husband wouldn't have broken his wedding vows."

"I know that. That's why I let my friendship with him fall by the wayside, even though that hurt. You two were trying to save your marriage and me being around would have made it harder. I didn't want you fighting about me on top of everything else."

It was on the tip of her tongue to ask him if that made him feel like some kind of noble hero, but she swallowed the bitterness. He was right. If she was going to accept his apology, she needed to let go of the anger and face the truth she'd been trying to deny for decades. "Blaming you made it easier to forgive my husband."

This time he *did* smile, but it was a sad one. "Like I said, I was young and stupid but I did, after a few years, figure that much out."

"And you never told anybody. I appreciate that."

"I saw how hard you and Earle fought for your marriage. Having the whole town weighing in on the matter wasn't going to help."

He'd been a good friend to Earle, even after she drove them apart. And that's why he wouldn't have told her what happened if Earle hadn't—not to be disrespectful to her, but to help his friend keep his family. She'd punished Andy by robbing him of one of his best friends just for being a stand-up guy. "I'll be cooking dinner tonight. You're welcome to stay."

"Thank you, Rose."

She went back inside and finished filling the sink to wash the breakfast dishes. Her hands were shaking a little, so she did the silverware before the glasses to calm herself. Even though the conversation had been hard on her nerves, she had to admit she felt better after setting down the decades' worth of bitterness she'd been carrying.

Mitch walked into the kitchen, yanked open the refrigerator and pulled out the pitcher of lemonade. After slamming a glass on the counter so hard she was surprised it didn't break, he filled it and then replaced the pitcher, slamming the fridge closed.

He'd been like that for two days now and she'd had just about enough. "You pull the door off that fridge, all the food will go bad."

"What do you care? It's not like you're going to cook it, anyway."

There was a line, and the tone crossed it. "Just who the hell do you think you're talking to, Mitchell Kowalski?"

The fight went out of him and his shoulders dropped. "I'm sorry, Rosie. That was rude and really uncalled for."

"What happened with Paige?" When he shrugged, she pointed to a chair and he sat. "Tell me."

"She said it's been fun and it's time to move on. That's all."

That wasn't all. Any idiot could see that. "Isn't that the way you like to do things?"

"Yeah, it is. But...I guess I wasn't expecting it quite yet."

"So if she'd broken it off next week, you wouldn't be like this?" If he was willing to talk, she was willing to listen, but she was going to keep him honest.

"She cried. She said it wasn't just fun for her anymore and she wanted me to walk away before she got in any deeper, but I couldn't. I just stood there, so she walked away from me."

"Why do either of you have to walk away?"

He blew out a breath, shoving a hand through his hair. "We don't want the same things in life, Rosie. Look what happened to Drew and Mallory."

"So you both compromise."

"Being here for six weeks, you all see the guy I am *here*. It's like being on vacation, but I'm not this guy when I'm not here. I'm focused on my work and I travel constantly and I live out of suitcases. And I *like* it. One of us would have to give up too much and things would go downhill from here. The truth is, we have two totally different lives that just happened to intersect for a few weeks."

"If you want her enough, you'll find a way to make it work."

Mitch stared at the table for a long time, then slowly shook his head in a way that broke Rosie's heart. "Trying to make it work and failing would just hurt her more. It's better if I do what she asked and walk away now before we get any deeper."

"Honey, love isn't like rappelling into a cave, where

you can control your descent and how deep you go. It's just falling into the hole."

"Well, right now it's probably a shallow hole, so we'll both get out a little skinned up but with nothing broken."

Nothing but their hearts, Rosie thought as Mitch got up and went out the back door. She'd known him all but the first few years of his life and, whether he wanted to admit it or not, the hole he'd fallen into wasn't as shallow as he thought.

IT WAS THE big day. Mitch tossed Josh's crutches in the back of the truck and they headed to the clinic to get his cast off.

"You're still going to have to take it easy for a while," Mitch said once they were checked in and hanging out in the waiting room.

"Which I know because you've reminded me of that a dozen times. And I'm pretty sure Rosie's cross-stitching it on a pillow for me right this very minute."

"Now that we have a plan for the lodge, I don't want you to overdo it trying to get everything done. Ryan's going to be coming up for a while next month, so leave the heavy lifting to him and most of the other stuff to Andy."

Josh gave him a lazy salute. "Yes, sir."

"Smart-ass."

A woman with a clipboard poked her head into the waiting room. "Josh? We're ready for you now."

Once the nurse led Josh away, Mitch leaned his head back against the wall and closed his eyes. If all went well back there, he'd be free to leave. He could go back to his apartment, pack his suitcases and head to wherever Northern Star Demolition took him.

Chicago, probably. It was a big job and he'd feel better if he checked on Scott's prep work, without looking as if he was checking up on him. Then he'd head to Philadelphia to finalize the contracts to drop some old tenement buildings and then head to Miami for a while. He had excellent people working for him, but his fingers itched to hold the reins again.

He wasn't worried about things having gone to hell while he was gone. He was worried about the possibility—no, the probability—that once he was back, his fingers would itch to hold Paige again. He'd never worried about that before. A kiss goodbye and a smile and that was that.

He was going to miss Paige. He knew it already and he was trying like hell not to think about it. But every time he closed his eyes, he saw her tears. He heard her coming *so* close to telling him she loved him, and he lay awake at night wondering if she had said those words, whether he would have thrown everything else away for the chance to hear her say them every day for the rest of his life.

In the harsh light of day, though, he remembered the responsibilities and the people who worked for him and the satisfaction of being damn good at what he did. And he could picture Paige in her diner or in her trailer, not only happy with her life, but proud of the fact she'd done it all herself. And he knew it was time to walk away.

Everything went smoothly with the doctor, and Mitch spent the next couple of days getting ready to go. He boxed up everything but the necessities that fit in the bike's saddlebags and shipped the boxes back to his apartment. He spent a lot of time talking to Josh, with Ryan on speakerphone, about how they'd proceed with the lodge. They'd decided Josh would talk to Sean and Liz about the possibility of selling and then they'd see how Rosie felt about it.

Though he was still supposed to use the crutches as much as possible, Josh was back on his feet, emotionally and mentally as much as physically, and much too soon Mitch found himself sitting on the porch with his cell phone in his hand.

He dialed Paige's number, trying not to hold his breath as he waited to hear her voice for the first time in days. It was a good thing he didn't, because all he got was the bland, stock voice telling him he could leave a message.

Maybe he should go into town. Try to see her one more time before he left and tell her…nothing. There was nothing he could say to make this any better. The phone beeped, ready to take his message.

"Hi, it's Mitch. I'm leaving today and…I know I said I wouldn't call or text, but it doesn't feel right to not at least say goodbye, so…" He couldn't find the words he wanted to say. That he *could* say, without making everything so much harder.

I wish I could find a way to make this work.

I'll miss you.

I think I might be in love with you.

"So, anyway…goodbye, Paige." He hit the end button and jerked his arm back to hurl the phone across the yard before common sense kicked in and he tucked it back in his pocket.

It was over. Nothing left to do but say goodbye to Josh and Rosie, then hit the road. He'd already stopped in at the police station to say goodbye to Drew, who was burying himself in work to take his mind off the end of his marriage.

"Stay off the ladders," he told Josh when he and Rose came out to see him off.

"You worry about blowing shit up. Leave everything else to me." They hugged, Mitch slapping Josh's back and thankful to have his youngest brother back.

Then it was Rosie's turn. As expected, she was weepy and didn't want to let him go. "Don't be gone three years this time."

"I won't." Though he'd end up like Ryan, sticking close to the lodge and avoiding town because the memories sucked.

He let her fuss over him for a few more minutes, then he straddled the bike and fired the engine. They stood and waved as he went down the drive and he beeped the horn before he left the Northern Star Lodge behind him and headed into the heart of Whitford.

Mitch let the Harley roll to a stop at the intersection, then stood there, balancing the machine between his legs. Straight ahead lay the open road and New York City. Northern Star Demolition. Suitcases waiting to be packed for the next job.

To the left was the municipal parking lot, which was small, but plenty big enough for him to turn the bike around and point it back in the direction of the diner.

He could convince Paige to leave Whitford with him. She cared about him—maybe even loved him—and if he told her he wanted her to be a part of his life, she might leave the diner and her little trailer behind. But it would be *his* life they'd be living from then on.

Just make sure you both want the same thing in life, because it hurts like hell when you find out years into it that you don't. The words Drew had said to him his first morning back in town echoed through his mind.

To Mitch, what Paige had was a job and a place to sleep. But to Paige, the diner and her trailer—and Whitford itself—were a dream she'd put her heart and soul into making come true.

A car Mitch hadn't heard pull up behind him honked and he got the motorcycle rolling. Straight through the intersection and out of town.

CHAPTER NINETEEN

THERE *WERE* WORSE things than people speculating on whether or not you were sleeping with a much-beloved hometown boy. The pitying glances were worse. The whispering behind hands was worse. The occasional pat on the hand. The often repeated refrain of *it's his loss*. In the week since he'd left, she'd had to put up with it everywhere she went, even—or especially—at work.

Mitch Kowalski had broken Paige Sullivan's heart and all of Whitford knew it.

Or thought they knew it, she fumed as she walked down the street with her library tote. Her heart wasn't broken. Badly dented maybe, but not broken. For goodness' sake, they were all acting like he'd jilted her at the altar.

Unfortunately, it was a hot and humid day and the tote was heavy since she'd gotten more books than usual—mostly thrillers and *no* romances—so she detoured into the park to rest for a few minutes. Of course, as soon as her butt met the bench she was hit by the memory of the day Mitch had sat down next to her and she'd thought he might kiss her.

So maybe her heart had a few cracks to go with the dents. And it certainly hadn't helped when Josh and Andy showed up for breakfast that morning. With the blue eyes and the voice that was so similar to his brother's, she found it painful to wait on Josh and, to make it worse, she could tell he realized that possibility too late. She'd put on her best smile, though, because she didn't want Josh to feel awkward about eating at the diner. Or Ryan, who'd be spending some time in Whitford in the near future.

She'd been sitting there about five minutes, trying not to think about Mitch, when her cell phone rang. When she saw her mother's name come up on the screen, she almost didn't answer it. She really didn't have the energy today. But it had been a while since they'd talked, so she answered it. "Hello."

"You'll never guess where I'm calling you from!"

Some kind of mental and/or emotional rehab center? "Where?"

"Costa Rica! Steven and I arrived this morning and it was such a whirlwind trip I didn't have time to call you until now."

"Who is Steven?"

"Oh, I didn't tell you?" Donna's nervous laugh sounded tinny over the phone. "Corey was starting to be neglectful—I think I told you about that—and I met Steven at a benefit dinner-dance and he said I was the most stunning woman in the room. Two weeks later, he asked me to come to Costa Rica with him. Oh, Paige, honey, I think he's the one."

Of course he was. The one after the guy before him and the one before the guy who'd come after him. "That's wonderful. I hope he is."

There was a long pause and she wondered if her mother had set the phone down and then forgotten she was talking to her daughter. Sadly, it wouldn't be the first time. "You sound a little funny, sweetheart. Is everything okay?"

The rare moment of awareness was almost Paige's undoing. For a moment she imagined having a mother like everybody else seemed to—one who put her daughter's feelings above everything else and would do anything to soothe away her hurts. "It turned out *my* guy wasn't the one."

"Oh, good Lord, I didn't even know you had a guy! Well, it's his loss, honey. You need to put on some makeup and a nice dress and go find yourself another one, and the sooner the better."

There was the Donna she knew and loved. "Yeah, I'll keep an eye out for one."

The subject turned back to Steven, the accountant, and his gorgeous house in Costa Rica and Paige said a quick, silent prayer her mother's newest relationship wouldn't end with a subpoena. Donna sure knew how to pick them.

A few minutes later she was able to end the call with a relieved sigh, and she picked up her tote and walked the rest of the way back to her trailer. Hailey was picking her up in an hour and they were going to drive down to the city and see a movie. As long as they could find something that didn't end with a mushy, smooching couple living happily ever after, Paige didn't care what they saw. She just needed the distraction.

When Hailey finally showed up, she tilted her head and frowned at Paige. "It looks like you brushed your hair, but a little mascara and lip gloss wouldn't hurt."

"I've already gotten the 'Look pretty and everything will be okay' advice today."

"Donna call?"

Paige rolled her eyes. "She's in a Costa Rica with a new guy. He's the one."

"Yeah, for now. You ready?"

"Let's go."

Hailey waited until she was held hostage in the car, buzzing down the main road, before asking the big question Paige had known was coming but dreaded hearing. "Have you talked to Mitch?"

"No, and I'm not going to." That was the deal and Hailey knew it as well as she did. "What's playing at the theater? I'm in the mood for an action movie. Or horror."

"No horror. The last time you dragged me to a horror movie, I woke up crying for my mommy in the middle of the night. Thank God I live alone."

Paige laughed, letting Hailey lighten her mood. She and Mitch had both laid it out there in the beginning. He wouldn't call or text, and she wouldn't mope. And she didn't need to put on lipstick and a dancing dress and rush out to find another man. She didn't need another man in her life.

And there was no other man she wanted.

"YOU'VE DONE ONE hell of a job, Scott." Mitch tapped the pile of papers he'd gone through to neaten the edges, then tucked them in the folder. "I appreciate you taking up the slack while I was in Maine."

"It's what you pay me for." Scott Burns sat back in the armchair and picked up the tumbler of scotch sitting on the end table next to him. "And to be honest, it was nice to have the challenge. We all got to step it up a notch for a while."

Mitch picked up his own scotch, then leaned back

against the sofa and put his feet on the coffee table. The gesture reminded him of the night he'd sat on Paige's couch and touched the bathroom wall with his toes, and he downed the drink in one gulp. His suite was mid-level and nothing too fancy, but it probably still had more square footage than that trailer.

He forced his focus back onto Scott. "Is that your way of telling me you guys don't need me around anymore?"

"It's my way of saying…maybe you can take the time to resolve whatever it is you left unresolved back at home."

Mitch thought he'd done a good job of hiding the fact he'd returned from Whitford a changed man, but maybe not. Still, he could hedge a little. "My brother wants to sell the lodge."

"Really? How do you feel about that?"

"I'm not sure yet. I can't imagine it not being our home but, on the flip side, I sure as hell don't want to run the place."

"Ah. Youngest kid got stuck holding the bag?"

"Yup."

Scott swirled the scotch in the bottom of the glass and then looked Mitch in the eye. "And the woman?"

"What woman?"

"Oh, come on. I've known you a long time."

"Her name is Paige." It hurt just to say it out loud. "She reopened the old diner and she's…amazing. But, you know, I have a business and she has a business and I travel and she loves Whitford. So it was pretty much doomed from the beginning."

"Wait. You left this woman because of the company?"

"What was I supposed to do, Scott? Walk away

from it and hang everything and everybody—including you—out to dry?"

His right-hand man laughed at him. "You know I'm married, right? That I have two kids?"

"What the hell does that matter?"

"It's not an either/or situation. I'm traveling right now because I need to be on-site for this phase of the job, but then I'll go home. To *them*. And I'll work from home until I need to be on-site somewhere again, and they'll kiss me goodbye and then I'll call every night to tell them I love them. It's compromise." Mitch started to say something, but Scott wasn't done. "And don't even tell me it's different because you own the company. You and I share a pretty equal workload. As a matter of fact, if we split up the jobs on a more even basis now that we've all proven we won't sink your company by running amok when you're away, we could both have more time at home."

"I'm almost never home. It wouldn't be fair."

"You *choose* to live this way. Almost everything you're going to do for the next ten days to two weeks, you could do from New York. The planning, running the prints, projections. A shitload of computer work. And if you can do it from New York, you can do it from Maine. Oh wait…kind of like you've been doing for the last six weeks?"

"I should have fired you five years ago when you had the flu and forgot to call in sick."

Scott snorted. "You missed your chance, buddy. And speaking of working from home, since I've wrapped up everything that can only be done on-site for the time being, I'm catching an early flight in the morning so I can spend the next two weeks with my wife and kids.

You know, like normal married people whose work involves travel do."

"Screw you."

"Good to have you back, boss." Scott stood and reached out to shake his hand.

"Thanks for not sinking the company."

Once Scott was gone, Mitch poured himself another scotch and walked over to the window. He didn't have much of a view, but it was something to look at, at least, while he turned the problem of Paige Sullivan over and over in his mind.

It wasn't Paige who was the problem. It was him. She'd been living a wonderful life doing what she wanted, where she wanted. He'd blown into town, swept her off her feet—and been swept off his by her—and then he was gone.

And here he was in Chicago, doing what he loved and sleeping in a bed big enough for four people, and all he could think about was Paige. How he wanted to wake up with her in that bed. Every time he took a shower in the spacious bathroom, he thought of her. *Everything* made him think of her. And miss her painfully.

He'd thought it would ease up after the first day or two, but every time his phone rang and he hoped it was her or he thought of something he wanted to tell her, losing her hit him like a wrecking ball all over again. He had the feeling it would be a long time before he got over that. If ever.

The question was what was he going to do about it?

PAIGE HEARD THE quiet purr of a car's engine and the crunch of its tires on the gravel at the same time headlights cut through the darkness of her bedroom.

There was no reason for a vehicle to be in the lot between the diner and her trailer at almost midnight, so she pulled her phone off the charger and slid out of bed, her thumb hovering over the nine.

By the time she got to the window, the engine had stopped and she heard a car door slam. Not trying to be quiet, then. With her heart pounding, she peeked out through a crack in the curtains, careful not to disturb the fabric, ready to dial for help if she didn't recognize the driver.

She recognized him, though, which did nothing to calm her racing pulse. It was Mitch, standing in the parking lot with his hands shoved in his pockets, staring at her door.

The seconds felt like long minutes as she watched him, neither of them moving. He looked tired. And, even though he'd shown up in the middle of the night, she got the impression he wasn't totally happy about being there. She knew she should open the door, but she was afraid if she left the window—if she lost sight of him—he might change his mind about whatever had brought him there, and leave.

It wasn't until his shoulders lifted and fell on a deep breath and he took a few steps toward the trailer that she moved. There wasn't much she could do about the fact she was wearing a T-shirt that should already be a few years into its second life as a dust rag, but she tried to smooth down her hair. Then she flipped on the light and pulled open the door as she heard his footfalls on the steps.

He stopped when the light washed over him and simply looked at her. She drank in the sight of him, forced to finally admit to herself she'd been terrified of never seeing him again. "Hi."

"I don't know what to do, Paige."

"About what?"

"Us. I don't know what to do about us. I can't walk away from Northern Star Demolition. I have obligations. I have dozens of people—and their families—depending on me for work. I have to travel. And I built that company from nothing. I'm not walking away from it."

He was going to ask her to go with him. Paige tried to brace herself, but the shock of the choice she was about to face almost stole her breath. She could have Mitch. All she had to do was give up her home. Her business. Her friends. And that meant she was about to get her heart broken all over again, because she couldn't do it. *Wouldn't* do it.

"But I can't ask you to walk away from this," he said, and she let out a breath she hadn't realized she was holding. "You bought this trailer and you've brought that old diner back to life. You've made Whitford your home. So I don't know what to do."

"I don't know what to say."

He gave her a small smile, rocking back on his heels. "I was hoping you'd know what to do."

She desperately wished she did. "What is it you want?"

"You. I want you and I don't want to be a luxury. I want you to need me. I want you to not be able to concentrate because you're thinking about me. I want you to reach for your phone because you thought of something you have to share with me. I want you to not even be able to breathe at the thought of never seeing me again, because that's how I feel about you, Paige. I want to be a necessity."

Tears welled up in her eyes. "I do need you, because I love you and you make me happy. I can live my life just fine on my own, but it will be so much better if I live it with you."

"I love you. And we can make this work. I'll try to cut back on my traveling and delegate a little better, which I'm willing to do if it means more time at home with you. As long as you're waiting for me."

"Always." He kissed her until she could barely breathe, then held her for a long moment. "The women in this town are going to be so disappointed you're off the market."

"There are other women in this town besides you?"

"Nice one."

"I'm trying to soften you up for the big question." His face grew serious and he took one of her hands in his. "Do you think we can get a bigger bed?"

Laughing, she pulled her hand away. "There goes all that lovely floor space."

"All three square feet of it. And maybe a TV?"

She tilted her head and smiled. "There you go trying to change everything."

"And maybe if I have to make a quick trip just to check on something and you can get somebody to cover your shifts, you could go with me so we can have sex in the hotel shower."

"We'll have to put your computer on the stove and live off microwave meals." This time, she was the one who turned serious. "Or, we could find a house together. One with a giant bathroom so we don't *have* to have sex in hotel showers. I'd like to stay close enough to town so I can walk everywhere, but there are a few to choose from."

"I know how much this home means to you, Paige."

"And I'll keep it. Rent it out. But the house we pick together will mean even more to me."

"I want you to marry me. I want to have your ring on my finger so I can feel it when I'm away from home. I want to tell people, 'I'm going home to see my wife,' when I'm waiting to board my plane. And someday I'll tell them, 'I'm going home to see my wife and kids.'"

She threw her arms around his neck and said "yes" over and over, punctuating each time with a kiss.

"How about we go inside before somebody calls the cops on us."

"Are you kidding? They're taking notes—maybe even video—so they can get all the details right over coffee tomorrow."

He took her hand and led her into the trailer, where he kissed her long and slow. "The sooner we go to bed, the sooner I get the pleasure of waking up next to you. Or, you know, kind of under you, since we don't really fit side by side."

Laughing, she pulled him into the bedroom. "It's going to be fun, being your wife."

As he lowered her slowly to the bed, he kissed her and then said, "And I'm going to love being your husband."

* * * * *

*For more sexy, contemporary romance—
and more of the Kowalskis—don't miss BE MINE,
a special anthology featuring Jennifer Crusie,
Victoria Dahl and Shannon Stacey.
Turn the page for a sneak peek....*

SIZZLE
Jennifer Crusie

CHAPTER ONE

"But, I DON'T want a partner," Emily Tate said through her teeth. "I like working alone." She clenched her fists to pound them on the desk in front of her and then unclenched them and smoothed down the jacket of her business suit, instead. "I don't need a partner, George."

Her boss looked exasperated, and she automatically put her hand to her hair to make sure every strand was in place, that no dark curls had escaped from her tight French twist. Be cool, calm and detached, she told herself. I want to kill him for this.

"Look, Em." George tossed a folder across the table to her. "Those are the cost estimates from your Paradise project and the final costs after you brought the project in."

Emily winced and clasped her hands in front of her. "I know. I went way over. But we still showed a mammoth profit. In fact, Paradise was the biggest money-maker Evadne Inc. has ever had. The bottom line, George, is that we made money for the company." *I* made money for the company, she thought, but I can't say that. Be modest and cooperative, Emily.

"Yeah, we did." George Bartlett leaned back in his chair, looking up at her.

I hate it when he does that, Emily thought. He's short, fat and balding, and he doesn't have a quarter of my brains, but he's the one leaning back in the chair while I stand at attention. I want to be the one leaning back in the chair. Except I wouldn't. It would be rude. She sighed.

"Listen to me, Emily," George said. "You almost lost your job over this last project."

"You got a promotion because of this last project," Emily said.

"Yeah, because of the profit. If it hadn't made a profit, we'd have both been canned. Henry wasn't happy."

Henry Evadne was never happy, Emily thought. It didn't have anything to do with her.

George leaned forward. "I don't want to lose you, Emily. You're smart, and you have a sixth sense about marketing that I'd kill to have. But you screw up the financial side on this next deal, and no profit is going to save you, no matter how big."

Emily swallowed. "I'll bring it in under budget."

"You're damn right you will, because you'll be working with Richard Parker."

"Who is Richard Parker?"

"He's a whiz kid from the Coast," George said. "He did an analysis of the Paradise project. It's in the folder, too. You ought to read it. He wasn't too complimentary."

"George, how much have we made on Paradise?" Emily demanded.

George looked smug. "Close to four million as of last month."

"Then why am I getting whiz kids from the Coast and nasty reviews in my project folders? Where's the champagne?"

George shook his head. "You could have flopped."

"I never flop."

"Well, someday you will," George said philosophically. "And when you do, you better flop under budget. Which is exactly what Richard Parker is here to guarantee. You're meeting him at eleven in his office."

"His office?"

"Next floor up," George said with a grin. "Two doors from the president. Nice view from up there, I'm told."

"Why not my office?"

"Emily, please."

"Is he in charge of this project? Because if so, I quit."

"No, no." George waved his hands at her. "Just the financial end. And you're not the only one he's working with. He's financial adviser for all our projects. It's still your baby, Em. He just watches the spending." He looked at her closely. She'd made her face a blank, but she knew the anger was still in her eyes. "Emily, please cooperate."

"His office at eleven," she said, clamping down on her rage.

"That's it," George said, relieved.

EMILY SLAMMED HER office door and slumped into her rolling desk chair. Jane, her secretary, followed her in more sedately and sat in the chair across from her. She broke a frozen almond Hershey bar in half and tossed the larger piece to her boss.

"I keep this in the coffee-room freezer for emergencies," she said. "And I've given you the biggest half. Greater love hath no friend."

"How do you keep people from stealing it?" Emily asked, pulling off the foil.

"They know I work for you," Jane said. "They know I could send you after them."

"No, really, how do you do it?"

"I keep it in a freezer container marked 'Asparagus,'" Jane said, sucking on the chocolate.

"And nobody asks what you're doing with asparagus at work?" Emily broke off a small piece of the chocolate and put it on her tongue. The richness spread through her mouth, and she sighed and sat back in her chair.

"They probably figure I keep it for you—you're the type who looks like you only put fruits and vegetables in your body." Jane studied her. "How come you never gain weight? We eat the same stuff, but I'm fighting ten extra pounds while you look like you're losing. And you've got nothing to lose."

"Frustration," Emily said, breaking off another tiny piece. "I'm working for narrow-minded patriarchal creeps."

"In the plural?" Jane finished her half and checked the foil for crumbs. "Did George clone himself?"

"Evidently," Emily said. "I now have a budget adviser to answer to. Some suit named Richard Parker."

"Oooh," Jane said. "Him I've seen. Things are looking up."

"Not a suit?"

"Oh, yeah, but what a suit. Too bad I'm happily married." Jane sighed. "Tall. Dark. Handsome. Cheekbones. Chiseled lips. Blue eyes to die for. Never smiles. The secretaries are lining up to be seduced and so are the female junior execs, but it's not happening."

"No?" Emily broke off another piece of chocolate.

"He's a workhorse. All he thinks about is finance. Karen says he's always still here working when she leaves."

"Karen?"

"That tiny little blonde on the twelfth floor. She's his secretary now."

"Make good friends with Karen. We need a spy in the enemy camp."

"No problem," Jane said, licking her fingers to get the last of her chocolate. "She loooves to talk about the boss."

"Good, good," Emily said. "He could be a real problem for us."

"How so?"

"He's controlling the money."

"And we're not good with money." Jane nodded wisely. "Good thing Paradise took off like it did. It's been fun rising to the top with you, but I wasn't looking forward to hitting the bottom together when we went sailing over the budget."

"You wouldn't have hit bottom," Emily said. "George isn't dumb. He'd steal you as his own secretary."

"I'm not dumb, either," Jane said. "You and I stay together. I knew when I met you in high school that you were going places and taking me with you. President and secretary of the senior class. President and secretary of student council. President and secretary of our sorority in college. I'm hanging around until you make president of this dump." She threw her foil away and smiled smugly. "I've already made secretary."

"You're every bit as smart as I am," Emily said. "Why don't you let me get you into an executive-training program?"

"Because I'm smarter than you are," Jane said. "I'm making more than most executives here right now, and I don't have to kiss up to the boss. Are you going to eat the rest of that chocolate?"

"Yes," Emily said.

"So I gather you slammed the door in honor of Richard Parker?"

"Yes."

"I know how you can handle Richard Parker."

"How?" Emily broke off another piece of chocolate. She wasn't interested in handling Richard Parker. She wanted, in fact, to eliminate him, but she was always interested in Jane. She didn't insist that the company pay Jane a lavish salary just because they were friends; she insisted because Jane had a lot of ideas and none of them were dumb. If Emily did get to be

president, it would be due as much to Jane's brains
as to Emily's.

"I think you should seduce him," Jane said.

* * * * *

TOO FAST TO FALL
Victoria Dahl

CHAPTER ONE

THE COP GREW larger in Jenny's side mirror as he approached, his sunglasses glinting ominous light as she considered whether or not to make a run for it.

She might be able to escape. The highway was a nice, straight run here, and a gorgeous 350 V-8 engine purred beneath the hood of her 1978 Camaro, just waiting for her to punch the accelerator. The deputy would have to get all the way back to his SUV before he could even consider chasing her down. By then, she'd be a speck of bright yellow a mile down the asphalt. And hell, with the snow still five feet deep on either side of the road, she could just pull off onto any old trail and he might pass right by her.

Jenny flexed her fingers against the thin circle of the steering wheel. She was tempted. She knew how to run. It had always been her first instinct, and she'd pulled it off many times. But as she watched the cop's hard-hewn jaw begin to tic in anger, she sighed and slumped in her seat. Deputy Hendricks knew very well where she lived. He'd written her address down on three separate speeding tickets, not to mention two terse warnings.

"Good morning, Deputy Hendricks!" she said

brightly, as if she weren't easing her foot from a tempted hover above the gas pedal.

He didn't return her greeting. He didn't say anything at all. He just...*loomed, his sharp cheekbones and hard-edged jaw a warning of danger.* His lean body a threat of strength. The mountains looked small behind him.

Jenny made a valiant attempt not to squirm. "I thought I had a few more days on my tags."

His hands were loose by his sides in a pose she recognized from the other five times he'd pulled her over. One hand near his gun. One near his baton. He'd never reached for, either, thank God, but this time, both his hands spasmed into brief fists before relaxing into readiness again.

"End of the month, right?" she squeaked. She'd found him pretty cute on previous stops. Now she only felt nervous.

His hands closed one more time, and then he eased them open with deliberate slowness. "Ms. Stone," he said, grinding out her name.

She aimed a big smile up at him, though her lips felt stiff. "That's me."

"Unfortunately, I'm well aware of that."

"I—"

"Just as I assume you're well aware of why I've stopped you today."

"Is it—?"

"And *no*," he barked. "It has nothing to do with your damn tags."

She flinched at the way his voice filled her car.

In response, he cleared his throat and rolled his neck.

"Excuse me," he said in a much quieter tone, though the ends of the words were clipped enough to sound razor sharp, "while I run your information to see if you've acquired any warrants for your arrest since the last time I stopped you."

His heel scraped against the asphalt. Jenny leaned out. "Don't you need my license and—?"

He threw a hand up to stop her words and muttered something she didn't quite catch. Apparently he was more than familiar with her name and birth date.

"Shit," she groaned as she ducked back into her seat. He'd been lenient in the past, but last time he'd clocked her going eighty in a fifty-five, he'd been clear that his tolerance had worn thin.

"One more ticket, Ms. Stone, and you'll be called before a judge. You'll lose your license for thirty days, at best. At worst, you'll be charged with reckless endangerment."

"Of what?" she muttered to her steering wheel. "Chipmunks?" It had been November. Too cold for Yellowstone tourists and not snowy enough for skiers. She rolled her eyes as she heard the door of his truck open, but immediately after he slammed it, his footsteps sounded again. She watched him approach in her mirror, just as he had a few minutes before, but this time, she sank down a little in defense.

"Do you know how dangerous this is?" he growled before he even reached her window. "It's the middle of winter, damn it! You could hit a patch of ice! You could—"

"It hasn't snowed in two weeks," she argued. "The roads have been bone-dry for days!"

"Are you kidding me? There's snowmelt streaming across the road everywhere! And what if you'd suddenly come up on an elk? Or some stupid tourist stopped in the road to take a picture of a stupid elk? Are you… just…are you…?"

"Stupid?" she volunteered, hunching farther down in her seat. If she lost her license, she'd go mad. She couldn't live without her car. Or rather, she couldn't live without driving. It felt like flying to her. It felt like freedom. And it had been, three times now.

"Yes!" Deputy Hendricks yelled. "Stupid!"

"I'm sorry," she whispered. He'd never, ever lost his temper before.

He was silent for a long moment. A gas tanker drove past them, sucking the air through her open window, then hurling it back in.

Jenny shook her head. "I'm really sorry." She meant it. He'd been kind to her and she'd promised not to speed again. And now here she was.

He took a deep breath. His clenched teeth looked very white against his tan skin. "Jenny," he said, the only time he'd used her first name since she'd invited him to three tickets ago. She glanced up but couldn't puzzle out his expression behind his sunglasses. She'd never seen him with his glasses off. She worked at the saloon at night, so all her joyrides occurred during daylight hours. All she knew of him was his dark skin and sculpted jaw and wide mouth. Under his hat, his hair looked deep brown. The wide shoulders beneath his uniform jacket eased the insult of the tickets, and the cheekbones didn't hurt, either, but for all she knew he had bug eyes that wandered in different directions and brows like a twitchy mad scientist.

But probably not.

* * * * *

ALONE WITH YOU
Shannon Stacey

CHAPTER ONE

"Ashgabat." The sexy stranger's breath blew warm over her neck as he whispered the word near her ear, and Darcy Vaughn chased a full-body shiver with a big gulp of martini.

"Ashgabat," she repeated for the trivia host, since he hadn't been wrong yet.

"That's correct!" The other teams around the bar all groaned, and Darcy smiled sweetly at Kent and Vanessa, formerly the reigning know-it-alls of Tuesday night trivia.

She and her sexy font of random facts were kicking butt tonight.

Her regular partner hadn't called to cancel until after Darcy had ordered her margarita and nachos, so she'd left it to the waitress serving as trivia host to pair her with another customer flying solo. She hadn't expected the guy rocking the scruffy, blue-collar look to raise his hand and join the academic fun, but figured he'd contribute on the sports questions. Despite working at a sports bar, Darcy wasn't much of a fan.

But now she knew a few things about her trivia partner. His name was Jake. He had brown eyes the same shade as his close-cut hair, smelled delicious and had a body made for selling charity calendars. He also knew a little something about which capital city sat between the Kara-Kum Desert and the Kopet Dag Mountains. Being able to cough up Turkmenistan trivia was almost as sexy as the way he rested his arm across the back of her bar stool every time he leaned in to whisper an answer in her ear.

"Ten-minute break," the host announced.

After hitting the restrooms, the teams eventually settled back on their bar stools to wait for the host, who'd disappeared into the kitchen. When the silence stretched toward awkward, Darcy turned to Jake. "So, let me guess. You're taking a break from exploring the world after an expedition to Turkmenistan to find an ancient, possibly cursed relic went bad."

His smile should've been illegal. "And that must make you the Russian spy sent to charm the relic's location out of me with your knowledge of U.S. presidents and the Periodic Table of Elements."

"I have ways of making you talk," she joked, though it came out a little more suggestively than she'd intended.

"I bet you do."

Darcy realized, with the way they were gradually leaning in closer to each other and the innuendo, they were in heavy flirting territory and she panicked a little. Guys didn't usually come on to her in bars. At Jasper's Bar & Grille, where she waited tables and occasionally worked the bar, most of the guys were looking at Paulie, who managed the place. She was tall, had a killer body—including great breasts—and knew everything and anything about sports.

Darcy was on the short side of average. Her breasts were on the small side of average. She pretty much ran just left of average overall. Her hair was nice, though.

Dark and thick, with just enough wave to keep it cute in a ponytail.

"So, Darcy, what do you really do when you're not answering trivia questions or charming Indiana Jones types out of their relics?"

"I wait tables." She shrugged. "It's a good cover. Lots of eavesdropping opportunities. What do you do when you're not sifting through ancient ruins?"

"Some business consulting. Boring stuff."

"Do you get to travel a lot?"

He shook his head. "Honestly, I don't fly, so a few sledding trips to Canada and a really misguided summer in Florida during my youth are the extent of my travel. Not trusting airplanes to stay in the sky killed my dreams of being Indiana Jones when I grew up."

"Yeah, well, my Russian accent sucks." They were laughing as the trivia host stepped back into the horseshoe center of the bar and poured them all another round before continuing the game.

After Kent and Vanessa got an economics history question right and the next couple blew it on geography, the host turned to them. "What famous player, inducted into the Baseball Hall of Fame in 1972, was known for the phrase 'It ain't over till it's over'?"

As Jake leaned in to whisper in her ear, Darcy blocked him with her hand. "Wait. I know this one, dammit. Finally a sports question I know the answer to."

"We should talk about it."

"Why? Don't you think women can answer sports questions?"

His mouth brushed her ear as his arm pressed against her back. "I just like having an excuse to whisper in your ear."

"Yogi Berra," she told the trivia host in a surprisingly normal voice, considering how on the inside she was a shivery, breathless mess.

A couple of drinks and a few rounds later, Jake and Darcy were declared the winners. The grand prize was nothing more than bragging rights and the his-and-hers puckered looks Kent and Vanessa sported as they went out the door.

"How are you getting home?" Jake asked as he held Darcy's sweater so she could slip her arms in. Such a gentleman.

It was an innocent enough question, but Darcy's overheated, alcohol-fueled imagination added a pronounced ungentlemanly slant to his words. "I'm walking."

"Alone?"

"It's not far."

"You've had a bit to drink." A bit more than she usually did, actually. "I'd feel a lot better if you let me walk you home."

He didn't know it yet but, unless she'd totally misread his signals, he'd feel a *lot* better because if he got as far as her front door, she was going to drag him inside and have her way with him. She wasn't in the habit of bringing men home after the first date—and random trivia partnership was stretching the definition of date—but she was going to roll the dice on this sexy, smart guy with a sense of humor. They were rare. Plus, she just really, really wanted him.

* * * * *

New York Times bestselling author

KRISTAN HIGGINS

asks: How far would you go to get over a guy?

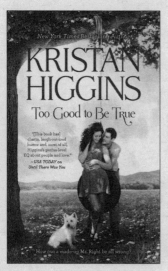

When Grace Emerson's ex-fiancé starts dating her younger sister, extreme measures are called for. To keep everyone from obsessing about her love life, Grace announces that she's seeing someone. Someone wonderful. Someone handsome. Someone completely made up. Who is this Mr. Right? Someone… exactly unlike her renegade neighbor Callahan O'Shea. Well, someone with his looks, maybe. His hot body. His knife-sharp sense of humor. His smarts and big heart.

Whoa. No. Callahan O'Shea is not her perfect man! Not with his unsavory past. So why does Mr. Wrong feel so…right?

Available wherever books are sold!

HARLEQUIN® HQN™
www.Harlequin.com

The "First Lady of the West," #1 *New York Times*
bestselling author

LINDA LAEL MILLER

brings you to Parable, Montana—where love awaits

Sheriff Boone Taylor has his job, friends, a run-down but decent
ranch, two faithful dogs and a good horse. He doesn't want
romance—the widowed Montanan has loved and lost enough
for a lifetime. But when a city woman buys the spread next door,
Boone's peace and quiet are in serious jeopardy.

www.LindaLaelMiller.com

Available in stores now.

The truth can't stay buried forever...

#1 *New York Times* bestselling author

LISA JACKSON

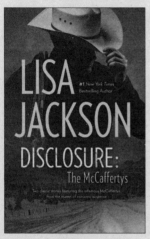

The McCaffertys: Slade

Slade McCafferty was a bachelor through and through—too busy raising hell to settle down. Case in point: fifteen years ago daredevil Slade had taken wild child Jamie Parsons's innocence, and then had broken her heart. But Jamie is back in town, a lawyer, all confidence and polished professionalism. And seeing her again is setting off a tidal wave of emotions Slade thought he'd dammed up ages ago. Back then, as now, there had been something about Jamie that made Slade ache for more. A hell of a lot more...

The McCaffertys: Randi

Is hiding the identity of her child's father worth risking her life? Randi McCafferty seems to think so, but investigator Kurt Striker is hell-bent on changing her mind. Hired by her well-meaning but overbearing brothers to keep Randi and her son safe, Kurt knows the only way to eliminate the danger is to reveal Randi's darkest secret...any way he can. Yet when protection leads to desire, will Randi and Kurt's explosive affair leave them vulnerable to the threats whispering in the shadows?

Available wherever books are sold!

REQUEST YOUR FREE BOOKS!

2 FREE NOVELS
FROM THE ROMANCE COLLECTION
PLUS 2 FREE GIFTS!

YES! Please send me 2 FREE novels from the Romance Collection and my 2 FREE gifts (gifts are worth about $10). After receiving them, if I don't wish to receive any more books, I can return the shipping statement marked "cancel." If I don't cancel, I will receive 4 brand-new novels every month and be billed just $5.99 per book in the U.S. or $6.49 per book in Canada. That's a savings of at least 25% off the cover price. It's quite a bargain! Shipping and handling is just 50¢ per book in the U.S. and 75¢ per book in Canada.* I understand that accepting the 2 free books and gifts places me under no obligation to buy anything. I can always return a shipment and cancel at any time. Even if I never buy another book, the two free books and gifts are mine to keep forever.

194/394 MDN FVU7

Name	(PLEASE PRINT)
Address	Apt. #
City	State/Prov. Zip/Postal Code

Signature (if under 18, a parent or guardian must sign)

Mail to the Harlequin® Reader Service:
IN U.S.A.: P.O. Box 1867, Buffalo, NY 14240-1867
IN CANADA: P.O. Box 609, Fort Erie, Ontario L2A 5X3

Want to try two free books from another line?
Call 1-800-873-8635 or visit www.ReaderService.com.

* Terms and prices subject to change without notice. Prices do not include applicable taxes. Sales tax applicable in N.Y. Canadian residents will be charged applicable taxes. Offer not valid in Quebec. This offer is limited to one order per household. Not valid for current subscribers to the Romance Collection or the Romance/Suspense Collection. All orders subject to credit approval. Credit or debit balances in a customer's account(s) may be offset by any other outstanding balance owed by or to the customer. Please allow 4 to 6 weeks for delivery. Offer available while quantities last.

Your Privacy—The Harlequin® Reader Service is committed to protecting your privacy. Our Privacy Policy is available online at www.ReaderService.com or upon request from the Harlequin Reader Service.

We make a portion of our mailing list available to reputable third parties that offer products we believe may interest you. If you prefer that we not exchange your name with third parties, or if you wish to clarify or modify your communication preferences, please visit us at www.ReaderService.com/consumerschoice or write to us at Harlequin Reader Service Preference Service, P.O. Box 9062, Buffalo, NY 14269. Include your complete name and address.

ROM13

**Two timeless tales of romantic suspense
from award-winning and *New York Times* and
USA TODAY bestselling author**

LINDA HOWARD

The Cutting Edge

Brett Rutland is a bull. As the top troubleshooter at Carter Engineering, he's used to getting his way. When he's tasked with cracking an internal embezzlement case, he meets firm accountant Tessa Conway. She's beautiful and interested, but falling for her will not only test Brett's control, it may also jeopardize the case—especially since she's the prime suspect.

White Lies

Jay Granger is shocked when the FBI shows up on her doorstep, saying her ex-husband has been in a terrible accident. She keeps a bedside vigil, but when Steve Crossfield awakes from his coma, he is nothing like the man Jay married. Ironically, she finds herself more drawn to him than ever. She can't help but wonder who this man really is, and whether the revelation of his true identity will shatter their newly discovered passion.

Available wherever books are sold!

8/14 (4)

shannon stacey

77686	YOURS TO KEEP	___ $7.99 U.S.	___ $9.99 CAN.
77685	UNDENIABLY YOURS	___ $7.99 U.S.	___ $9.99 CAN.
77678	EXCLUSIVELY YOURS	___ $7.99 U.S.	___ $9.99 CAN.

(limited quantities available)

TOTAL AMOUNT $ _____
POSTAGE & HANDLING $ _____
($1.00 FOR 1 BOOK, 50¢ for each additional)
APPLICABLE TAXES* $ _____
TOTAL PAYABLE $ _____

(check or money order—please do not send cash)

To order, complete this form and send it, along with a check or money order for the total above, payable to HQN Books, to: **In the U.S.:** 3010 Walden Avenue, P.O. Box 9077, Buffalo, NY 14269-9077; **In Canada:** P.O. Box 636, Fort Erie, Ontario, L2A 5X3.

Name: _____
Address: _____ City: _____
State/Prov.: _____ Zip/Postal Code: _____
Account Number (if applicable): _____

075 CSAS

*New York residents remit applicable sales taxes.
*Canadian residents remit applicable GST and provincial taxes.

HARLEQUIN® HQN™
www.Harlequin.com

PHSS0113BL